MW00440389

Amish Knitting Circle: Smicksburg Tales One

Karen Anna Vogel

He restores my soul

ISBN-13: 978-0615908007
ISBN-10: 0615908004

Dedication

. To the real Amish women who inspire the character of
Granny Weaver.
My husband, children, family and friends who believe in
my 'writing mission' of seeing women spun together and
then spun out into a hurting world, giving hope.

&

To Jesus Christ,
the One
who keeps me spun together
in His love.
Psalm 139

Karen Anna Vogel

Karen Anna Vogel

TABLE OF CONTENTS

INTRODUCTION

Pickwick Papers (Charles Dickens), *Adventures of Sherlock Holmes* (Conan Coyle),and *Anne of Green Gables* (Lucy Maud Montgomery), have two things in common; they started as continuing short stories and became classics. I've always felt we should learn from the best, and to me, a continuing short story invited readers to participate in the storyline, helping the author see their blind sides.

Amish Knitting Circle would have been a different story had it not been for reader input. The character, Maryann, would have been terminated if my younger sister hadn't clucked her tongue and said, "You can't kill her!" There are characters that were going to move away from Smicksburg, but readers protested. Then there's the character of Lavina, who was going to be in just one episode. Readers just loved this hurting teenager, so I made her a major character.

The story seemed to really take on deeper meaning when readers started to call themselves, "one of Granny's girls". Many said they didn't have a granny they could talk to, and were prompted to go to other older woman for advice. This is the Amish way of thinking, and I hope our culture shifts to make it an American way again. Respect for the elderly and the sage advice they give needs to be restored.

Granny also taught many how to pray. Her "casting off prayers" became popular as each episode ended with Granny Weaver casting her cares on the Lord. This became a mainstay, since so many told me they learned to pray; Granny is frank and talks to God like she would a friend.

I'm so encouraged because other readers are reaching out to women they see hurting, like Granny Weaver, believing women are stronger spun together. Oh women, we do need each other. We are more beautiful spun together; we are the nurturers of the world, and are needed.

AMISH-ENGLISH DICTIONARY

Ach – oh

Boppli – baby

Brieder - brothers

Daed - dad

Danki – thank you

Dawdyhaus – grandparent's house

Dochder – daughter

Gmay - community

Goot – good

Guder mariyer – Good morning

Jah - yes

Kapp- cap; Amish women's head covering

Kinner – children

Loblied - The second song sung in a church service, sometimes twenty-five minutes long.

Nee- no

Mamm – mom

Oma – grandma

Opa –grandfather

Ordnung – order; set of unwritten rules

Rumspringa – running around years, starting at sixteen, when Amish youth experience the outsiders' way of life before joining the church.

Wunderbar – wonderful

Yinz – plural for you, common among Western Pennsylvania Amish and English. A Pittsburghese word, meaning 'you ones' or 'you two'

EPISODE 1

Beginnings

Granny Weaver took a piece of wool and fed it to her spinning wheel, watching it form a long strand of sturdy yarn. She thought of the women she'd been praying for; they were like separate pieces of wool that needed to come together as one strand. On their own they were easy to pull apart, like the wool sitting in her basket. White, brown, black and cream wool blended together made pretty yarn. She thought women could have more beautiful lives if they came together like yarn.

Truth be told, she needed spun tighter with some women folk too. She still missed Abigail, her dear daughter-in-law, taken too soon. Her son, Roman, warned her not to take route 954 into Smicksburg, but she did. She breathed a prayer of thanks that none of the girls were in the buggy with her. With Abigail gone, Granny was like their *mamm*, and exhausted...

Roman and Abigail had worked hard to make her old age special. They built a little *dawdyhaus* cattycorner to the big old white farmhouse and it was easy to maintain. They had a team of men dig a large fishing hole behind the house for her husband Jeb and it kept him smiling. The wraparound porch made a wonderful trellis for her climbing red roses. She sat with Jeb many nights on the porch swing taking in the aroma. Now it was mingled with the scents of dried cornstalks and apples that the wind blew in from the fields.

She took the last of the wool from her basket and fed it to her wheel. Her black lab, Jack, darted off the porch to make his daily run. He could hear the girls little feet as soon as they started walking the quarter mile gravel driveway that led to the house. Tillie and Millie seemed like they were just in diapers, and here they were, coming home from kindergarten. Jenny was only in second grade but like a little *mamm* to her sisters.

Granny soon heard the sound of laughter and turned to see the girls. Her precious girls. Jenny was a picture of her Abigail. Blond hair and light blue eyes. Millie and Tillie looked like their *daed*, chestnut color hair and brown eyes. They were identical and only a dimple apart, her Jeb said. Millie was kissed on one cheek by an angel, forming one dent, but Tillie on both. Jeb knew how to encourage timid Tillie.

"*Oma*, school is so fun," Millie said as she ran up the stairs and hugged her grandma.

"Wait 'til you have to learn multiplication," Jenny sighed. She kissed her grandma's cheek and plopped on one of the hickory Amish rockers on the porch. Tillie was still walking up the driveway, her hands full of goldenrod, Queen Anne's lace and daisies. Jack panted close behind her. Granny felt that same gnawing feeling in her *goot*. She didn't feel capable of being a *mamm* to these girls. Why hadn't Roman found a wife yet? Why wasn't he paying any attention to Lizzie?

"What's wrong *Oma*?" Jenny asked.

Granny playfully pulled on one of Jenny's braids. "I'd

feel better if you'd help me make cinnamon flop for dessert. I have a craving for it this time of year. It washes down good with apple cider."

~*~

Later that night Granny sat at her oak kitchen table and took out her finest embossed floral stationery. She would start this knitting circle. She'd put it off long enough. Most women's calendars in November were empty except for Tuesday or Thursday weddings. Knitting could start on Wednesday at seven o'clock. She fidgeted with her pen as she decided who to invite. She thought of Maryann. She looked too tired and needed a break. Ruth seemed to need a break too, from that husband of hers. Should she invite Ella? She just got such bad news? If Fannie came would she feel comfortable? Anxiety filled her, but she thought of the Amish proverb: Courage is fear that has said its prayers. She bowed her head for a few minutes of silent prayer and then picked up her pen and simply wrote the same thing on each card:
Dear friend,

I bought this beautiful floral stationary and couldn't wait to use it. I have an abundance of yarn and would like to knit shawls to send to tornado victims of Joplin, Missouri. I've contacted our people at Christian Aid Ministries in Berlin, OH. They'll distribute all shawls and assure me there is great need. We'll start at seven on Wednesday Nov. 2nd I. I do hope you can make it.

Love, Deborah Weaver

She'd decide who to mail them to in the morning, when everything seemed fresh.

Maryann

Stirring the pot of venison stew with one hand, Maryann, held the letter her daughter just gave her. "What on earth could she be thinking?"

Becca, her oldest daughter, rolling out dough at the kitchen table looked up at her. "What's wrong, *Mamm*?"

"Granny Weaver wants to start a knitting circle and wants me to come. Every week? *Ach,* she must be lonely, but I have too much to do."

"*Mamm*, I think you should try it. I am fourteen and can manage here."

Maryann looked at her daughter fondly. She was growing into a woman. She could be married in four or five years, and she suspected it would be Gilbert Miller. "You like tending to the home, don't you."

"*Jah,* it's all I've ever wanted. To have a large family like you, *mamm.*"

"And you feel you need practice? Running the home alone?"

Becca dusted the dough with more flour. "*Mamm*, I don't need practice. I have plenty of that helping you with the *kinner.* I just think you need a break. You look tired."

"That's what other folks are saying," she said. "But, I do have eight *kinner.*"

"The lady in the yarn shop in town said knitting is goot for you. Helps you relax."

"But I nurse the *boppli*. What if she gets hungry?"

She saw her daughter give her a wry look. "You feed her before you go to Wal-Mart in Indiana. Why don't you want to go?"

"Well, I can't knit very *goot* for one thing. I haven't used a knitting loom in ages. I have your *oma's* but never use it. It's up in the attic."

"I'd love to learn how to knit on *Oma's* loom. It would be such a link to her."

Maryann puckered her lips and put her pointer finger on her cheek. "Why don't you go to the knitting circle? Granny would teach you to spin wool too."

"*Mamm,* are you sure?"

Maryann collapsed on her rocker. "I'm sure."

Ella

Ella started the long walk down the gravel road to get her mail. She missed going barefoot already. Autumn always meant shoes, but it was her favorite season. Selling pumpkins, Indian corn, and gourds at their roadside stand was a family tradition growing up, and when she married Zach five years ago, he built theirs, knowing how much it meant to her.

Since no one was around, she took off her bonnet and took a spin on the tire swing Zach had tied to the old oak tree by the pond. She leaned back and admired the yellow and orange leaves that swirled overhead. She closed her eyes and breathed in deeply, taking in the crisp air. She brought the swing to a halt and the silence of the day made her feel like she was in a sacred place. She bowed her head and whispered, "Lord, I love all this beauty you've made. It's a wonder to behold."

She continued to sit quietly for a few minutes. Something welled up in her and she brushed away a tear.

"A baby is a beautiful thing too. Seems like you created me to not have one." She took the corner of her white apron and dabbed her eyes. "Zach made this swing hoping to see *kinner* on it, but it just won't be. Help me to carry this burden Lord. Help my dear Zach too."

She got off the swing and continued to the mailbox. When she opened the box, she wasn't surprised to see a letter from Granny. She wrote often with some scripture or word of encouragement. The red roses that dotted the envelope made her grin. She ripped it open and quickly read the short note. "A knitting circle…but who would be there? Women and their *kinner?* A sharp pain ran through her stomach. At twenty-seven, it was getting harder to carry on a conversation with other women. Everyone talked about their *kinner.* Tears misted her eyes and she looked up to the clear blue sky. God had a plan, unique for her. She put the card in her apron pocket and headed back to her house. She'd go to that knitting circle. Maybe Granny asked her so she could get to know her *grandkinner* better, and help them learn women things. She could be like a *mamm* to them. God worked in mysterious ways, for sure and for certain.

Fannie

Fannie pulled her buggy out of Miller's Variety Store. She looked at the list her *mamm* made. She was sure she forgot something. Oatmeal, sugar, cinnamon, butter, yeast, cream of wheat, baking powder, salt, molasses, and honey. Yes, she got it all. She clicked her tongue, signaling her horse to move. Living so close to the food co-op made life easier; seeing Jonas Miller try to run the store, struggling to walk using his arm crutches, made her count her blessings. Seeing his daughter Lizzie as an old maidel made her shiver though. Would that be her someday? Always living at home?

If she didn't have a figure the size of their milk cow she'd have a husband. She'd have Hezekiah, the one she had her heart set on. But word had it he was taking home skinny little Lottie after Sunday singings. She could feel her teeth starting to grind and opened her mouth to make herself stop. Why were some women as thin as a rail and others fat? Oh, her *mamm* said she was big boned, but she heard the emphasis on BIG.

She looked at all the Black Angus cows behind the barbwire fence as she drove the short distance to her house. She usually walked since they lived two farms down, but the bags were too heavy this time. Several cows meandered toward the road and mooed at her. Birds of a feather flock together, she thought. Oh, why didn't the delicate little hummingbirds at her feeder flock toward her? No, cows did. They thought she was one of them, most likely.

She pulled into the gravel driveway and stopped the buggy. She bounded out to get the mail. She opened the mailbox and took the floral card and ripped it open. Granny always wrote her encouraging letters. She read the note, and sighed. What if Lottie's at this knitting circle? Or Lavina Yoder, who was smaller yet? She'd look ridiculous hovering over her knitting loom if she sat between them.

She skimmed through the short letter. Joplin,

Missouri. She had kin in Missouri who wrote and told of the devastation the tornadoes left behind. Winters got cold there too, and a wool shawl would warm a body, Amish or not. She had a friend who volunteered at Christian Aid Ministries in Ohio. She told her they flew cows into a Romanian orphanage. How could you fly a cow? Wouldn't it be too heavy?

She slipped it in her apron pocket. She'd go, only because it was for a good cause.

Ruth

Ruth put two year old Mica down for a nap and went down to her kitchen. She pumped water into her stainless steel kettle. Most women had gravity fed water with modern plumbing in the home; her husband Luke thought things were making life too easy for the Amish. How he'd rant that soon the community would be New Order. She knew from letters from her cousins in Lancaster they were still very old-fashioned. No diesel tractors being pulled by horses here in Smicksburg. No gas powered modern refrigerators too. She looked over at her icebox. Maybe the ways of Lancaster Amish were better. No need to haul ice to the chest. Most men gladly replenished the ice for their wives, but not Luke.

She looked out the window at her birdfeeder. Yellow and brown finches peacefully perched on their cylinder feeder. They didn't squawk at each other like the cardinals and blue jays that fought over the sunflower seeds in their large wooden feeder. She and Luke were like cardinals and blue jays. Why couldn't they be like finches? She wasn't the quiet girl Luke thought he married. He wasn't charming either. She looked again at the birds. Why couldn't I fly away too?

She heard the kettle whistle and sighed. The sweetest moment of the day was her afternoon tea, when all was quiet. She made her way over to the assortment of teas she kept in a little basket. Chamomile soothed her nerves. She plopped the bag into a mug of hot water and sat down again at the window. She took a sip and closed her eyes. She soon heard a buggy come up the driveway. Maybe her mamm had come to visit. She heard loud footsteps and turned to see Luke come in the side door.

"*Ach*, so this is what you do all day. Sip tea and watch your bird friends?"

Ruth pursed her lips, willing them to stay shut. She saw fire in her husband's eyes. Why was he home? She looked in horror as he walked across her linoleum kitchen floor with his work boots on. Muddy footprints followed. She could hear her heart throb in her ears. He walked over and threw a card in her lap. She froze as he drew closer. "Time to sip tea but always too tired to tend to my needs."

She shivered. He acted like a wild animal at times. She felt his sweaty hand pull at her prayer *kapp*. He slid it down to the back of her neck and roughly pulled the strings. She smelled his foul breath as he drew closer. She could remain silent no more. "Wash up and then approach me." She felt his fingers dig into her arms as he pulled her out of the chair and started to jerk her. She closed her eyes, afraid to look in his eyes. Yes, she said no last night, but she was tired. Was this his way of making her pay? The pain in her arms increased and she screamed. Soon she heard Mica crying upstairs. She felt him release her and she collapsed into her chair. Through her sobs she heard the side door slam shut. She leaned over, feeling nausea wash over her. Through blurry eyes she saw a card on the floor. It had red roses on it. It was from Granny. She picked up the letter, held it to her chest, and wept.

Lizzie

Lizzie took a scoop of dried peas and put them in the bowl at the top of the scale. One pound exactly. She slid them into a plastic bag and took a white sticker and a black pen to write the label, then stuck it on the bag. She looked over at her *daed* who was struggling to put cornflakes on one of the wooden shelves that lined their little food co-op. A box fell but he didn't lose time in retrieving it. He took his right arm crutch and pushed the box against his leg and inched it up his side, and grabbed it.

She admired his stubborn persistence. The way he got himself into their buggy took longer, but he'd never let anyone help. When he was told he'd never have his own chicken business, it only made him try harder. With the click of a generator button, all the water and feed were pumped in to his beloved hens. Collecting eggs was a bit tricky, so he hired the neighbor boy.

She thought of Fannie's recent visit. "*Daed,* I don't think Fannie's fat, do you?"

"*Nee,* she's just got a round face, but she's a mighty pretty girl. Those big green eyes will catch her a husband soon."

"She's always talking about how fat she is and makes fun of herself. I don't think she realizes she's turning them away."

"What about you, Lizzie? What do you do to turn Roman away?"

His bluntness shocked her. Yes, Roman came over more than he needed, sometimes buying only one item, although he did have a weakness for her whoopee pies. She put the box full of bagged dried peas in their place and went back to the scale to measure oatmeal.

"Lizzie. Roman is a *goot* man. Why not talk to him more when he comes in? I think he's here to see you."

"He made his choice long ago." She shoved oatmeal in a plastic bag.

"*Nee*, you made it for him. You postponed your marriage and he met Abigail. That man liked you since you were both in diapers. How long did you expect him to wait? And for what?"

She rubbed her temples, feeling tension starting to mount. "You needed me after *mamm* passed on."

"But it still doesn't make sense to me. If you'd wed Roman years ago, you could have built a *dawdyhaus* for me attached to the main house. We'd still be together."

She saw him make his way over to her, and she sheepishly looked across the scale and met his dark black eyes. "You were so sad about *mamm*, I didn't think it was time for anything to change."

His eyes misted. "Oh, Lizzie, is that the truth?"

"*Jah*, but it's not your fault. Roman didn't love me enough to wait." She came from around the corner and kissed her *daed* on the cheek. "We both came though the fire though, *jah*?"

"The house fire was before you *mamm's* death."

"*Ach*, I mean the fiery trials the Bible talks about."

Jonas winked at his daughter. "I get these trials mixed up."

She heard a car honk. It was the mailman with a package too big to put in the mailbox. "I'll get it." She ran barefoot out the door a short distance to the road to collected their package and mail. She looked at the box; more coloring books for the store. She leafed through the mail and saw a floral envelope. She sniffed the envelope. No scent? Granny usually rubbed a rose petal on her stationary. She opened it and read about the knitting circle. She felt heat rise to her cheeks. She'd see Roman once a week if she went. How would she tell Granny she couldn't go?

~*~

Granny enjoyed sitting on the porch swing with Jeb to wind down the day. She looked out over the vast field of golden rod then at the shades of pink across the evening sky. She took Jeb's hand. "I appreciate you letting us take up the house every Wednesday night. What will you do tomorrow?"

He pulled at his lengthy gray beard. "Well, most likely go to Roman's and play with the girls. Think I'll go over to Millers and buy some coloring books and crayons."

"Let Roman do it."

"Deborah, you need to stop sending that boy over

there. You and your whoopee pie cravings. You're not kidding anyone. You make them better than Lizzie."

"I don't have the time with all this wool. Two sheep would have been enough. Six is too many. *Ach*, I can't keep up."

She felt her husband's eyes on her, needing a confession. She looked at him evenly, and then tried to hide her grin. "You know me well, old man. Why can't Roman see he still cares for Lizzie?"

"Maybe he doesn't, that's why. Maybe he has his eye on someone else."

"Like who?"

"Well, he does say he stops by and chats with Fannie on the way back from Millers."

She's only twenty-one. He's thirty-two. *Ach*, your mind's gone mad."

"Fannie's a pretty girl and single. Not been seen in any courting buggy. Why not?"

She crossed her arms. "Roman and Lizzie courted before he met Abigail, and he needs a wife who's mature. And because I've been planning his wedding to Lizzie since he was a *kinner*."

"He chose Abigail. You aren't regretting that, are you?"

"Course not. I loved her like my own. I've just known Lizzie since birth, and watching those two together, so much in love, they sure got my hopes up. They still look at each other in that special way…at church."

"He most likely can't even see her. He's on the men's

side."

They both listened to the chain on the porch swing squeak. A ruby throated hummingbird came and perched on the red feeder hung from the porch rafter. The wind whipped and she took her shawl and pulled it over her shoulders. She felt her husband's arm around her. "Anyhow, even if Roman was looking over Lizzie's way, maybe it was Fannie he was eying."

She hit his knee. "Quit that teasing of yours. I sit in the back and it has its advantages. When all the weddings were announced last week, it was no surprise to me, the way those young loves glance over at each other."

She heard tiny footsteps come up the stairs that led to the front of the house. Soon the girls came around the corner. She was glad the swing was on the side of the house away from Roman's. They needed privacy.

"*Opa*, can you tell us a story?" Millie asked. "The one about the deer by the pond?"

She got off the swing and let the *kinner* sit with Jeb. Another nightly ritual a good wife for Roman would be doing. She took a deep breath and looked out at the forest beyond the pond. Crimson and yellow leaves swirled off the trees as the wind picked up. Lord, help Roman see he needs Lizzie.

~*~

The next day, Granny wiped down the cedar bench Roman and Jeb brought in from the porch. She put four rockers in a semi-circle across from it. "If all the women show up, we have plenty of room." She looked over at Roman and searched his tender brown eyes. "What's

22

wrong, son?"

"Abby went to a knitting circle out in Volant, when she was in her teens. She talked about it often."

She took a break and sat in a rocker. "Sit down, Roman."

"*Mamm*, I don't mean to sound short, but don't need another talk. I know it's been three years and I should move on."

"Then what's keeping you? Abigail would want you to be happy."

"I am. Just haven't met a girl I love like Abby, is all."

"What do you think of Fannie?"

His eyebrows furrowed. "She a nice girl. Easy to talk to. Why?"

"Your *daed* thinks you have eyes for her. Is that true?"

He leaned over and pulled his chin. "Haven't thought of her...I'm so much older."

She felt her mouth grow dry. "What about Lizzie?"

"*Ach*, she's always too busy to talk when I see her at the store." He stood up, took off his straw hat and ran his fingers though his hair. "*Mamm,* the cow needs milked. I *gotta* run."

She gripped both sides of her rocker tight. She nodded and he headed out the door. Why was Lizzie acting this way?

She got up to take the cinnamon flop out of the oven. She'd made three pie plates full. She heard voices on the front porch. It was Roman talking to a woman. She went over to the window to see him smiling at Fannie. She hid behind the white tie back curtains and watched. She'd never seen Fannie's eyes glow before. She studied her son. He was yapping up a storm, and he was usually reserved. She saw Lizzie come over from the big house. The girls circled around her as she chatted with them. When they got to her front steps, she saw Roman nod his head, to acknowledge her, but turn back to Fannie to talk. What on earth?

The Circle Begins

Granny hurried to get the cinnamon flop out of the oven as she welcomed Fannie and Lizzie. They both brought apple pies. "We'll need to do hard labor on Thursdays after eating so much here on Wednesday."

"No amount of labor will take off these pounds," Fannie sighed.

Lizzie rolled her eyes. "You're not even heavy. Sometimes I wish we had those big long mirrors so you could really see yourself. Our little ones just show our faces."

Fannie put both hands in the air. "I see my face in my mirror. It's fat."

Granny cleared her throat. "When you go to Wal-Mart, take a look at yourself in one of their mirrors. You'll see you're trim."

Fannie went over to hug Grannie. "You're always making me feel better about myself."

Granny took Fannie by the waist and squeezed. "I can almost get my hands around your middle. I don't flatter to make you feel better. That's deceitful. You're just plain not fat." She looked over Fannie's shoulder to see Ella and Becca come in. "Becca, where's your *mamm?*"

"She's sends her love but feels too tired to come. It's okay I came, right?"

Granny took the raisin pie from Becca and the pumpkin pie from Ella. "Of course you're welcome to come. Maybe in a few weeks your *mamm* can join us too."

Ella shifted her weight. "I stopped by Ruth's to see if she needed a ride. Luke came out and said he wouldn't have it."

Granny stomped her foot. "I'll have him. The girl is too cooped up and looks depressed."

Ella's eyes misted. "I saw Ruth peeking out the window, like a caged bird. The fire in Luke's eyes scared me."

"I agree," Becca said. "He looked at us like a rabid raccoon."

"I'll go sit on him," laughed Fannie. "I'll straighten him out. Leave it to me."

Becca burst out laughing. Granny put her hand up. "Ladies, let's sit down, shall we?"

The five women took seats and Granny folded her hands in her lap. "We're here to knit, not gossip, but are you serious about Luke?" She turned to Ella. "I've heard other people talk."

Ella bowed her head. "Maybe I'm afraid of Luke because…he's Zach's brother and my husband…knows more. We both know more."

Silence echoed around the room as the ladies stared at Ella. "Like what?" Lizzie asked.

Ella fidgeted with her white prayer *kapp* strings.

25

"Maybe I've said too much. Let me talk to my husband and he can talk to Luke. Make him realize his wife needs to get out with friends more."

"Sounds like a good idea," Granny said. "Now, next week, we need to decide who's bringing dessert. We have too much for one night..." Her jaw dropped when she saw Roman enter the house. "What's wrong? Are the girl's, okay?"

"They're fine, *Mamm*. Just came in to see if you'd like some apple cider. The girls said they'd come over with some if you'd like." He looked over at Fannie and grinned.

Granny furrowed her brow. She was known for her hospitality. Did her son think she was daft?

"I'll help the girls bring the cider over," Fannie said. She jumped out of her chair and joined Roman at the door. "We'll be right back. Need to get to that knitting we came here for in the first place."

Granny slouched. What was going on between Roman and Fannie? She looked over at Lizzie. She was clearly hurt by the attention Fannie was getting compared to the way he ignored her. She sighed. Her hopes were unraveling concerning those two.

~*~

Dear Readers,

Here is the first recipe my Amish friends in NY gave me. As a mother of 4 preschoolers, long ago, I needed a quick and easy dessert. They said cinnamon flop was my answer. I call it the lazy way of making cinnamon rolls. They taste the same but made in no time. Little hands love to poke the dough too....

Cinnamon Flop

3 tablespoons melted butter or margarine

1 1/2 cups sugar

2 eggs, well beaten

2 1/2 cups all-purpose flour

2 teaspoons baking powder

1 cup milk

1 cup light brown sugar

1/4 cup butter

Cinnamon

Directions

Cream butter with sugar.

Beat in eggs.

Sift flour with baking powder and add alternately with the milk.

Pour into well-buttered 9-inch pie plate.

Sprinkle top with brown sugar, dot with butter, and sprinkle with lots of ground cinnamon.

Bake in preheated hot oven (375° F.) for approximately 30 minutes.

Enjoy!

EPISODE 2

Wedding Season

Roman put another log in the black cast-iron stove, and then grabbed *The Budget* to read while having his morning coffee. He dreaded the November edition, just like he did last year; wedding announcements published across the country. He thought of his Abbey, and how she cut out the clipping of their engagement and taped it in her scrapbook. He knew it was still in her hope chest, but he couldn't look in it, even after three years. He wasn't afraid of remembering her, his precious bride, but how he'd never asked her forgiveness. On their wedding day, half his heart still belonged to Lizzie. He loved two women on that sacred day, Lord help him.

He chugged down some coffee and took a bite of raisin crumb pie, his favorite breakfast food. His mind wandered to the day Lizzie told him they needed to postpone their wedding. Her big brown eyes didn't beg him to understand; she just evenly said her *daed's* MS was flaring up. It was like being splashed with cold water on a winter day. Lizzie expressed little emotion.

Roman remembered showing her the blueprints for a *dawdyhaus* to be built next to his parents. She said her *daed* needed to be in his own house, where he was comfortable. He knew Jonas, his soon to be father-in-law, was looking forward to sharing a fishing hole with his *daed*. When Lizzie dug in her heels and refused to move, Roman even agreed to let one of his brothers have the family house and live in Lizzie's and have an attached *dawdyhaus* for Jonas.

It didn't make sense. Nothing he proposed was acceptable to her, so she postponed the wedding. *Why was Lizzie so stubborn?* Heat rose into his face. Why did Lizzie still bother him? When he saw her he still blushed like he did in sixth grade, when he first started to like her. He ran his fingers through his chestnut brown hair. Why did such foolish ideas flood his mind?

He heard little footsteps coming down the steps.

"*Guder mariyer*, Daed," Jenny said as she ran over to hug his neck. She was a picture of Abbey and behaved like her too, full of life and love.

"*Guder mariyer*, Honey Bear. I don't hear the twins."

"I felt Tillie's head and she's warm. Millie said her head hurts."

"*Ach*, it could be allergies to the golden rod."

Jenny pursed her lips. "We need to tell *Oma*. She'll know what to do."

"*Nee*, she's gone. Went to help clean up after the Byler wedding. Tonight she has that knitting circle of hers." Roman stood up while shoving the last piece of pie in his mouth. "Go tell *Opa* to come over. I'll get some medicine at Miller's Variety."

"Ask Lizzie what to do. She's a woman."

Roman groaned inwardly, not wanting to talk to Lizzie. He looked with pride at his daughter though. She was as level-headed as Abbey.

~*~

Granny Weaver arched her back and cracked her neck. So much cleaning up after a wedding, but she was so happy for Noah and Annie. She looked over at the newlyweds as they pitched in to help. What love in their eyes. She looked across the kitchen at Fannie, still drying dishes. Did she see tears falling or was water splashing? She walked over to take a look. Tears ran from Fannie's beautiful green eyes.

"*Ach*, what's wrong?" Granny hugged her from the side with both arms.

"Happy for Noah and Annie, is all." She sniffed. "My cousin married a *goot* man. Noah adores her."

Granny reached up and took Fannie by the shoulders. "I'm not too old to see. Those are tears of sorrow."

Fannie's chin quivered. "With age comes wisdom." She tried to smile. "Just wondering if Hezekiah will ever look my way, silly of me."

"Why is it silly?"

Fannie put down the dry white plate and put both hands on her hips. "Look at me. Do I look like someone he'd want to court? *Nee*, he wants a little thing like Lottie."

Granny had to confess she was relieved Fannie wasn't keen on Roman. Her imagination had run wild with that thought, her husband, Jeb, feeding it fuel. What nonsense. She looked at Fannie. "What'd you say about Lottie?"

"She's a skinny twig and Hezekiah likes, well, twigs."

"Who said that? Hezekiah?"

"*Nee*, not out loud, but I caught him staring at her quite a bit at the wedding yesterday. He tried to sit next to her when the cake was served too."

Granny pulled at her chin. "I watched the young folk and didn't notice. I'll remember to look for it at church."

"At church?"

"*Ach*, you know, I sit in the back with the girls. I notice things, not that I'm not paying attention, heaven forbid." She looked past Fannie and noticed Roman walk in the side door. "What's wrong?"

"The twins have colds or allergies. I'm headed over to Miller's Variety to get some medicine. Wanted to stop by real quick to let you know." He turned to Fannie. "Hi Fannie. Why so sad?" He walked closer to her and put a hand on her shoulder. "You've been crying."

Tears welled up in Fannie's eyes. "Wedding season makes me, well, emotional."

"I know what you mean. Maybe we can cheer each other up."

Granny gasped. Maybe what Jeb had been saying about Roman being keen on Fannie was true. She grabbed the edge of the counter when she heard Fannie ask if she could go to Miller's Variety with Roman to pick out medicine. Granny didn't wait for Roman to answer. "Lizzie's so *goot* at that, let her help you. She's older too. With age comes wisdom."

"*Mamm*, Fannie can help if she wants to —"

"Let Lizzie help. She and Jonas know all about herbal remedies too. The girls could be deathly ill."

Roman cocked his head. "Are you okay, *Mamm*?"

"She's just overworked," Fannie said. "Roman, I was going to ask you the same thing. You look so pale. Are you okay?"

"Feel cold, but it is November. I'm fine."

Granny went over to feel his forehead. "You're fine. Best be going to Lizzie's, Son, and get that medicine for the girls. She'll know what to give you."

Granny watched as her son rolled his eyes and groaned. What did that mean? Was he disappointed that Fannie couldn't go with him? Was he really sick? What on earth?

~*~

Ella squeezed her husband's hand after he knocked on his brother's door. She'd prayed to the *goot* Lord to help her be quiet and let Zach deal with Luke. She only came to be a comfort to Ruth. She froze when she saw Luke's icy-cold blue eyes. He looked so much like her husband, blond hair and dark blue eyes, but Zach's eyes were loving and gentle. She said a silent prayer of thanks to the *goot* Lord for her beloved husband.

"We're busy here," Luke snapped. "Did Ruth invite you over?"

"We need to talk. Can you take a walk?" Zach asked.

"It's cold out… not in the mood for a walk." He smirked. "Came home for lunch and I'm hungry."

His crazed eyes sent a chill down Ella's spine. He wasn't talking about food.

"I came home for lunch so I could pick up Ella so we could visit. We need to talk."

"I said I'm hungry," he snarled.

Zach took the basket from Ella. "We brought food. Let's eat together." He pushed Luke aside and entered the living room.

Ella followed, close by her husband. She heard Ruth crying and wanted to slap Luke, but willed herself to calm down. "Where's Ruth?"

"Upstairs," Luke snapped.

"I'll go up and visit for a spell."

She started for the steps but Luke grabbed her arm. She yelped in pain. Before she knew it Zach charged at Luke, pushing him up against the wall. "Don't you ever touch my wife, you hear me?"

Luke let out a hideous laugh. "Why would I do that when I have Ruth?" He looked over at Ella. "She sure is pretty though…"

Zach took Luke by the scruff of the neck and pushed him until he was out on the porch. "I'm Amish to the core, and non-resistant, but if you touch Ella again, God forgive me….I'll…."

"You'd break your Amish oath to be a pacifist?"

Zach rubbed the back of his neck and took a deep breath. "Daed would be ashamed of you if he were alive. He raised you to be a real man. To love your wife in the right way, just like he treated *Mamm*. With respect...you..."

"Go ahead and say it again, Zach. I act like Uncle Otis. Crazy Uncle Otis. That's what *Daed* said all the time."

"Well you do!" Zach shouted. He shoved a finger in Luke's face. "Ella's going to Granny Weaver's tonight and she *will* be picking up Ruth. Understand me? Tell Ruth that Ella will be here at six-thirty."

Ella clung to the door as she heard Luke laugh like a madman.

~*~

Lizzie put little plastic bags full of raisins on the shelf, but stopped when she heard Roman's voice asking her if she needed help. She turned to him, nervously straightening her black apron. She tucked lose brown hair back under her *kapp*, and then met his eyes, that were oddly cool. "Is something wrong?"

"My twins are sick and I came for medicine."

His nearness made her lose her train of thought. She struggled for words. "Sick? How sick are they?"

"Just have a cold or could be allergies. Can't tell."

Lizzie could take this closeness no longer and picked up the empty box beside her and started walking toward the register. "I'll get my daed. He's the expert."

"You always used to say that when – "

Lizzie's eyes met his. "When what?"

"When we were courting." He shook his head. "Don't know what made me think of that..."

Lizzie felt sweat form in her palms and her mouth grow dry. Why did Roman say such a thing? They'd never spoken of their courtship since Abbey died. Why now?

"You didn't listen to his expert advice though," Roman added, a bit sarcastic.

"Roman, what's wrong with you? Are you coming down with something too?"

"Nothing medicine can cure."

She lowered her jaw in shock. "Roman, say plainly what you mean…"

She saw him look around the room, then back to her. "You never listened to your daed's advice about building him a *dawdyhaus* next to us. There I said it. And now you know I'm still angry." He wiped sweat that was forming on his brow. "I'm still angry."

"But you chose Abigail…"

"I'm not regretting it either. She *loved* me."

"And I didn't? Is that what you think?"

She noticed Roman's face was too flushed. She was relieved to see her daed come in from the back room.

"Roman, what can I get you today?" Jonas asked.

Roman clung to the counter and put his head down. "I'm not feeling *goot.*"

"Daed, where's the thermometer?" Lizzie asked.

"In the top drawer of the dresser."

She ran across the store and opened the door that led to the house. *Roman's delirious; no wonder he was talking such nonsense.* She quickly retrieved the thermometer from the dresser that was in the living room and ran back to the store. She commanded Roman to sit down, and he obeyed. She placed the thermometer under his tongue and put her hand against his forehead. "*Ach*, he's burning up." When she heard the thermometer make its ringing sound, she quickly read it. "You have a fever of 103 degrees."

Jonas made his way over to the medicine and started to clumsily get two bottles. "Roman, you need to take these pills. Lizzie will make you some tea and show you where you can lay down."

"I have to go. I need medicine for the twins." Roman groaned.

"You listen to Daed, Roman." She let out a nervous laugh. "He's the expert, remember? Just lay down a spell."

She watched as Roman staggered toward the door. "I need to get home."

Lizzie looked at her daed, puzzled over what to do, and then she found herself running toward Roman and putting her arms around him, turning him to go into the house with her. He didn't resist.

~*~

Granny looked at her husband's hunched shoulders. "Jeb, you're exhausted and worried sick. The girls only have a cold."

He fingered his long gray beard. "Their temperatures are climbing. Where's Roman? It never takes this long to go to Miller's Variety and back."

Granny took her knitting loom off her lap and leaned it against the wall. She'd learned over the years to trust his instincts. The girls were getting sicker and needed medicine now. "Want me to go over and get medicine myself?"

"*Ach*, you're exhausted from cleaning up after the wedding and we have another one tomorrow. Wedding season. <u>Humph</u>. Really cuts into my fishing time."

"Jebediah, that is no way to talk. Marriage is sacred and every ounce of effort put into it is worth it."

"But the fish are just calling to me," he grinned. "Who's getting married tomorrow?"

"Levi and Marie. Dear couple they are."

"You sure you should be having your knitting circle with the girls sick?"

"Can't get word out this late if I cancel. Besides, we'll be at our place, not over here."

Granny heard Jack bark, a sure sign someone was coming up the driveway. Was Jenny home from school so early? She pulled back the white curtains and her heart flooded with joy. She saw her black lab following a buggy with Roman and Lizzie in it. She remembered all the times they slowly came down that lane. She narrowed her eyes as they got closer. Roman had his arm around Lizzie!

"Jeb, come look at this. *Ach*, praise be. I told you so...old man."

She watched as Jeb peered out the window, his brow furrowed. "He's leaning against her because he looks sick."

Granny clenched her fists. When would her husband admit she was right? She ran down the stairs and opened the front door to greet the young lovers, but was horrified to see Lizzie driving and Roman leaning on her for support, just like Jeb said.

Lizzie stopped the buggy. "Help me get him in bed. He insisted on coming home for the girls."

"*Ach*, he's sick too?" Jeb asked.

"*Jah*. His temperature was going down when I placed vinegar on his forehead, and he felt as right as rain to come home. On the way over, it spiked again."

Jeb ran to help Roman out of the buggy and get him onto the long cedar bench in the living room. Granny put a pillow under his head. Roman shot her a look of fear. "My girls. How are they?"

"Upstairs. They're fine." Granny winked at Jeb. "They were just asking for their medicine. Did you get it?"

Lizzie handed her a brown bag. "The directions are on the bottle. My daed said to follow them exactly."

Jeb grabbed the bag and ran upstairs. Granny watched as Lizzie pulled up a rocker next to Roman, fear in her eyes. "I'll stay and help Roman...and the girls."

Granny grinned. "Praise be." She went upstairs to help Jeb and told him Lizzie would be staying to help care for Roman and the girls.

Jeb looked at her in disbelief. "She can tend to the girls but not Roman. It's not done. Men tend to men and women to women."

Granny picked a piece of lint off of Jeb's black vest. "Maryann realized Colonial Brandon was the one for her because he nursed her back to health...when she was on death's door..."

Jeb groaned. "Deborah, are you reading those Jane Austen books again? Is it allowed?"

"As allowed as your *Pennsylvania Field and Stream* magazine. Course it is…old man."

Jeb collapsed into the chair between the girls' twin beds. He looked at Millie and then Tillie. "So precious when they sleep. Like angels." He smiled at Deborah. "As precious as you, Love." He held out his arms and she sat in his lap. "Means a lot to you that Roman sees Lizzie again, huh?"

Granny put her arms around her husband's neck. "*Jah*, it does."

Jeb gave her a squeeze. "Okay, we'll let Lizzie help the girls and Roman and I'll keep an eye on them…men should be taking care of men though….Old Woman."

~*~

Granny sat at the table and took the tea towel off the left-over raisin crumb pie from yesterday's wedding. She thought of her *mamm* teaching her to make this pie as a child, and smiled. She didn't have a picture of her *mamm*, since the Amish didn't believe in such things, but she had a clear image of her in her heart. Granny cut a piece and then got up and opened her woodstove to check on the pineapple upside down cake she had in the oven. She'd be taking something different to the wedding tomorrow. She was tired and thanked God for Betty Crocker who made wedding season so much easier. She heard Jack bark outside, and looked to see Fannie appear in the doorway.

"Hi Granny. I brought raisin crumb pie."

Granny opened her arms to embrace Fannie and pinched her cheek. "Feeling better?"

"Another wedding tomorrow, at Hezekiah's house, of all places. He'll be drooling all over Lottie. I don't want to go."

Granny sat on the bench and patted a seat next to her. "Sit down. I've wanted to share something with you."

Fannie sat beside her and took Granny's hand that was offered her.

"Do you think I'm fat?" Granny asked.

Fannie's eyes grew round. "Heavens no, you're thin."

"I feel fat though," Granny said. "Fatter than you."

"Come on Granny. Quit pulling my leg."

"Pull up your skirt and show your thigh."

"What?"

"You heard me."

Fannie obeyed. Granny sat closer to her. "See, we're the same size. So if you think I'm thin, why do you think you're fat?"

Fannie's eyes brimmed with tears. "I don't know. I have a fat face."

"You have a beautiful round face, the shape God intended."

Fannie embraced Granny. "You make me feel better, but it doesn't last long. I'm always thinking about my weight and how...fat I am compared to skinny girls like Lottie."

"You're taller than most women, and thank God for it. Quit comparing yourself to other women. Maybe

Lottie's at home right now wishing she was as tall as you."

"I doubt that. She's probably not home at all. Most likely Hezekiah asked her to come over to help prepare for the wedding. Didn't ask me."

"Can we come in Granny?" Ella asked through the screen door. "Looks like a private conversation…"

Granny stood up. "Ella, you brought Ruth. *Ach*, I'm tickled pink." She opened the door and gave Ruth a bear hug. She noticed that Ruth winced from pain. Most likely Luke had bruised her arms. Heat rose to her face until she felt like she was on fire. She turned to go to the kitchen for a glass of water.

"Granny, what's wrong?"

"Hot flashes," she said.

Ella laughed. "You're over the change of life, aren't you?"

Granny fumbled for words. "*Ach*, hormone imbalance is the blessing us women folk get until the day we die." She looked over at Ruth, whose head was down. She knew the truth. Why she was so hot…with anger. Looking to turn the conversation, she said, "Let's play a game tomorrow at the wedding. We'll keep an eye on Fannie and count how many young men look her way."

"Granny! What are you doing?" Fannie asked, hand on her heart.

"Trying to recondition that mind of yours. You feel like no men are attracted to you and it's just not true."

Ella chimed in. "It's true Fannie. I notice men practically gawking at you."

"You're just saying that to make me feel better."

Ruth put her hand up. "Ella doesn't say things to make people feel better, take it from me. She sees truth...truth we don't like to see."

Ella turned to her and gently embraced her. "I didn't mean to make trouble."

A sob escaped Ruth. "You and Zach did the right thing."

"Let's all have some pie and you can tell us what happened, Ruth. We can pray for you."

"Ella's praying, and she prays *goot*. No need for everyone to know."

Granny put plates and forks on the table and asked the girls to sit down. Soon they were all enjoying pie, when Granny ventured to probe Ruth further. "Luke acts like someone I knew long ago...Otis, his uncle. Actually, we courted for a spell."

"See Granny, the men liked you." Fannie sighed.

Granny rolled her eyes. "Yes, there were others beside Jeb, but when I met that man of mine, there were no others."

"How romantic," Ella said. "I feel the same about Zach. I couldn't have dreamt him up."

"Zach's a wonderful man," Granny said, "unlike his Uncle Otis, I'm sorry to say. He had a temper."

"D-Did he yell a lot?" Ruth asked.

Granny poked at her pie. "He did once and scared me to death. We were out on a buggy ride after a singing and I just kept quiet until I got home. Then I told my brothers and they had words with him."

"Like Zach did with Luke," Ella said.

Ruth gasped. "Ella, it's a secret."

Ella turned to Ruth and put her hand on her shoulder. "I am so sorry. It slipped."

Granny huffed. "No need to keep things like this hidden. I'm glad Zach confronted Luke. Faithful are the wounds of a friend, the Good Book says." She looked tenderly at Ruth. "We'll be praying for Luke, don't you worry. God sees a woman's broken heart and fill the cracks with His love."

Ruth turned as red as beets. "How would you know? You're not married to a….I can't say."

"I'm sorry, Ruth. You're right. I can't say how you feel or what the *goot* Lord will do, but I know he hears a cry for help. I have experience with that."

Ruth reached across the table for Granny's hand and she took it. "*Danki*, Granny. I plan to be here every Wednesday night for knitting. Luke said Zach helped him see I need women folk." She took a piece of pie. "He's mean one minute, then sorry the next and real nice. It's nerve wracking."

"We need your fingers too. You knit so quickly." Fannie said. "There's supposed to be a cold winter in Joplin." She looked over at Granny. "Where's Maryann and Lizzie?"

"*Ach*, I almost forgot. Maryann's exhausted from the wedding yesterday and is resting up for the one tomorrow," Ella said.

Granny took a bite of pie. "Lizzie's over at Roman's nursing them all back to health. Jeb was helping, but started to feel sick too. He's resting in our bedroom."

"So Lizzie's nursing Roman by herself?" Fannie gasped. "I best go over and help and —"

"You stay here," Granny said abruptly. "Lizzie's mighty capable since her dear daed's an herbalist. She knows what to do." Granny noticed the women looking at each other, bewildered. "Shall we start to knit? I do have so much yarn."

~*~

Roman grasped for Lizzie's hand. "Abbey, it that you?"

Lizzie didn't know to do. She'd read never to wake someone sleep walking. She remained silent.

"Abbey, I'm so glad you're here. Why don't you kiss me? Come lay beside me?"

Lizzie now understood why the Amish had a rule that men cared for men. She looked at Roman evenly. "It's me, Lizzie. Can't you see?"

Roman held his hand out to her. "I'm so sorry…Abbey. I should have told you. But I loved you more in the end."

Lizzie put a fresh washcloth in the bowl of ice water and placed it on Roman's forehead. He caught her hand. "Why are you being so cold to me? You don't forgive me, do you?"

Lizzie felt anger come from within her. His wife had been gone for three years. Abigail would always occupy his every waking hour, even when he was delirious. He released her hand and turned away from her. She thought of Melvin Yoder. He'd liked her since they were little and remained faithful to his words. It was almost unheard of for a man who was thirty to never be married. He said he'd tried to find love, even moving to Ohio for a spell, but he said he'd never be able to love anyone but her. She straightened her shoulders. For three years she'd hoped Roman would come around with no results; Roman actually acted cool toward her now. She was determined. She could learn to love Melvin, even if he was two years younger and seemed like a younger brother.

~*~

Granny couldn't sleep, so she slowly got out of bed, hoping not to wake up Jeb. She tip toed barefoot downstairs to her rocker and looked outside at the crescent-shaped moon. Clouds were moving quickly across the sky, sometimes obscuring her view of the moon. She thought of Ruth and how she was hiding her problems, then Fannie...how she hid her insecurities. Tears filled her eyes and she bowed her head in prayer:

Lord, you know I love these girls. I saw them grow up, but life is snuffing out their joy. I know I tease Jeb too much, but I thank you for that man. He's my strength and anchor in stormy seas, like you are Lord...only Jeb has skin on. I do pray you'll change Luke's heart. He's not right in the head. And help dear Fannie find love. She's so deserving of a fine man...if it's Roman, your will be done, but it's hard Lord to see things Your way sometimes. I still think Roman and Lizzie need to be together.

She opened her eyes and sat quietly, looking up at the moon. Peace flooded her. She'd cast her burden on

Christ, like the Good Book said to do. *Cast your cares upon the Lord for He cares for you*....she thought of each word of the scripture, especially '*cast*'. How many times did Jeb cast his fishing line until he caught a fish? Hundreds? She'd be casting this care on God again, she was sure. She did love these dear girls in her little knitting circle.

~*~

Maryann smiled as she watched Levi and Marie exchange vows. So young and innocent. She looked across the large living room to the men's side at her husband and love filled her heart. Her wedding day was sunny and cold, just like today. Weather good for cuddling, her Michael always said. Her love for him was so much sweeter and richer than the day they wed. The more they walked through life, side by side, in good times and in bad, made their union all the stronger.

She noticed Marie picked powder blue for her and her two attendants to wear. It fit her, having blue eyes. Her white apron and prayer *kapp* looked so crisp and fresh. Maryann's dress was mauve and neatly stored away until the day the *goot* Lord took her home. She mused. So much work to be worn only twice, the day you're married and the day you die.

When the vows were exchanged and the bishop blessed them, he announced them as man and wife. Everyone got up and the men started lining tables up against the outer walls. A special table in the corner for the bride and groom and their attendants was put up first. She felt a hand on her shoulder, and turned to see Michael.

"Remember when we sat in the *eck* table like that, having enough privacy for me to give you a peck?"

She winked. "A peck in the *eck*."

He kissed her cheek. "Why don't you go sit down and not overdo it in the kitchen. You've been too tired."

"We're related. We have to help. Now go help the men and quit fussing over me." She hugged him around the middle, and then headed toward the women in the kitchen. Granny Weaver met her on the way.

"We sure missed you last night. How come your Becca couldn't come?"

"I told Ella to tell you. Becca stayed overnight here to help."

Granny put her arm around Maryann. "Ella didn't tell us. She had other things on her mind and forgot."

Maryann felt like the room was beginning to spin. She grabbed on to Granny.

"What's wrong child?"

"I'm dizzy again. *Ach*, getting old."

"Then I'm a fossil. Maryann, you need to see a doctor. The fatigue and other symptoms you've been telling me about are your body's way of screaming for help. Listen to your body."

"I have eight *kinner* to tend to. I don't have time." She leaned harder on Granny.

"Fannie, come here. Help me. Maryann's ready to faint."

"I am not. You're embarrassing me."

Maryann put her hand up in protest, but was no match for Fannie. "You sit down and I'll do your chores in the kitchen. Understand?"

Granny giggled. "You can't win when Fannie's determined."

Maryann let Granny lead her to a bench along the wall. She leaned her head back and took a deep breath. She soon felt something cool in her hand. Ella had gotten her a glass of root beer. She drank the cool substance and within a few minutes the dizzy spell was over.

"You should get your blood sugar level checked," Ella said. "You may have hypoglycemia. I do and know all the symptoms."

"Or she may have the twenty-four hour bug like Roman and the twins. At death's door yesterday and right as rain now, having fun at a wedding." Granny clapped her hand and laughed. "Ten!"

"Granny, what on earth are you doing?" Ella asked.

"Remember? We're counting how many young men gawk over Fannie. Ten and counting."

Maryann chuckled. "How do you do it? You can make a game out of everything."

"I'm not playing a game, just trying to help Fannie rethink herself."

"Rethink herself?"

"You know, renew her mind, like it says to do in the Bible. To think of the good and not the bad."

"You mean have hope?" Ella asked.

"*Nee*, hope is expecting something *goot* is going to happen. I'd say she needs to see the truth. She's deceived somehow, thinking she's fat."

"Did anyone ever tease her as a child?" Maryann took another sip of root beer. "I know someone made fun of Becca when she was a wee one and she kept it locked up in her heart, until one day we talked about it. There's a root to Fannie's feeling. Best we find it and pull it out."

Granny took her hand. "Maryann, your girls are blessed to have such a *goot mamm*. I had five sons and always wanted a girl."

Maryann noticed Ella's honey-hazel eyes tear up. "Sit down beside me, Ella. We know the doctor gave you such sad news and here we are talking about our *kinner*. You were brave to go to the doctor."

Ella brushed away a tear that trickled down her cheek. "The truth sets you free, *jah*? Now Zach and I can plan our future better. We're looking into foster parenting."

Granny clasped her hands and smiled. "*Ach*, Ella, you and Zach will make the best parents for hurting *kinner*."

"*Danki* Granny. When I come by for knitting or just to pick up more yarn, I see Roman's darling *kinner* and the desire gets stronger to have our own. Just because I can't have them doesn't mean I can't love someone else's."

Maryann squeezed Ella's hand. "You see sunshine when God sends clouds, don't you?"

"She has hope," Granny said. "She expects the *goot* it going to happen, *jah*?"

Ella laughed. "*Jah*, I do."

Maryann looked over at Granny. "Twelve. I've counted twelve men staring at Fannie."

Ruth walked over and sat next to Ella. She whispered something Maryann couldn't make out, but she knew Ruth wasn't happy. She wished all married couples could be as happy as she and Michael were.

After a few minutes, Luke came over and demanded for Ruth to get in the buggy. She said she wanted to stay and said Ella and Zach would take her home. Maryann bowed her head in silent prayer for Ruth, but was jarred by Granny's voice. "Luke, Ruth and I have *lots* to chat about. Jeb and I *will* take her home. *Understand?*"

Maryann saw the shock on Luke's face. "I'm taking her home. She's my wife."

"Do I need to turn you over my knee like I did when you were a child?" Granny asked, her voice shaking.

Maryann knew her prayer was answered when Jeb came over and put his arm on Luke's shoulder. He whispered something in Luke's ear. Soon Zach came over and spoke in muffled tones to Jeb, and then the three men walked to the back door and went outside.

Maryann heard Granny gasp and she turned to her. "Your husband's doing the right thing."

"I know. I'm just shocked. Lizzie just put her arm through Melvin's."

"Well, it's about time! What's wrong with that?"

"Everything…" Granny whispered.

"Thirteen!" Maryann squealed. "Your Roman's staring at Fannie. Who would have guessed?" She heard Granny moan and watched as the dear woman leaned over and put her head in her hands, eyes closed, as if praying. She put a hand on her back. "*Ach*, come on, Granny, Roman needs to move on sometime."

~*~

Here is a recipe for raisin crumb pie, by Rebecca Byler from Smicksburg, PA ~ Enjoy!

Raisin Crumb Pie

¾ cup raisin

2 cups water

1 cup brown sugar

1 tablespoon vinegar

2 tablespoons cornstarch

Pinch salt

Bring all ingredients to a boil using cornstarch for thickening.

Cool. Pour into unbaked pie crust and top with crumb topping below.

CRUMB TOPPING

1 cup flour

½ cup brown sugar

¼ cup lard (or butter)

½ teaspoon baking soda

Bake until done.

Note: Many Amish recipes simply say, "bake." My daughter is a pastry chef and says most pies can be baked at 400 degrees for the first 15 minutes and then you need to reduce the temperature to 350 degrees and bake for another 45 minutes. I bake my pies at 350 degrees for an hour, afraid I'll forget to turn down the temperature. I get sucked into a good novel or knit when I bake and lose track of time. ;)

Lazy Wife Pie Crust

1 cup flour

3 tablespoons powdered sugar

½ cup oleo (Crisco or margarine)

Mix ingredients to make crumbs. Press into pie pan. Bake for 10 minutes until done.

EPISODE 3

Thanksgiving

Ella reached across the table to take her husband's hand, and they bowed their heads in silent prayer. She tied her loose prayer *kapp* strings and looked up. Concern was etched on Zach's brow. "What's wrong?"

"If we could have *kinner*, they might look like you…"

"A child's a gift from God, not matter how it comes to us. Let's look over the papers one more time. Are we forgetting anything?"

Zach clenched his pen and marked off the boxes again. "I think there's something we need to confess to the social worker. Luke's behavior."

"He doesn't live here. Whatever for?"

"Well, they want to know if anyone could be a threat to our foster child. You see how little Mica fears his *daed*."

Ella's jaw stiffened every time Zach's brother was mentioned. "Luke should be ashamed of himself. I'll make sure the child is never alone with him."

Zach's blue eyes brimmed with tears. "I'm so sorry you married into my crazy family."

Ella got up and sat on Zach's lap. "Your parents are gone but they were *goot* people. Luke's the only problem."

"And Uncle Otis."

"He lives in Ohio…"

"If he comes out to visit, he can't stay here."

Ella put both arms around Zach's neck. "Is that your only concern, or is it something else?"

Zach squeezed her tight. "Sometimes I think Luke's really crazy. I mean, he's mean as a bear caught in a trap one day and then fine the next."

"We need to have them over for dinner. Have a nice meal, and maybe if he sees your concern, he'll open up. Tell you what's wrong."

"I'm off Thursday and Friday for Thanksgiving, since it's an English holiday." He kissed Ella's cheek. "Luke works for the English, too. He'll be off…"

"Okay, so let's have them over on Thursday. I don't think there's a wedding that day either." Ella got up and ran to get her cookbook. "I've always wanted to make a Thanksgiving dinner. We could go to the Dayton auction and buy a turkey. *Nee,* I can't. Wednesday's knitting circle. Should we invite other families?"

Zach smiled, accenting his chiseled jawline. "I'll go to the auction and get a turkey. You love having company, don't you?"

"*Jah,* I do. I want to cook for a big family." She planted her pointer finger in a dimple. "We could take in more than one foster child. The case worker said siblings need to stay together."

Zach grinned and scribbled something on the foster parent application form. He handed it to Ella and she laughed. "Eight *kinner*? Are you serious?"

"Why not? There's lots of *kinner* that need a *goot mamm*

like you."

~*~

Granny put on a wool shawl and took a walk over to Roman's woodworking shop on the other side of his house. The wind whipped at her skirt and she thought of how the shawls sent to Joplin must be a real comfort. So many more to make, though.

When she entered the shop, she felt her knees grow weak. "Fannie, I didn't know you were here. Are you needing some rocking chairs?"

Fannie ran over to embrace Granny. "My sister, Eliza, is going to have a baby! We just got word. I wanted to order a little hickory baby rocker."

"*Ach,* you came the whole way over here for that? You could have placed an order tonight at the knitting circle."

Roman stopped fiddling with a piece of wood. "I brought Fannie here on the way back from Miller's Variety. We're going out to dinner at the Country Junction. I'll have her back here by seven for knitting, though."

Granny looked at Fannie, who was beaming. She'd been praying for this dear girl who was so pretty and thin, yet thought she was ugly and fat. Was Roman the answer to her prayer? She saw Roman's gaze was on Fannie. Was he looking at her like he did his dear deceased wife? But Fannie was only twenty-one. Surely Lizzie was the one for Roman. She remembered her "casting off" prayer and bowed her head and quickly cast this worry on the Lord.

"Well, you're welcome to eat with Jeb and me. I'm making stuffed cabbage rolls. Plenty to go around."

Roman looked at Fannie. "*Mamm's* a *goot* cook. Would you mind? We can take a buggy ride after dinner."

"*Ach*, I don't care. As long as we get to talk."

Granny held on to the side of the wall. So we can talk? What was going on?

~*~

Ruth rolled out dough to make biscuits. She jumped when Luke grabbed her by the waist. "Gotcha. You didn't even see me in the room."

"*Nee*, I didn't. Supper will be ready soon."

Luke sat at the round oak table. "So, are you looking forward to the knitting circle tonight?"

Ruth wasn't sure how to answer his question. It was tinged with sarcasm. "It's for a *goot* cause. *Jah*. I am."

"Sit down, Ruth. Supper can wait a few minutes."

Ruth turned to look at Luke. She thought of the November weather, warm one day and freezing cold the next; it matched her husband's moods exactly. She took a seat at the table opposite him.

He cleared his throat. "Jeb and Zach showed me something in the Bible I've never seen." He took a new pocket-size Bible from his pocket and took out a paper marker. "In Ephesians it says for wives to submit to their husbands."

Ruth felt her cheeks burn. How many times he'd reminded her of this scripture.

"But I never read the whole chapter. It says later for a husband to love his wife and not be harsh with her...or God won't answer his prayers." He lowered his head. "I'm sorry, Ruth. I see the bruises on your arms, but I don't do it on purpose. It's like I'm...possessed."

Ruth was glad of his confession, but it did little to make her feel safe in the future. He was saying he couldn't help himself. "So what are you going to do so this never happens again?" She pulled up her sleeve to reveal bruises on her wrists. "This happened after Jeb and Zach talked to you at the wedding and gave you that Bible."

"I'll just never do it again, is all. I'm trying to apologize."

Ruth looked into Luke's mellow blue eyes. He looked so much like his brother, Zach, when he was being kind. But one thing was missing. Sincerity. Or was she jaded toward him? After two years of being married to a man who treated her so cruelly, did she now have a hard heart? She turned away, hoping he couldn't read her mind. "I need to finish the stew. Mica will be hungry."

"I'm hungry, too." Luke came around the table and encircled her in his arms. She hated how he referred to a loving, intimate act like he was an animal. And at the most inconvenient times. She recoiled and felt his hand dig in her wrist. When she yelped, he surprised her by backing off, putting both hands up. "Did that hurt? Honestly?"

"*Jah!*"

He gently took her wrist and kissed it. "I don't know my strength, I suppose."

She looked into his eyes, and hints of the man she used to love punctured her heart. He was genuinely sorry. He drew near to kiss her, but she turned her head.

He kissed her cheek softly. "You'll see over time...I've changed." He walked away into the living room. She heard the melting snow drip into the rain barrel outside. Could God soften Luke's heart permanently? Deep down she missed that man she'd married.

~*~

Lizzie shoved more dried beans into a bag and put it on the scale. Two pounds exactly. She ripped off a plastic bag from the roll and tried to open it, but such force tore the bag. She sat down in the chair behind the counter, glad her daed and no customers were in the store.

The thought of Fannie's outright flirting with Roman, talking and laughing so much, she couldn't get a word in edgewise. And what audacity she had to ask Roman to take her to his shop to pick out a rocker. Lizzie clenched her fists. Why couldn't she open up to Roman, like Fannie? In no time, Fannie would have Roman proposing if she didn't open up and tell him why she'd called off their engagement years ago. But something told her it would make Roman despise her.

She heard her *daed* come into the store. He always had a smile on his face after being with his chickens, but now he was smiling about something else. "Look who stopped by again. Two times in one day." Someone opened the door and her *daed* swung in on his hand crutches.

Lizzie looked up to see Melvin. This tall, lanky man held hope in his erect shoulders. His green eyes edged with shaggy brown hair twinkled. She wondered if he'd look older as a married man, having to wear a beard.

Melvin strode over to the counter. "How'd you like to

go out to the Country Junction for dinner?"

"I, ah, I have chicken in the oven, Melvin," she said. "You can join us, though."

Her *daed* clapped his mangled hands together. "*Jah*, Melvin. Lizzie's a *wunderbar goot* cook. She'd make someone a fine wife."

"*Daed!*"

"*Ach*, I'm only teasing you, in a way." He looked at Melvin. "I guess I just feel guilty sometimes, having her all to myself. Lizzie should open one of those bed and breakfasts for tourist."

"That's a *goo*t idea," Melvin said, staring at Lizzie. "Your neighbors next door will have their farm up for auction. The *Englishers* who live there didn't pay their mortgage."

"Troutmans? Are you sure?" Jonas sat in a chair. "They're *goot* friends. Bill never mentioned anything to me."

"I suppose he was trying to work it out with the bank. They just told me when I delivered a clock." He turned to Lizzie. "I thought of Lizzie, and decided to stop in again…"

Lizzie was truly touched. Melvin had a loving heart, and didn't seem like the pesky little boy who liked her in grade school. He was thirty now and she thirty-two. It all seemed very…practical.

"Well, I'd like to know how much they want for that house," Jonas quipped. "Lizzie, I do think you could run one of those little hotels. You'd give it a woman's touch."

"*Daed*, we're debt-free. Why would we want a

mortgage?"

"I get bored with the store at times. Would be nice talking to folk from all across the country."

Lizzie had to admit the store was monotonous at times. Same customers and same dry goods to stock, day in and day out. She could also decorate a bed and breakfast with fancy curtains, like the ones she saw in Lancaster. The bishop gave her cousin special permission to use electricity, too. *Ach*, to have such luxuries, especially for her aging *daed*, who suffered from MS, would be a blessing. "*Daed*, if the price is right, I think we should do it."

Melvin looked at her and winked. "If you buy the place, I'll make a grandfather clock for it."

Lizzie's heart melted at Melvin's kind offer. She was seeing such fine qualities in him, now that she was trying to turn her attention away from Roman.

~*~

Granny pursed her lips as Jeb bent over and laughed. He hit his knee and laughed some more. "I told you so...Old Woman."

She shoved the wooden spoon into the large pot to swish the liquid around the stuffed cabbages. "I think they're just friends."

"And when was the last time our son had a *goot* female friend? Deborah, you have to admit I'm right."

"You put the idea in the boys' head, is all. He ran with it to please you." As soon as she said this, she knew she was digging a deeper hole. Their son never did anything he didn't want to. He was headstrong.

"What's wrong with Fannie?" Jeb asked. "She's already like a *dochder* to you."

"*Nee*, she's twenty-one. She calls me Granny for a reason. I'm old enough to be her granny. I could be Lizzie's *mamm*, though."

"But Colonel Brandon was twice the age of Maryann…" Jeb said.

Granny's eyes softened. "You're reading my books? *Ach*, and Sense and Sensibility at that?" She went over to her husband and got on her tiptoes to kiss his cheek. "Isn't it *goot*?"

"I flipped through it. Didn't really read it." He cleared his throat. "I read though that she was a preacher's *dochder* who grew up poor. Lived a real simple life."

Granny's eyebrows furrowed. "Where'd you read that?"

"Now don't get mad, Deborah, but I was over at the yarn shop in town. To buy you some colored yarn, and well, I asked Suzy to look up that lady on the Internet."

"Jeb, you fool. We're not allowed to use it."

"I didn't. Suzy did. I needed to make sure this Austen lady was a *goot* woman, since you're reading her books." He shifted his weight. "I ordered you another book, too."

Granny pushed at his chest. "Still don't make it right…what'd you get?"

"Well, Suzy recommended Pride and Prejudice, and I thought it would do you a heap of good. You're so prejudiced against Fannie, always saying Lizzie's the right one for Roman. It shows too much pride."

Fannie smiled across the table at Granny. "Supper was

so *goot. Danki.* Let me do the dishes." She got up and started to clear the table.

"I'll help," Jenny said. "I used to help my *Mamm.*"

"I can help, too," Millie said.

Fannie bent over and put her hand on Tillie's shoulder. "Do you want to help, too?"

Tillie nodded her head.

She put her hand on Granny's shoulder. "Now, you go relax before the women come for knitting."

Roman watched Fannie's green eyes sparkle as she talked to his girls. She was a natural *Mamm.* Why someone hadn't snatched her up yet was a mystery to him. He thought of his *Daed's* advice; to spend time with Fannie and see if he's drawn toward her. Nothing yet, only images of Lizzie flashed through his mind most days that gave him a wagon full of guilt. He should have told Abby before their wedding he still cared for Lizzie, but just couldn't risk losing her, too.

He walked over to his house to check the woodstove. After throwing a log in, he sat in his Amish rocker and closed his eyes. He needed to go out to the barn for the cow's second milking, but needed to rest a spell. Roman thought again of Abby's hope chest upstairs. He'd mentioned it to Fannie on their buddy ride, and she encouraged him to open it. He could tell Fannie about his guilty feelings for some reason. She was so easy to talk to and full of good advice.

When she said a woman's heart can be divided, too, some never getting over their first boyfriend, he was shocked. Was he too hard on himself? Should he go upstairs and read Abby's journal? Maybe she never got over the first man she courted. It seemed disrespectful, but Fannie encouraged him; even offered to look through it with him.

He tried to get the idea out of his mind, and closed his eyes to fall asleep, but the sound of buggies coming up the driveway and Jack barking kept him awake. He heard a man's voice call to his horse. Roman got up to look out the window, hoping it wasn't Luke. He'd made it clear he didn't want him coming around his girls with such a quick temper. His eyes widened when he saw Melvin helping Lizzie out of the buggy. Through the twilight, he could see she flashed him a smile that lit up her whole face. She'd never looked at him like that; she was so reserved around him. He felt silly spying but continued to watch. Lizzie looked so beautiful when she smiled; he'd almost forgotten. It was her warmth and love that had captured his heart, but she was showing affection to Melvin as they continued to talk in the driveway. What had he done wrong all those years ago to cause her to break off their engagement?

He watched as Lizzie kissed Melvin on the cheek and headed toward his *mamm's* house. Melvin watched her as she walked up to the porch. Jenny flew out the door and into Lizzie's arms. Roman's heart went into his throat. How his daughters needed a *mamm*.

~*~

"Well, Lord be praised, you're all here. And Maryann, you brought your Becca."

Becca beamed. "No relatives getting married this

week, and I'm glad."

Granny chuckled. "We depend on the young girls to help too much maybe, but you can do twice as much as us old folk." She looked around at the other women. "I'm talking about myself being old, not *yinz*."

Maryann put up her hand. "I'll admit I'm old. Forty – five and feeling it. So tired all the time."

"Too young to be so tired," Granny said.

Ella looked up from her loom. "Did you make a doctor's appointment yet? See if you have low blood sugar, like me?"

"I don't have time…"

"Make the time," Ruth said, coolly.

Granny's jaw dropped at Ruth's bluntness. She'd noticed a tougher spirit in her, and feared bitterness was taking root

"You have one child, Ruth. I have eight," Maryann said. "When you have more *kinner*, you'll understand."

"Don't want any more *kinner*." Ruth got up to pour hot water from the tea kettle. She fumbled to open a tea bag and ripped it in half, spilling lose black tea all over the counter. Lizzie got up to help her. "I did this today at the store. I kept ripping bags. I've been so edgy lately."

"Melvin on your mind?" Fannie teased.

Granny watched Lizzie's face intently. It was how people reacted that she took to heart. Anyone could put on a show. When Lizzie had no twinkle in her eye when talking about Melvin, she wanted to leap for joy. A woman's eyes couldn't hide a thing. She looked at Lizzie more intently. "I know Roman stopped by today. Did he do something to unnerve you?"

Granny watched with delight as Lizzie's face reddened and she fumbled for words. "*Nee,* ah, he just came in, ah, to buy a whoopie pie. He said you don't make pumpkin ones like I do."

Now Granny had to get up and make some tea. She wanted to dance over to the counter. She didn't even ask Roman to go and get her a pie. He went on his own. Praise be. He was seeing the light. Lizzie was the one for him.

"I'd like the recipe," Ella said. "I collect pumpkin recipes, since I have so much filling put up."

"*Ach,* I have a recipe for pumpkin cheesecake," Granny said. "I'll write it down before you go."

"I'll take it. *Danki,* Granny."

Becca looked up from her knitting loom. "Ella, when can we have another baking day?"

Ella smiled at her across the room. "*Ach,* soon I hope. I may need you as a little *mamm's* helper, too."

All the women stopped knitting and gawked at Ella. "*Nee,* I'm not pregnant, but we are applying for foster kids…lots of them."

"Will they be little or teenagers like me?" Becca asked. "I'd love for you to get a girl my age. We'd have fun."

"She'd be in school all day. The English go to school up through twelfth grade."

"I'm glad we only have to go up to eighth grade." Becca sighed. "All I want is to bake all day, anyhow."

Granny always marveled at Becca's tender heart. At fourteen, she was responsible enough to raise a family.

"You'd be *goot* with little ones and a friend to any teens that they may get."

Becca looked over at her *mamm*, and then whispered into Granny's ear. "Kind of tired of little ones."

Granny hid a giggle. Having been the oldest girl in her family, she understood. She looked over at Maryann and noticed the woman was barely staying awake. "I'm making a doctor's appointment for you and I'll make sure Suzy can drive you. I'll go, too."

Maryann looked at her. *"Danki.* I'm so tired and dizzy again."

Fannie got up to make a cup of tea. "Have *yinz* ever heard of 'Black Friday'?"

"Sounds spooky," Ella laughed. "What on earth is it?"

"It's what the English call the day after Thanksgiving. I got a flier in the mail. All yarn and craft supplies are seventy-five percent off at Punxsy-Mart if you go early in the morning." She snickered. "The English think five in the morning is early. I say we go and get things on our winter craft lists."

Granny clapped her hands. *"Wunderbar goot* idea. I need some canvas to do needlepoint."

Ella sighed. "I need embroidery thread. I'm working on a baby quilt, just in case we get an infant. I want to embroider kittens on each square."

"Ach, like the one in Emma's quilt shop?" Granny asked.

"Jah," Ella said. "It's red and white. I think it's dear."

"I made that," Granny said. "I can help you." She looked over at Fannie. "Do you think we can get a driver that early?"

"And to take all of us?" Ella asked.

"*Jah*, Suzy has a van. I'll ask."

"I won't be going," Ruth snapped. "No money in the budget for crafts."

Ella turned to her. "Have you asked Luke?"

"*Nee*, what's the point? He says the same thing every time I ask for craft money. 'It's a waste of hard earned cash'."

Granny cringed at the coldness in Ruth's voice. "Sugar makes medicine sweet," she said. "Why not put some sweetness in your asking?"

Ruth looked across the room at her evenly. "Granny, you think a few words to my husband by your Jeb and Zach will cure everything, don't you? Well, it doesn't. Luke's broken my heart, and there's no cure."

"*The Lord is nigh unto them that are of a broken heart...Psalm 34:18*," Maryann said. "I've meditated on that verse and it seems like God's not close to the ones who are suffering for no reason. But He wants to help...to heal."

Ruth put her head down. "You think He'd help me, even though my faith teeters all over the place?"

"He wants to help you more because your faith waivers, I think," Ella said.

"*Jah*, I agree," Granny said. "He leaves the ninety-nine sheep and goes to look for one that is lost." Granny got up walked over to Ruth. She cupped her cheeks in her hands. "We're not only praying for you, dear girl. We're here to hold you up." Granny soon felt tears on her hands and bent down to hug Ruth. The other women got up and one by one embraced her. Granny stood back and thanked God He gave her the idea to have this little knitting circle.

~*~

Ella took the turkey out of the oven and stuck the meat thermometer in it. It needed to cook longer, so she popped it back in the oven and turned the egg timer to fifteen minutes. She put a toothpick in the pumpkin cheesecake and looked at it carefully. It was clean, so the pie was done. Ella went to her pantry to get two cans of cranberry sauce and grabbed the hand can opener. She went over to her china closet to get a fancy bowl and after opening the store-bought cans of chunky cranberries, dumped them in. When the clock chimed twelve-thirty, she panicked. She didn't even have the mashed potatoes done yet. When Zach came into the room with his white shirt and black pants and vest, she couldn't hide her smile. "You're wearing your for *goot* clothes?"

"*Jah*, it's a special day. Are you ready?"

"I was going to wear what I have on. Should I put on my *goot* dress? I don't have time. I don't have the mashed potatoes done."

Zach went to her and planted a kiss on her cheek. "I'll finish the potatoes."

She hugged him quickly. "*Danki.*"

Ella ran upstairs and quickly changed into her burgundy dress and put on a fresh white apron. Why hadn't Ruth and Luke come to help, like planned? She sat for a minute to collect herself. Luke always made her feel so nervous. She'd never said a word to anyone, except Granny, that it seemed like Luke lusted after other women...after her. Did Ruth ever notice her husband's eyes on other women, even after church? She bowed her head and silently prayed the Lord would give her strength to get through this meal. That she and Zach, and Granny and Jeb, could teach by example how to love your spouse. And she added a special Thanksgiving prayer that Becca could come. Ella wasn't old enough to be her *mamm*, but Becca treated her like one, and she filled a void in her life.

She heard the clip-clop of horse hoofs and ran downstairs. Luke would laugh in Zach's face if he found him helping in the kitchen. She was relieved to see it was Granny and Jeb. She opened the side door and welcomed them in.

When Jeb saw Zach smashing the potatoes, he looked at Granny and grinned. "I thought I was the only man in town that helped cook."

"You're *goot* to a tired old woman." Granny pinched his cheek. "Maybe we will all rub off on Luke and Ruth, *jah*?"

Zach looked puzzled. "Ruth? It's Luke that needs to change."

"Well, I suppose you're right. I just want to see them both loving and respecting each other. Ruth has such a broken heart that's getting nippy."

Ella heard more wagon wheels and looked out the window. It was Michael, dropping off Becca. Ella opened the door and even though a cold draft flew in, her heart was warmed by Becca's embrace.

"*Danki* for asking me to come." She picked up the basket at her feet. "I made two pies, all by myself."

"*Ach*, you run circles around me," Granny said. "Let me take them and warm them in the oven."

Ella looked at the clock. It was almost one. Luke and Ruth said they'd be over by noon. Zach was looking forward to shooting clay pigeons with Luke like they used to when they were boys...try to bond over old times...goot times.

~*~

"There's no need to feel guilty," Fannie said. "Go ahead and open the chest."

Roman sighed. "I know, but why do I feel so nervous?"

"Because you're afraid. When you open that, all the memories you held dear with Abby will come back...but she's not here. You might miss her more."

Roman took Fannie's hand. "How'd you grow up so fast? I remember when you came as a mother's helper, but now you're a...woman."

"*Jah*, I was fourteen when Jenny was born and I remember running for diapers when Abigail called. Seems like yesterday."

"Seems like a lifetime ago to me. Raising these girls alone has been hard."

"Thank the *goot* Lord you have your *mamm*."

"I am thankful, but the girls need a real *mamm*." His eyes locked with hers, but she looked away.

"Are you ready?" she asked.

They both reached for the latch of the chest and his hand rested on hers. He felt heat rise like a schoolboy. Why?

Fannie opened the chest, and laying on the top was an old phonebook. She gently opened it to find pressed wildflowers. She lifted one up. "The petals look like butterfly wings."

Roman felt oddly peaceful. He remembered how much Abby loved to press purple flowers. This was a craft his girls could easily learn. "I should have opened this before. I'll show the girls the flowers and tell them how their *mamm* did this."

Fannie gasped. "Her knitting loom! *Ach*, Roman. Your girls will treasure this always, like Becca does her *Oma's*."

Roman took the knitting loom and ran his fingers over the smooth oak wood. Abby's *opa* had made her this loom; another treasure for his girls. A stab of guilt ran through him. It was selfish to not open this chest sooner; he was protecting his heart, but what about the hearts of his daughters? They needed to know more about their *mamm*.

Soon Fannie handed him a floral quilted journal. He put up his hand. "I can't read that."

She put a hand on her hip. "*Ach*, yes, you can. I bet you'll find Abby loved someone before you, and all this guilt over having loved Lizzie on your wedding day is sheer nonsense. Maybe she left part of her heart back home in Volant, too."

Roman knew Abby had courted other fellows before him. Was Fannie right? He took the journal.

Ella heard a bang on the door and jumped with a start. She hadn't heard a buggy pull up. She ran to the side door and saw Luke, Ruth, and Mica. "Our buggy slipped on some ice and we lost a wheel. A nice Englisher gave us a ride," Luke said, dusting the snow off his black wool hat.

"Where's the buggy now?" Zach asked.

"Well, it happened over by Rueben Byler's and they said they'd shoe the horse for me. Just need to pick her up."

"That was kind," Ella said. "Take off your coats and hang them on the pegboard. We need to eat before the food gets cold."

"Sorry I couldn't help," Ruth said, head down.

"*Jah*, it's embarrassing to come empty handed," Luke added sarcastically, "but Ruth can't make pies like yours anyhow, Ella."

Ruth continued to look down and Ella felt Luke's eyes on her.

"Luke, why not sit down at the table?" she asked, evenly. She was relieved when he nodded and headed toward the table. She led Ruth into the utility room and took her by the chin and looked in her eyes. "What's wrong?"

"We've been fighting all day. I burnt a pie and he ridiculed me, then when the horse lost its shoe, I told him it needed looked at last week. I did tell him that but he doesn't pay attention." She tucked stray brown hair into her kapp. "I am so sick of him."

Ella flinched at the coldness in Ruth's jet black eyes. Was her heart broken beyond repair, like she'd said? She led Ruth out to the table; Ruth did not sit by Luke, but slid on the bench next to Granny.

~*~

"Well, I can still shoot clay pigeons better than *yinz* 'boys'," Jeb said with a snicker. "*Ach*, hunting and fishing, it makes me feel whole."

"You say Deborah encourages you to fish?" Luke asked. "Hunt too?"

"It's important to me. Of course she does." He cleared his throat. "That's what love is…putting the others needs before your own."

"Well, Ruth doesn't encourage me to do anything but work and fix stuff around the house."

"Do you encourage her to do anything?" Zach snapped.

"Jah, the knitting circle she goes to."

"*Ach*, remember, I insisted she go."

Jeb readjusted his black wool hat. "Hey, there's times when Deborah gives all the encouragement because of my blind side, but she doesn't keep a record of wrongs, like the Good Book says to do." He stroked his long gray beard. "Luke, what made you marry Ruth?"

Luke's eyes grew round. "We dated since I was sixteen and she was fifteen. It was only right that we got married when we were older."

"But why'd you pick her? There're lots of girls at singings. What made you go up to her and ask her to go riding after a singing?"

"I didn't. She asked me."

Jeb coughed to hide laughter. "Okay, so she asked you.

What made you say yes?"

"I don't know. She's kind of pretty, although quiet."

"So she was quiet, yet she asked you to go riding? So you liked her tenacity?"

"*Jah*, maybe I liked how daring she was. Over the years I've tried to tame her, though."

Zach sighed. "Say what?"

"She's too outspoken. I'm taming her."

"You're breaking her spirit…"

Jeb put his hand on Zach's shoulder. "Luke, Deborah's as spunky as they come. I loved that about her since the day we met. It's her God given personality."

Luke's eyes were as round and big as wagon wheels. "What if she tries to rule over me?"

"Okay, now I think we're finding the root to your iron fist," Zach said. "You're afraid if you give an inch she'll take a yard?"

"*Jah*, she needs to know I'm the boss and what I say goes. How else is there order in the home?"

"By loving your wife!" Jeb shouted, surprising himself. "When I see Ruth I see a locked up bird, flying against the metal bar of a cage…the cage you've made for her. You need to let her fly."

Luke turned to go but Jeb and Zach stopped him. Jeb pulled out a leather book from his pocket. "I want you to read this. It's a little book of scriptures and things I've learned over forty-some years of marriage. I wrote it out for you to use. Add to it if you want." He sighed. "I don't want you getting a warning from the bishop."

Luke looked at him with wild eyes. "A warning for

what?

"Abusing your wife. We know about the bruises on her arms."

Luke slammed the book to the ground, his chin quivering. "She bruises easily. I don't hit her."

Jeb put his hand on his heart. "You bruise her in here, where it's harder to heal. Now we're your friends, but we won't be covering for your behavior." He picked up the book. "You read this and come to me if you have a problem."

Zach put his hand on Luke's shoulder. "You can come to me, too."

Jeb said a prayer of thanks when he saw Luke bow his head and heard him sob. He knew something deep in him, something cold and icy, was cracking and beginning to thaw.

~*~

Granny watched as Fannie, and her short, red-haired English friend, Suzy, nearly skipped down the aisle at Punxsy-Mart, straight to the craft section. Granny wondered why Fannie was so chipper at four in the morning. Was she was excited to get a good deal on embroidery thread? Or did she have a secret romance going on...with her son? Granny grimaced inwardly. How many times was she going to have to cast this need to see Roman and Lizzie married on the Lord?

She looked over at Maryann. "I'm so glad you and Becca could make it."

Maryann gave Granny a side hug. "I've been feeling better since I started that hypoglycemia diet."

"When? Yesterday? *Ach*, you need to go to the doctor, not just guess what's wrong."

"Well, I feel a real change. Isn't it kind of clear low blood sugar's my problem?"

"*Ach*, Maryann, you avoid the doctor like the plague."

Becca pushed past them and Maryann chided her. "Don't act like these crazy *Englishers*, grabbing at things like chickens do their corn."

"*Mamm*, I'm just catching up to Fannie and Suzy."

Maryann turned back to Ella and Ruth. "I've only seen Punxsutawney packed like this on Ground Hog Day. I don't like crowds…they make me nervous."

"I think it's exciting," Ella said, as she took Ruth's hand to try to catch up to Becca.

Granny noticed Lizzie stayed behind, and she offered her hand to her. "What's ailing you, child?"

"Nothing. Not used to all this noise, is all."

Granny's eyes narrowed. "You look sad. Now what's wrong?"

"You're embarrassing me," Lizzie whispered.

Granny told the rest of the group that she and Lizzie were going to look at cookbooks. When Lizzie protested, she gripped her hand and hauled her toward the book section. "I'm old but not daft. You've been crying."

Lizzie pulled away. "I'm coming down with a cold. I'm fine."

"It's the craft season, right?" Granny said. "If you were to marry in early spring, you might be buying material for a new dress."

Lizzie put her head down. "I know. And I might

be…"

Granny put her hand on her heart. "Be what?"

"Getting new material today. Melvin and I are courting and he said we're not spring chickens anymore."

Granny felt a knot in her stomach, then a sharp pain. She grabbed at her middle, and felt Lizzie's arm under hers, leading her to a bench. "Granny, are you sick?"

"*Nee,* just shocked. Are you engaged to Melvin?"

"Not yet, but we're talking about a future together."

Granny stared at the magazines and then looked at Lizzie evenly. "Marriage is for a long time. Do you love Melvin?"

Lizzie pursed her lips. "I like him a lot. He's goot to me."

"*Ach*, Lizzie, I could say the same of my dog, Jack. Do you have romantic feelings for him?"

"Romantic feelings died long ago."

Granny noticed Lizzie stiffened and her eyes looked like a wounded deer's. She put her hand on hers. "Lizzie, what is it?"

"Granny, I see how you and Jeb are, even after all these years. I don't have the love in my heart to love like you do."

"Nonsense," Granny said, patting Lizzie's hand. "I see lots of love in that big heart of yours. The way you care for your Daed, and how you nursed your *mamm* when she was ill."

"We're talking about romantic love, and I've been…hurt over the years."

Granny felt heat rise in her cheeks. "You broke off the

engagement with Roman and he was hurt, but moved on. It's been eleven years since –"

"You can't understand what I've been through, Granny," Lizzie snapped. "Now I need to get some material and embroidery thread. I won't talk about this anymore."

Lizzie got up and headed toward the craft section, and Granny felt the life run out of her. What could have hurt Lizzie so badly that she hadn't healed yet? Was she bitter toward Roman, like he'd said?

She was so tired and wondered why she agreed to come shopping. She stared at the aisle in front of her. Granny spied some fishing magazines and thought she'd get one for Jeb, but froze when she saw Fannie race down the magazine aisle and snatch a magazine. A glamour magazine? She cleared her throat loudly and Fannie looked her way.

Like a child, Fannie put the magazine behind her back. "There're great recipes in here."

Granny put her hand out as Fannie reluctantly gave her the magazine. She flipped through the glossy pages and gasped. "These women are half naked." She shook her head in disgust. She heard Suzy's voice but didn't look up, shocked at the images in front of her. "Have they no modesty?"

Suzy sat by Granny and looked at the pictures. "The worst part is that those women aren't as skinny as they look. Their bodies are changed by a computer."

"How?" Fannie asked.

"I can show you from my computer how it's done."

Suzy put her nose in the magazine. "No one looks this good. Perfect body, perfect skin. It puts pressure on us women to look like them."

"Not if we don't look at them," Granny said, eying Fannie. "We're allowed to look at magazines that are pure and beautiful and true, like the Good Book says. But this isn't true, is it Suzy?"

"Heavens no. And lots of women who look at them get eating disorders, starving themselves to be this ridiculously thin."

Granny slowly looked up at Fannie. "How long have you been looking at magazines like this?"

Fannie's chin quivered. "A few years now."

Suzy got up and put an arm around Fannie. "Is that why you're always saying you're fat?"

"I don't know…"

Suzy led her over to a full length mirror and Granny followed. "Look in this mirror. You can see you're not fat, right?"

Granny watched in horror as tears welled up in Fannie's eyes, then spilt down over her cheeks. "*Nee*, I don't see I'm thin at all. I have huge hips and fat legs. Bigger than I thought."

Suzy took Fannie by the shoulders. "You're coming to my place after we're done shopping. I'll show you how this is done and you'll see how deceived you are. The truth will set you free."

~*~

Granny sat in her rocker, gazing up at the full moon. Another restless night, where she needed to do more casting off prayers. The wind rattled the windows and she pulled her shawl up over her shoulders. She couldn't get the images Suzy brought up on the computer out of her mind. The before and after pictures were downright deceitful. Women's waists where shaved down to an unnatural size and their skin was too perfect.

Her heart sank, thinking Fannie had compared herself to these women for years. She opened her well-worn Bible to the verse that helped her feelings of insecurity in her courting days. She ran her finger down the page until she found 2 Corinthians 10:12:

For we dare not class ourselves or compare ourselves with those who commend themselves. But they, measuring themselves by themselves, and comparing themselves among themselves, are not wise.

She'd make Fannie memorize this verse and meditate on it until it got into her heart. Fannie needed to guard her heart, like the Good Book said.

Granny leaned her head back and her eyes misted. She thought of the day she'd caught Jeb's eye. He made her feel like she was the best thing since ice cream, and still did. As she aged and wrinkles etched her face, Jeb joked and told her another angel had kissed her, like they did to make Tillie and Millie's dimples. Jeb's love had made all fear of rejection go away. Granny knew there was healing in being loved by a good mate, like Jeb.

She bowed her head to pray:

Lord, I love Fannie like my own. Speak to her heart about how beautiful she is, and if it be Your will, bring someone along who can bring healing, like my Jeb did for me…even if it's Roman.

And Lord, give Luke a loving heart toward Ruth. Help him get to the root of why he treats women with so much disrespect.

I'm here casting my cares on You, Lord, because I know You care about me. I'm so thankful that our little knitting circle is getting close knit, but it seems the closer we're spun together, the more burdens I see…Give me strength to keep encouraging the girls, as You knit our hearts together, in love.

In Jesus Name,

Amen

~*~

Here is a recipe you can make for Thanksgiving. Enjoy!

Pumpkin Cheese Pie

8 oz. cream cheese

¾ cup sugar

2 Tbsp. flour

1 tsp. cinnamon

¼ tsp. nutmeg

½ tsp. ginger

¼ tsp. vanilla

3 eggs

2 cups pumpkin puree

Beat cream cheese, sugar and flour in a large bowl. Add remaining ingredients, and beat until smooth. Pour into pie crust and back at 350 degrees for 50-55 minutes. Pie is ready when a fork is inserted into center of pie and it comes out clean. Serve warm.

EPISODE 4

Snowflakes

Fannie walked out of Granny's little house, shaking her head. She seemed to be encouraging her to get to know Roman more. Why? Yes, Roman was a handsome widower, but a decade older, with three kids. Was Granny so tired of helping with the girls that she was trying to get him a wife?

She pulled her black cape around her to shield her from the December chill and snowflakes swirling around, and walked over to Roman's. When he greeted her at the door, she did what Granny asked.

"Hi Roman. Your *mamm* said you needed help sprucing your house up."

Roman tilted his head to one side. "Does she think my house is dirty? I'm as clean as they come."

"She said you needed a woman's touch. Anyhow, maybe we can look in Abigail's hope chest again."

Roman motioned for her to come in. "I'm glad you talked me into going through her things. For three years I've been so selfish. The girls are going through all those pressed flowers we found and making pictures."

"How?"

"Give me your cape and bonnet and I'll show you." He motioned for her to come into the kitchen. "Do you want some hot chocolate or anything?"

"*Nee*, I just had some at your *mamm's* and don't want to get fat."

Roman narrowed his eyes. "Fannie, *Mamm* told me you've been looking at those magazines at Punsxy-Mart. I've seen the covers; can't help it when you're in the checkout line. No one looks like that."

"So she keeps telling me…"

"Well, I think you're pretty and don't let anyone dampen that spirit of yours. Promise?"

Roman thought she was pretty? Was he just saying that because he felt sorry for her? "*Danki*, Roman. No more glamour magazines."

Roman grinned and grabbed a paper off the basket that hung on the wall. "Look what the girls made you."

Fannie took the card covered with pressed flower. On the top read it read, Sisters Day. She opened the card and read:

Dear Fannie,

We see mamms taking their girls out on Sisters Day. We don't have a mamm. Can you take us? We can't drive the buggy. And you're fun.

Jenny, Tillie and Millie

She held the card to her chest. "Those precious girls of yours. They're going to make me cry. What an honor to be picked."

"You're their favorite of all the women who go to the

knitting circle. Glad they see more of you."

Fannie felt tears well up. "Well, I love them like my own, if I was married and had my own." She forced herself to stop fumbling with words. She needed to recondition her mind like Granny said. She was a catch for any Amish man and would have her own *kinner* someday.

"Well, where do I start cleaning?" she asked.

"Ach, we fooled you. The card was a surprise."

"Why didn't Granny just give it to me, or the girls?"

"I don't know. She told me to give it to you in private. Maybe she thought since I'm their *daed*?" He smiled at her broadly. "I think you're just what my girls need."

Was it her imagination, or was Roman looking at her in a romantic way? She felt heat on her cheeks. "Want to look in Abigail's hope chest?"

"I was hoping you'd be with me again to look inside. It's pretty unnerving. Do you have the time?"

"I'll make the time," Fannie grinned.

~*~

Granny thanked God that Ella could go to Maryann's doctor's appointment with them. Ella was a burst of sunshine in the dead of winter and Maryann seemed so glum. Suzy pulled her car up to the doctor's office and said she'd be back soon; she had to get some groceries. Ella and Granny sat on either side of Maryann in the waiting room.

"You know *yinz* are overreacting. I'm fine," Maryann said. "There's a billion things I could be doing today. It's Tuesday – Laundry Day, remember?"

"Ruth and Lizzie are helping with your wash," Granny grinned. "Our knitting circle is a force to be reckoned with, *jah*?"

"*Jah*, that's for sure. But my baby needs fed."

Ella rolled her eyes. "Becca's fourteen, not five. I remember helping my *mamm* bottle-feed babies. Store bought milk won't kill your *kinner*."

"But Dan Miller's against it, and he's the best naturopath around."

Granny knew this was going to be a long, unpleasant visit to a much needed doctor's appointment, but held her tongue. She looked at some of the others in the office. Some looked like they had the flu and fear shot through her. The flu at her age wasn't good. Should she get a flu shot like Jeb encouraged her to do? Maybe Maryann's demise of going to doctors bothered her, because she was the same. *Nee.* She'd lived to be in her seventies by good eating and not being idle.

Soon a nurse called for Maryann and they followed her into a room where the doctor would see her. The nurse cocked her head. "Are you related?"

"*Nee*," Maryann said. "They made me come."

The nurse bit her lower lip, and Granny noticed she was trying to hide laughter. "You see other stubborn people here, too, don't you, Nurse?" Granny asked.

"Oh, yes." She turned to Maryann. "You should be glad you have friends who care."

Maryann put her head down. "I'm afraid."

"Why?" Granny probed. "Is it because you've been hiding other symptoms?"

"*Jah*, I have."

The nurse looked at Maryann's chart. "Well, maybe it's nothing at all. You're raising eight children and that would be stressful. Giving birth to so many can deplete you of minerals. You may just need a supplement." She turned to Granny and then Ella. "Let's hope for the best. And ladies, you've made my day. It's so nice to see friends who really care about each other. I live here and barely have time to see my sisters."

"Ach, have a Sister Day," Ella encouraged.

"Sister Day?"

"*Jah,* don't the English have a day where you just go out and catch up with your sisters?"

The nurse pursed her lips. "No. But that needs to change, huh? Great idea." She looked at her watch. "I'm on break soon. I'm going to email my sisters to see when we can put it on the calendar." She beamed. "I'm glad to be working here in Punxsutawney and meeting so many Amish people. Sometimes I wish I were Amish."

~*~

Self-pity threatened to choke Ruth. The Bishop was coming to talk to her husband, but Ella chose to be with Maryann instead of her. She needed Ella's support. Two men against one woman would be unfair.

She looked out at her birds to try to calm down. The mourning doves mated for life. Is that why they mourned? She put her hand on her heart. I am becoming so calloused towards marriage. Help me, Lord.

She heard a buggy pull in and looked out to see Luke. Fury was etched into his face, and fear gripped her heart.

When he opened the side door and marched in, leaving a trail of dirt and snow all over her clean floor, Ruth gripped the sides of her rocker, but said nothing.

"This better be important to have me take a half day off at work."

"*Jah*, the Bishop said it couldn't wait."

Luke collapsed in an Amish rocker across from her. "He needs to hear my side. I'm glad he's coming. All your yackin' is giving me a bad reputation. She will do him good and no evil all the days of her life...the Bible says that's the woman's lot. You nag too much."

Ruth wanted to slap him, but soon heard a buggy pull in. She went to her kitchen to put water in the tea kettle and looked at her basket to see chamomile on hand. *Goot* for my nerves. She heard Luke answer the door and turned to see the Bishop. Ruth nodded and looked deeper into his eyes. Did she see pity?

"Would you like some tea to warm you up, Bishop?" she asked.

"*Nee*. I have a thermos full of hot chocolate in the buggy. Let's talk."

They all took a seat in the living room. Ruth sat on one side and Luke on the other. The Bishop asked them to sit on the bench together, so he could speak to them easier. He looked at Luke. "I've heard some disturbing reports of how you treat your wife."

Luke put both hands behind his shoulders and slouched. "Well, I'm glad you're here, Bishop. Now you can hear my side."

"Your wife has bruises on her arm, is that right? To

me, there is no other side!" the Bishop boomed.

Luke shot up. "It says in Proverbs there's two sides to a coin."

The Bishop groaned. "Sit down and tell me your so called side."

"Well, she's a nag. Always pestering me…provoking me to anger, like the Bible says not to do. Fix this and do that, on and on, drip, drip, drip."

"About what?"

"Getting indoor plumbing for starters. My *mamm* lived with a hand cranked pump, and she never complained."

"I made sure Sarah had a gravity fed spigot. She washes too many dishes and it makes her tired. I think a goot husband would want to help carry his wife's burdens before anyone else's."

"I don't have money for all that plumbing. And that's not the only thing. She burns so much food, we're nearly starved."

"Luke, I see something in Ruth's eyes. She's a nervous wreck and most likely is very distracted." He turned toward Ruth. "Is that true?"

She didn't know if she should tell the Bishop about how tired she was, and how hard it was to focus. He might think something was wrong with her. But something inside her rose up; desperation. She needed help. "I'm, ah, tired all the time and forgetful."

"I've seen this before," the Bishop said. "It's too much stress, Ruth. Go to the doctors to rule out anything else, but stress and fear are written all over your face. Come here, child."

Ruth felt her chin start to shake, and then her body as she went toward the Bishop.

"Can I see your arms?"

"That's not fair! She bruises too easy," Luke shouted.

Ruth rolled up her sleeves and held them out for the Bishop to see.

The Bishop took her hands and fire came out of his eyes. He shot a look at Luke. "You have six weeks to repent, or you'll be under the ban. You're to love your wife, not abuse her."

"Show me in the *Ordnung*! We all agreed on those rules," Luke yelled.

The Bishop stood up and walked over to Luke and sat next to him. "Are you so daft to think our *Ordnung* is more important than what the Bible teaches? *Nee*, never. I married *yinz*, and you vowed to love and cherish and not be harsh with your wife. You broke an oath." He took off his black wool hat and placed it next to him. "Jeb gave you a little book to read. Did you read it?"

"*Nee*, I don't need to. I know what I live with and –"

"Luke! Are you saying you have no intention to repent? To get help from men like Jeb and Zach, who have *goot* marriages?"

"*Jah*, that's what I'm saying. I won't have Ruth and her meddling knitting friends rule over me. This all started because of them and they yacked to their husbands."

"I'll give you two days to reconsider. I have no other choice than to put you under the ban if you don't change your decision." He rubbed his temples. "I came prepared for the worst. Ruth is one of my sheep, and we all know a wounded sheep needs oil put on its bruises. I'm asking you to leave to give her time to heal."

"*Nee*, I built this house. It's mine."

"I also know there are counseling centers in Lancaster. We feel you need help...with your emotions. We're willing to pay any expense."

"Who's we? Ruth and her gossiping knit pickers?"

The Bishop coughed uncontrollably. Ruth ran to get him a glass of water.

"*Danki*," he said, taking a sip. "I promised Sarah I wouldn't get worked up. My ticker isn't too *goot*." He looked up at Luke. "Our *Gmay* will pay for counseling for you."

"Ruth, your big mouth....your slanderous mouth...has everyone turned against me."

The Bishop put his hand up. "Only the elders know and they made the decision. You need help." He turned to Ruth. "You and Mica are coming with me."

~*~

Samuel will always have a part of her heart? Roman read the words over again in disbelief, and then looked over at Fannie. "You're right. She did have a boyfriend before me. Looks like he moved to Colorado when she was seventeen. She never told me about him."

Fannie sat on the floor beside him, sorting Abby's embroidery thread and yarn. "She was human. Do you feel less guilty now for thinking of Lizzie on your wedding day?"

Roman took a deep breath and got up and looked at the snow flying outside. "*Jah*, I do. It was so silly of me to feel so guilty."

"Roman, I hope you don't think I'm being *nebby*, but do you think you feel guilty because you've never stopped loving Lizzie?"

"I loved Abby with all my heart..."

"And now that she's gone?"

Roman looked again in Abby's journal. Sometimes feelings never die. "I think a part of me will always care about Lizzie. My heart is free to love another..." He looked over at Fannie and thought of his *Daed's* encouragement to give this girl a try. Maybe it just took a lot longer to have feelings that were steadfast and true. A house wasn't built in one day and neither was love, like his *mamm* said. He'd let nature take its course. If he felt for Fannie someday, *wunderbar*, if not, there was someone out there to be a *mamm* for his girls...and to warm his heart like his dear deceased wife had done.

~*~

Lizzie measured a pound of chocolate chips and took the bag off the scale to label it. She heard the door jingle and saw it was Fannie, who was simply radiant. Her green eyes danced as she came near the counter.

"Lizzie, I stopped by on my way home to show you something." She held up what appeared to be a coloring book. "It's something Roman and I found in Abigail's hope chest. A book full of patterns on how to make paper snowflakes, and some that Abigail made."

Lizzie felt the room spin and sat on the stool behind her. Any thought of Abigail's hope chest made her ill. It used to be hers and she returned it when she broke off her courtship to Roman. Anger filled her, but Lizzie had learned to hide it by smiling. "So, why were you looking at Abigail's hope chest?"

"Well, Roman's had his head in the sand for three years. I convinced him to open it and see what's inside and he's so glad he did. He found Abigail's knitting loom, her pressed flowers, and now this book."

"That's it?" Lizzie asked.

"We're going through it slowly. I'm taking this book home so I can practice making snowflakes with the girls. We're celebrating Sisters Day together." She put her hand on her heart. "Those girls picked me to take them out. Can you believe it? They think I'm fun!"

Lizzie felt like she was a pressure canner ready to blow its top off. She needed so badly to let off some steam. "Fannie, are you...ah...chasing Roman?

"Chasing him? Lizzie, how degrading. I'd never chase a man." She stomped her foot. "And even if I was, I am beautiful enough to get him. Do you think he sits home pining for you?"

"Ach, I'm sorry Fannie. I don't know what came over me."

Fannie's eyes softened. "I do..."

"What?"

"You still love him, don't you?"

Lizzie willed tears to not form in her eyes. Roman had made his choice long ago and she was moving forward...with Melvin. Roman didn't even attempt to stop their courtship, so she knew what happened years ago tainted him toward her. "I'm going to marry Melvin in early spring, before planting time."

"Do you love Melvin?"

"He's a *goot* man and he loves me." Lizzie heard the door to the house open and saw her *Daed* and was relieved. Maybe he would change the subject.

"Hi Jonas," Fannie said.

"Fannie, your smile's a mile long. You look, well, radiant."

Lizzie listened in horror as Fannie spoke on and on about Roman's *kinner*, but she seemed to light up more when she said Roman's name. This was the confirmation Lizzie needed. Obviously Roman had his eye on Fannie, so she'd make a life together with Melvin. Love was growing slowly in her heart toward him....

~*~

That night Granny sat in her rocker, dumbfounded. The doctor must think something's wrong with Maryann to order all those blood tests. And Ruth was living at her *mamm's*? Was Luke so hard-hearted, that after the Bishop offered to pay for counseling, he refused to get help or repent? If a man was shunned, his family couldn't eat with him at the same table, but apparently Ruth was in danger, or too afraid to live with such a man.

She remembered when she was young and her *goot* friend got abused by her husband, but it was all hush-hushed. Since English women didn't put up with such behavior, the Amish women were learning to open their mouths. On a rare occasion when an Amish woman was abused, she needed to speak up. Granny admired Ruth's tenacity.

She looked out into the night sky but saw no stars, only beautiful, chunky snowflakes. Granny leaned closer to the window. They melted in seconds, but she couldn't help but admire their shapes. She'd read that no one snowflake had the same pattern. It was to the glory of God, to show his handiwork.

Granny closed her eyes and prayed:

Dear Lord,

Here I am again, casting my cares on you, because you care. Help Fannie see she's as beautiful as these snowflakes. She's your handiwork, too. And Lord, I just can't stop worrying about Maryann. If there's something wrong, I'm trusting that you're in control and I cast my worry on you. But Lord, shake Luke up. Give him a whoopin' from on high. Put your arms around Ruth and protect her. Help that husband of hers to find the root to his bizarre behavior, 'cause I want to slap him silly.

In Jesus Name,

Amen.

~*~

Granny put down Pride and Prejudice and looked over at Jeb, drooling over his Pennsylvania Field and Stream magazine. "I am not prejudiced against Fannie....old man."

"Who said you were?"

Granny sighed. Was her husband's memory getting that bad? "You did. Remember? You thought the book was about, well, being proud and prejudiced." She leaned her head against the back of the rocker. "It's a love story, like Jane's other books, but when I pick it up, I still hear you accusing me of being prejudiced against Fannie."

"Well, you are, aren't you?" Jeb looked over at the clock on the living room wall. "Don't you have to get ready for company? Isn't your knitting circle at seven?"

"*Jah*, I just can't move. Feeling so tired."

Jeb got up and put his lips on his wife's forehead. "You're hot. Maybe you caught something at the doctors yesterday. I'm getting the thermometer."

Granny closed her eyes and felt her throat. She knew her glands were swollen but didn't want to say anything. Fatigue washed over her. Soon she felt a thermometer being put in her mouth. After a minute, she heard Jeb tell her to get in bed. The knitting circle would have to be at Romans'.

~*~

"Granny's sick?" Lizzie and Fannie asked simultaneously.

"*Jah*," Roman said. "I'm having the knitting circle here." He grinned. "I won't be knitting, but Jenny will." He turned to Fannie and smiled. "Could you teach her how to use Abbey's knitting loom?

"*Jah*," Fannie said. "So glad we went through that hope chest."

Lizzie took a deep breath and clung to the back of the bench in Roman's living room. Why was Roman asking Fannie? Why did he act like she wasn't even there? And the hope chest, why had he never even cared to respond to the message she put inside when she returned it? Shame and grief washed over her and Lizzie found she couldn't hold back the tears. She let out a gasp and felt Fannie's hand on her shoulder.

"Lizzie, what on earth? What's wrong?"

She couldn't speak. Having kept such a secret for years was too hard to bear, and ever so often she just couldn't cope. Lizzie turned to leave, but Roman stood in front of her and asked if he could talk to her in private. She nodded and followed Roman into the utility room off the kitchen. She felt him near her; that old familiar feeling that just wouldn't go away overwhelmed her…love for this man.

"Lizzie, I asked Fannie to help Jenny because my girls look at her like an older sister. Asked her to go out for Sister Day. It was no offense to you."

Lizzie kept her head down. "I didn't think it was…"

He put his hands on her shoulders. "Then why are you crying?"

She felt herself go as stiff as a board. "That hope chest. It belonged to me, remember?"

"*Jah.* Do you want it back?"

Lizzie looked at him evenly. "*Nee,* it brings back bad memories."

"Lizzie, our courtship was a *goot* memory to me, until you broke it off."

She pushed him aside. "You had the final say in that! You rejected me because…"

Roman tilted her chin up. "Lizzie. Look at me. I never rejected you. You don't make any sense."

She looked into Roman's eyes. He seemed sincere, as if he didn't know. "You read my letter, *jah*?"

"You sent me lots of letters. Which one?"

"My final one…"

"*Jah*, the one you put in the woodpecker hole, calling off our engagement."

She looked at him, startled. "Which tree?"

"*Ach*, we had so many trees and it's been so long...why?"

Lizzie gasped for air and ran to open the door. She didn't stop, but ran through the women sitting in the living room, outside to the porch. She felt Roman grab her arm. "Where are you going?"

"Home. I feel sick."

~*~

Fannie could see through the window that Roman had his arms on Lizzie's shoulders. She stared to see if he'd embrace her, but he didn't. Lizzie ran down the steps and he didn't follow. He came into the house and slammed the door shut; his face flushed. He looked at her and asked if she could get a ride home with Maryann. She nodded yes.

Fannie held Roman's eyes. "Is Lizzie alright?"

Roman shook his head. "Women," he mumbled and headed upstairs.

Maryann gasped. "I knew it. He still cares for Lizzie."

Ella looked up from her knitting. "I think so, too. The eyes are the windows to the heart, or soul, or something like that."

"But she's courting Melvin," Fannie said. "She mustn't care for Roman then." She put her hand over her mouth when she saw Roman appear at the bottom of the steps with his girls. "*Ach*, we need you girls at the circle tonight. Only three of us."

The girls ran over and hugged Maryann and Ella, but nestled all around Fannie.

"How are my girls tonight?" Fannie asked. "It's bedtime soon, *jah*?"

"We have a surprise," Jenny giggled. "Another one."

Fannie beamed and put her arms around Millie and Tillie, seated on either side of her.

Jenny stood before her with a piece of paper. "We wrote this poem for you," she said. "Well, actually, I wrote it and the girls helped."

"I put in the part about heaven," Millie protested.

Roman cleared his throat loudly. "All three girls wrote it."

Jenny smiled at Fannie, exposing her gapped teeth, and read:

Snowflakes come from heaven
A gift from God above
Shiny little crystals
Made with His love
You are like a snowflake
A gift from God above
Sparkling with beauty
Made with His love

Jenny folded the paper and ran to hug Fannie. "You're so pretty, just like the snowflakes *Mamm* made from paper."

Maryann clasped her chest. "Ach, you girls are so sweet."

"*Jah*, you sure are," Ella said.

Fannie felt the tears on her cheeks and couldn't speak. Was God speaking through these little angels? Was she really pretty?

Tillie brushed at her tears with her two little hands. "Why you crying?"

Fannie tried to laugh. "Ach, I'm just silly. So, you girls think I look like a snowflake. Why, because I'm round?"

Millie giggled. "You're so funny. I know my shapes now. You're not round; you're a…really long rectangle."

"*Jah,* like the ruler we use in school to measure things," Jenny said. "You're tall and skinny."

Fannie knew children always spoke as they saw things. Was she really that deceived? Granny said she needed to empty her mind of bad thoughts and fill them with good. From now on, she'd think of a ruler whenever she saw a circle. She embraced all three girls and let her tears fall freely.

~*~

Fannie pulled into Melvin's clock shop with her sister, Eliza, to order the cuckoo clock that their *mamm* had always wanted. She could hardly wait to see her face on Christmas morning when she saw the clock with carved squirrels on the bottom. When they walked into the shop, Fannie was once again in awe at the skill Melvin and his father possessed. Intricately carved cuckoo clocks lined the walls and she and her sister jumped when they all stuck their heads out and cuckooed nine times. She heard Melvin laughing and turned to him.

"This noise will wake up the dead," Fannie said, her

hand on her heart.

"*Jah*," Eliza said, putting both hands on her bulging stomach. "Made the baby kick."

"Can I help you with anything?"

"We'd like to buy a clock for our *mamm* for Christmas." Fannie pointed to the one she wanted and Melvin took it off the wall for her to hold. She ran her fingers over the little squirrels. "How do you do it, Melvin? They look so real."

"I've been carving since I was a wee boy. My *Daed* was a *goot* teacher, too."

Eliza took the clock and looked over it carefully. "We'd like to buy this clock, but can you keep it here until Christmas Eve? We have no place to hide it."

"No trouble at all," Melvin said, taking the clock from her.

Eliza grinned at Melvin. "Seeing Lizzie? I remember in school how much you liked her, even though she was two grades above us. I have to admit; I was jealous."

Melvin's green eyes danced. "And why's that?"

"Because I had a crush on you. But that was so long ago, when we were *kinner*."

Fannie cocked her head to one side. "Melvin, you've never liked anyone but Lizzie?"

"*Jah*, it sounds silly, but I've never really cared for anyone but her."

"Even when you lived in Ohio? No one caught your eye?"

"Well, someone did for a little while, but it didn't last." He walked behind the counter and put the clock in a box.

"Why so many questions?"

"I heard from Lizzie *yinz* are courting, *jah*?" Fannie asked.

"*Jah*," Melvin said, holding her gaze.

Fannie never noticed what a handsome man he was. So kind, too. But he seemed too old for her....

~*~

Ella sat in a rocker, white cotton square and red thread in hand. She got up and walked over to Granny's bed. "Do these stitches look even to you?

Granny looked into Ella's hope filled eyes. How she wanted a baby and the *goot* Lord was sure to give her her heart's desire. "Very even stitches. *Goot* job."

"Do you want more soup? There's lots of chicken soup simmering downstairs."

Granny didn't want anyone to know she still had no appetite. "I'll have some later. I'm awfully tired."

"I can read to you if you'd like."

Granny pulled the covers up to her chin. "I'd feel like a *boppli. Nee,* you go ahead and work on your quilt." The windows rattled loudly as the wind whipped outside, and Granny closed her eyes. She thanked the Lord she was in a warm home. A home not destroyed by tornadoes last summer. She thought of all the shawls they'd made to send to Missouri, to anyone in need, and the thought warmed her soul.

Granny heard the loud footsteps coming up the stairs and opened her eyes to see Zach. He ran to Ella and picked her up and twirled her around. He was telling her about a baby. A baby for them? Granny sat up, afraid she was dreaming.

"What's going on, Zach?" Granny asked.

"Word spread that we wanted a child. Amish grapevine. I got a letter from the settlement in Troutville. Teenage pregnancy and they're looking for a family to adopt the baby." Zach put his arm around his wife. "Ella, there's no guarantees, but we need to go up and visit the family. Take it from there. Are you up for this, or should we stick with foster care?"

Ella bit her shaking lips. "Is it legal to just take the baby?"

"'Course it is," Granny said. "It's the way it's always been done. You go on home with your husband, Ella. *Yinz* have a lot to talk about."

"*Nee,* Jeb said to stay until he got back."

"Where is he?" Zach asked.

Granny put her head back down. "He has an elder's meeting. The bishop called it. Looks like Luke's calmed down and repented of his sin, but Ruth won't go home. She's afraid."

"I don't blame her," Ella said, walking over to Granny, grabbing her hand. "You look too pale."

Granny heard footsteps again and soon saw Jeb. She could tell by his expression that he carried a heavy burden. He collapsed in the rocker and sighed.

"Sometimes I wish Luke were young enough to give a whoopin'. He says he's sorry, repented and all, but doesn't seem sincere to me. We can't blame Ruth for being fearful." He bent over and coughed loudly.

"Will he go to counseling?" Zach asked.

"*Jah,* when Ruth said she wasn't going home, he agreed to go. It's expensive, but we're in agreement; it's money well spent. He'll be going to Lancaster soon. Maybe stay with the Amish there for a spell."

"*Ach*, what a *goot* day! We'll have a baby by Christmas and my brother will get help."

Jeb's head spun toward Ella. "What? A baby by Christmas?"

Granny giggled. "old man, she's not giving birth to one. You okay?"

Jeb coughed again. "*Nee,* not feeling too well."

"Get in bed," Ella said, and then turned to Zach. "I'm staying here until they're better."

Zach winked at her. "You work on that baby quilt. We'll need it soon. I have a *goot* feeling about us getting this baby."

~*~

Lizzie threw a snowball at Melvin, hitting him right in the forehead. He fell down and didn't move. She ran over to him, remembering in her Bible the story of David and Goliath and how one little stone to his forehead killed him. In the twilight she couldn't see so well, but was sure he was knocked out, at least. She bent down and put his head in her lap. He was motionless. She patted his cheeks, and still no movement. "Ach, Lord, I killed him. Don't take him, Lord!"

Melvin's body started to move. He was laughing. He sat up and turned to her. "I gotcha. Least I know now if I was dead, you'd care."

Lizzie stood up. "What makes you say such a thing?

Of course I'd care!"

He stood up and dusted the snow off his black pants. "I was kidding…why so serious?"

"I was concerned, is all."

Melvin pulled her close. "Nice to know you care." He leaned forward to kiss her, but she turned her head. "Lizzie, if we're going to get married, we should kiss sometime. Nothing wrong with it."

"It leads to other things," she said, trying to pull from him. How many times did she have to tell him she didn't want to kiss until after marriage? She may be the only Amish woman who felt this way, but no other Amish woman had been through what she'd experienced. She looked into Melvin's dejected eyes. "We talked about this before."

"*Nee,* we never talked about it. You told me. Is this what it'll be like when we're married? You barking orders?"

Lizzie gasped in shock. Melvin had never acted so boldly before. "Seems like you've wanted to say that for a while. Anything else you want to say?"

Melvin readjusted his black wool hat. "Maybe…"

"And?"

"When you love someone, it's natural to kiss. Makes me wonder if you love me at all."

She didn't know what to say. If she said she loved him, it would be a lie. If she told him about the pain locked in her heart, he might reject her. If she said she still felt a little for Roman, it would break his heart. Lizzie froze where she stood, just like the snowman they'd built together, and watched him walk away. Hot tears blurred her vision, and once again, the pain of that dreadful night stabbed her like a knife.

~*~

Luke sat in Ruth's rocker and bit his lower lip. What was wrong with him? Were Ruth and Mica really too afraid to come home? Was he an animal, like Ruth said?

He heard wagon wheels and saw his brother pull the buggy through the deep snow. He'd forgotten to shovel the driveway, but then again, he didn't have Ruth by his side to remind him. He met Zach and let him in. "I'm talked out. Do you need something?"

Zach patted Luke on the shoulder. "I'm proud of you. Takes a strong man to go to counseling."

"Who said I'm going?"

"Jeb. Didn't you tell the Bishop and elders you'd go?"

"Well, *jah*, I did. But it'll be weeks before I can go and I'm hoping Ruth will wake up and come home before I have to."

Zach groaned and sat at the round oak table. "You gave your word, so you need to keep it, plain and simple. I came to tell you something else, too. We might be adopting a baby. Ella doesn't want you coming around. She's afraid of you."

Luke collapsed in the chair next to Zach. "Why? I've never yelled at Ella."

"When a man loses his temper...shows no self-control...it scares the women folk."

Luke put his head down. "Never knew that."

"Did Uncle Otis scare you when you worked for

him?"

"*Jah,* he did, but he made me listen."

"I worked for Smiley, and like his name, he never yelled. He made me listen." Zach shifted in the chair. "Maybe being around Uncle Otis so much growing up wasn't *goot.* Maybe he rubbed off on you."

Luke didn't know if he should tell his brother everything that went on over at their uncle's, but he didn't want to go to counseling either. "Did you ever see the magazines Uncle Otis had in his barn?"

"*Nee,* never. Why?"

Shame welled up in Luke. "He had stacks of girly magazines. Looked at them and let me take some home."

Zach shot out of his chair. "What? You mean pornography?"

Luke put his hands up. "I was only ten when I first looked." A sob caught in his throat. "I was only ten..." He put his head on the table to hide his face, but couldn't hold back the anger that rose in him. He slammed his fist on the table. How could his uncle expose him to such filth? He had a wife and *kinner!*

He felt Zach's hand on his back. No judgmental words? He'd feared telling someone his whole life and he could have told his *Daed* or Zach years ago. Ruth acting like she was locked up in a cage made him so angry because she really didn't know the prison cell he was in.

Luke turned to look up at his brother. He didn't know how to interpret the shock in Zach's eyes. Was he disgusted with him? "Maybe I should have kept my mouth shut."

"*Nee,* you did the right thing. I think we found out why you treat Ruth like you do. Pornography shows no respect for women."

"I thought it only fed my lustful thoughts."

Zach rubbed the back of his neck. "Do you look at those magazines still?"

Luke didn't know what to say now. He couldn't risk losing his job, but something made him open up to his brother. "*Jah,* on those phones with pictures. At work."

"Luke, you're only allowed to talk on a phone connected to a wall for a reason."

"Why's that?"

"Don't you pay attention when we have our vote on the *Ordnung*? Some other men have been lured into that trap of looking at porn on those new phones. The Bishop said only phones connected to a wall could be used. The ones with the big handles."

Luke put his head down. "I can't stop looking. It's like I'm possessed."

"Well, you did the right thing. You told someone, and now you're not carrying this burden alone. I'll go out to Lancaster with you when counseling starts. We'll get through this."

Luke let the tears flow and stood up to hug his brother. When he felt wrung out, he released him and looked at him and grinned. "I'll think talk about getting through things together. You sound like a girl."

Zach laughed nervously. "What do you mean?"

"Ruth's been saying how Granny Weaver talks about getting through life together. Maybe we should join the knitting circle."

Zach burst into laughter. "How about we start a chewing tobacco circle? We can spit in the same spittoon and gab."

Luke chuckled. "I'd like that."

~*~

Fannie slowed her buggy when she saw a man along the road. He staggered like a drunk. When she got closer, she realized it was Melvin. What on earth? She pulled back the reins. "Melvin, are you okay?"

"Just walking off some steam, is all," he said. "Best walk the other way than fight, *jah*?"

Fannie knew he was freezing. "I'll take you home. Get in."

"My horse and buggy are back at...Miller's Variety."

Fannie knew the store closed at five. "Melvin, how long have you been walking out here?"

"Not too long. Toes are feeling numb though."

"It's almost seven. The store closes —"

"I was visiting Lizzie...."

Fannie couldn't help but feel for this man because she knew the truth. Lizzie didn't love him and he probably figured it out. She knew what rejection felt like and her heart went out to him. "How about I take you to my place and give you a mug full of hot chocolate, and then we go get your horse at Lizzie's?"

The smile that flashed across Melvin's face, Fannie found totally adorable. He hopped in the buggy, and her heart skipped a beat. Why? Melvin brushed some snowflakes off her nose, and she thought she'd melt like a puddle right there.

~*~

Granny took Ella's hand. "*Danki*, honey, for taking care of us. You make me feel I can leave this world in good hands."

Ella leaned over and kissed Granny on the cheek. "You're not that sick. Only a bad cold."

"You don't know what I mean," Granny said. "You have a *mamm's* heart, and I know when I go to my reward, the girls will have you to look after them."

"I have time on my hands," Ella said, faintly. "But hopefully that will change."

"Until it does, maybe the Lord intended for this 'time on your hands'. You see more needs around you with no *kinner* to chase after." She patted Ella's hand. "You promise me you'll stay the way you are. People depend on you."

Ella's chin quivered. "No one's tells me I'm needed except Zach." A tear slid down her cheek. "I'm scared. What if we don't get that baby? I want to be a *mamm*."

"Did I ever tell you about my Aunt Anna? She couldn't have *kinner*, but she had more time for me than my own *mamm*. She's the one who taught me how to knit, crochet, and do embroidery. My *mamm* didn't have the time, having so many *kinner*, but Aunt Anna always did. She was my special gift from God."

"I couldn't be helping you here now if I had *kinner* at home...and Zach and I wouldn't be looking to adopt...or take in foster *kinner*..."

"It's a mystery," Granny said, "but God works

everything out for the *goot*. How he does it is a miracle."

Ella kissed her cheek. "You started the knitting circle because you're like your Aunt Anna in a way, aren't you? You never had *dochders*, but you're like a *mamm* to us."

Granny felt a lump in her throat. Ella always touched her heart so. "*Jah*, you girls are like *dochders* to me, since you were all *kinner*. So, I guess I'm like my Aunt Anna..."

~*~

Lizzie heard her *daed* call for her. She lit an oil lamp and made her way to his room. Was he in pain? Did he need his hot water bottle changed already? When she opened the door, she saw him in bed, sitting up reading a book. "What is it *Daed*?"

"Lizzie, come sit here a minute. We need to talk."

"About what?"

"About you. I've seen so much pain in those eyes of yours. Keeps me up at night, reading the Good Book for comfort. What's wrong?"

:Lizzie sat in the chair near his bed. "You saw Melvin walk away, didn't you?"

"*Nee*, I saw him and Fannie come get his buggy though..."

"Fannie? Brought him here?"

"*Jah*, it was late. You were sleeping."

Lizzie started to grind her teeth. Young, little green-eyed Fannie, who got such attention because she was always feeling sorry for herself. Roman, and now Melvin? "What did Melvin say?"

"Well, he looked mighty down, but Fannie cheered him up." Jonas took his *dochder's* hand. "Want to talk to your Pa?"

Love for her *daed* filled her heart. He was a *mamm* and *daed* wrapped up in one person. She could freely tell him anything, except the one thing that haunted her. "*Daed*, I need a woman to talk to about…"

"Why not talk to Granny Weaver. She looks at you like a *dochder*."

"*Daed*, are we still going to try to buy the house next door? Try to run a little bed and breakfast?"

"Lizzie, you're changing the subject…"

"*Nee*, I'm not. I need to get away. Maybe go out to visit relatives for Christmas in Lancaster and see one of those little hotels to get ideas."

"Not be with me on Christmas?"

"*Daed*, you could come. Surely we can find someone to look after the store while we're gone. When was the last time you had a vacation."

Jonas pulled at his long beard. "Women folk beat around the bush too much. So, you're trying to say you want to talk to one of your cousins about your problem, *jah*?"

Lizzie withdrew her hand from his and put her head down. "*Jah*, I do. But I also want to see a bed and breakfast. Are we buying Troutman's house or not?"

"It looks *goot*." Jonas yawned. "Let me sleep on this whole notion of leaving Smicksburg for Christmas. Things will look clearer in the morning."

~*~

Here is a very simple and cost effective hot chocolate

mix. I've given it as Christmas presents and it's always a hit. Put mix in a mason jar and wrap a ribbon around the top. Attach recipe to the ribbon by using a hole punch.

Homemade Hot Chocolate Mix
2 c. powdered milk

1 ¼ c white sugar

½ c unsweetened cocoa (bakers cocoa)

.

.

EPISODE 5

Christmas Cookies

Granny hugged Ella and Ruth as they entered her little *dawdyhaus*. She cringed when she looked into Ruth's eyes; Luke made a deep wound in the poor girl's heart. She took the trays of Christmas cookies they brought and put them on her long oak table. She heard buggy wheels spinning and looked out the window. Fannie and Lizzie were stuck in the snow. She saw her son, Roman, fly out of his house to help dig them out, and she couldn't help but notice again the coldness in Lizzie's eyes when she looked at Roman. What had her son done to her that eleven years couldn't heal?

Her heart leapt when Roman went to Lizzie's side first to help her out. Lizzie slipped on the icy driveway and Roman caught her. Her tray of cookies slipped and went all over the ice and her black lab, Jack, soon made them disappear. Granny noticed how Lizzie and Roman both laughed, while he still held her hand. How fickle Lizzie's emotions were toward Roman. But as she continued to watch them talk, hope rose in her. Oh, she loved Fannie and didn't care which woman her son chose, just so he chose someone. He had three years to grieve his wife's death, and it was time to move on. And his three little girls needed a *mamm*.

She noticed another buggy and saw Jack race toward it, snow flying up from his heels. Maryann and Becca were both coming to the knitting circle; Granny put her hand on her chest and thanked God that everyone could make it, since she had a Christmas present for them all.

She hugged each of her girls as they came in and shoved Roman out the door as this was a woman's only gathering. She had everyone put their cookies on the table and soon the oak top disappeared in a myriad of colors. The girls all hugged each other, but Granny noticed Maryann and Becca were not as warm toward Ruth as they should be. Yes, Ruth separated from her husband, almost unheard of, but the Bishop had a good plan and Granny was confident things would turn out in the end.

"Do you girls want to knit first or do the cookie exchange?" Granny asked.

"Let's talk," Fannie said. "Well, and knit too, *jah*?" She turned to Ella. "I want to hear about this Christmas baby."

Ella lifted both hands in the air. "I'm so excited; I could just, well, pop open! Zach and I will be going up to Troutville tomorrow to meet the little *boppli*."

They all took their normal seats on Granny's rockers or benches and picked up their needles to knit, and looked expectantly toward Ella.

"We've exchanged some letters with the *mamm*. She's sixteen and well…doesn't know who the father is…"

Maryann gasped. "How immoral."

"She's honest," Ella corrected. "She could have made up a story, but was very open in her letters. The *mamm* hasn't had the happiest life and seemed to be looking for love in lots of men's arms."

"And nothing satisfied, *jah*?" Granny asked.

"*Nee*, she's come to understand the love of God and isn't out there begging for love…"

Maryann huffed. "My *dochder* is here; are you forgetting? You're making excuses for this woman's sin."

Becca put her hands on her ever reddening cheeks. "*Mamm*, I'm sitting right here and I am fourteen, not a *boppli*."

Ella put down her knitting needles and looked across the circle at Maryann. "The *mamm* of this *boppli* is repentant. She did her kneel down confession in front of her whole *Gmay*. We're to forgive and restore. Like I said, I know things about this woman that are confidential. She was starved for love."

Ruth spoke but stared at her knitting. "I know how that feels…."

"But the Bishop has a plan, *jah*?" Granny asked.

Ruth shrugged her shoulders and remained silent.

Ella put her hand on Ruth's shoulder. "All of us are praying for you…"

All the women nodded in agreement. Granny realized Lizzie hadn't opened her mouth since she came in. "Lizzie, something ailing you?"

"Well, I won't be here for Christmas, and I'll miss everyone…"

Granny looked up from her knitting. "Why are you

visiting those little hotels in Lancaster on Christmas anyhow?"

"Well, I've always longed to see Lititz and their Moravian stars they have lit up all over town. And my cousin's bed and breakfast is so busy she said I'd be a great help."

Fannie put down her needles and beamed. "I'm going to take Lizzie's place at the store and I can't wait." She turned to Lizzie and smiled. "I just love your *Daed*. I hope I don't mess up too much."

Lizzie looked at Fannie fondly. "You'll do *wunderbar goot*. Melvin and Roman have also volunteered to help."

Granny studied Fannie's face. Were her cheeks growing pink just at the sound of Roman's name? She looked down at her cream and black shawl that was just about finished. The colors looked so pretty intertwined….her son would be happier if her were intertwined with a *goot* woman. She was a matchmaker. Granny pursed her lips to hide laughter as she thought of the surprise Jeb gave her last week; Emma to add to her Jane Austen collection. He was sure she'd learn from meddling Emma not to play matchmaker. It only made her want to try harder to see Roman with a *goot* wife.

"I heard from the doctor. I have low blood sugar for sure. Explains my fatigue and dizzy spells…" Maryann said.

"I read it causes mood swings, too, *Mamm*," Becca chimed in.

Maryann laughed out loud. "*Jah*, it does. *Dochder*, you don't miss a beat, do you?"

Becca giggled. "They say it's hereditary, so, *Mamm,* next time I'm moody, I'm going to say I have hypoglycemia, too."

Granny was relieved that Maryann laughed and didn't chide her daughter. Maryann did seem edgy.

"The doctor wants to do further testing though. She wasn't too happy to hear I've never had a mammogram." Maryann looked down to knit.

"Never?" Ella asked. "That's not *goot.*"

Granny didn't know if she should say anything, but did. "I've never had one."

Ella clucked her tongue. "Granny, you need to. What if you have breast cancer and don't know it?"

"Never thought to go, is all."

"Don't want to go, is all," Ruth corrected. "I had one when Mica was born. So embarrassing, but Luke insisted."

Granny felt tears well up in her eyes. What tenderness Luke had toward his wife at times, but then such cruelty. Her husband, Jeb, told her about Luke confessing to looking at pornography on the men's cell phones at work and how helpless he felt to stop. It was an ugly situation, but what a balm of healing oil her husband and the other elders where pouring over Luke's life.

"You need to go get one, Granny," Ruth said.

"Get what?"

"A mammogram."

"Why not come with me?" Maryann asked. "It would be a comfort."

Granny looked around the circle. "Anyone else not

ever get this test?"

Lizzie and Becca both raised their hands. Maryann took her daughter's hand and laughed. "You won't be needing one for a while. But Lizzie, you too? Never went?"

Lizzie bowed her head. "*Nee*...it's degrading."

"Only women give the tests," Maryann added.

"Let's talk about this some other time," Granny said. "It's our Christmas cookie exchange and I have a gift for everyone." She sprung from her seat and ran into her kitchen. She got the basket full of white bags she'd filled with her gifts. How she loved to give presents. Granny ran back and told each woman to take one. She heard the rustling of paper and looked as each bag was ripped open. Squeals of delight echoed around the room.

Ella got up to hug her. "Granny, *danki* for the scarf. How'd you have time?"

One by one the girls all hugged her and asked her the same question. "Ach, I didn't make them. I got them Black Friday at Punsxy-Mart. Remember when I said I was going out to see if Suzy was there to pick us up? I bought them then."

Laughter filled the room. Granny felt like her heart would explode with love for these dear women. She suggested that every time they put on their scarves, think of it as her giving them a hug around the neck. Granny noticed Ruth brushed away a tear, and put her arm around her, and suggested they start the cookies exchange. All the women headed toward the table, some arm in arm.

~*~

Luke threw a log in the woodstove and picked up Rules for a Godly Life, reading required by the Bishop. It was an easy read, but what the Bishop asked was too much. Quit his job? He made good money working for the lumber company. To survive off a small woodworking business would be hard. Jeb and the other elders thought it was clear cut; if your eye causes you to sin, pluck it out, just like the Bible said. So, they were bound to make his life miserable by not letting him near any English with one of those phones with pictures...that might have girly pictures on them.

He started to grind his teeth again, wishing he wouldn't have made such a fuss about going to counseling in Lancaster. It might have been easier. The Bishop found a local counselor and now Luke felt like an animal in a trap. Salt was only rubbed into his wound when he went to visit his son, and Ruth seemed happier living with her parents; she was better off without him. But the bishop warned this separation couldn't last long, maybe another two weeks at best. Then he'd have to leave his house and move into the *dawdyhaus* by his in-laws, so they could keep an eye on him. When he told his brother Zach how humiliating this was, he was surprised at his response...Ruth feels humiliated and betrayed... you broke your marriage vows to forsake all other. He'd never realized that...

~*~

Roman helped his girls across the icy driveway to the *dawdyhaus*. They needed to get to bed and wanted to give their homemade Christmas cards to all the women in the knitting circle. He opened the door and his eyes locked with Lizzie's. Holding her out in the snow after she slipped brought back raw emotion, even after so many years. He knew he gripped her hard, but the way she seemed to be repelled at his embrace cut to his heart. Why was she so cold toward him? Why did she say he rejected her, when she clearly called off their wedding a decade ago? Now she'd be gone for Christmas and he realized he'd become accustomed to seeing her around the holidays, and it pained him that she'd be gone.

He had to admit his heart filled with some hope when his *mamm* told her that Lizzie and Melvin were no longer courting, only being friends and seeing where the Lord led them. Roman felt a tug on his coat and looked down at Tillie. His little "Timid Tillie" was too shy to pass out her cards without his help. He patted her head and squeezed her hand, going from one woman to another as Tillie gave them a card and a kiss on the cheek. When they got to Lizzie, he was surprised that tears were in her eyes. He heard her tell Tillie how she would be gone for Christmas and how she needed to be in Lancaster. How she'd miss watching the school program on Christmas Eve. Was it his imagination, but was Lizzie trying to say good-bye for a longer time…much longer than a week?

~*~

Fannie crept down the wooden wide-plank stairs in her wool knit slippers to ward off the cold. She opened the large, black, wood burning stove and was glad to see there was still an ample fire going; she wouldn't have to fetch kindling and start a new one.

All was quiet at four in the morning except a lone owl hooting outside. Would she always be alone, just like that owl? She thought of Melvin and how easily she could talk to him. She'd have no reason to go over and check on her *mamm's* clock, unless she ordered another one…but for who? And with what money?

She looked over at the bags full of cookies she brought home from Granny's. They would taste so good with her morning coffee, and no one was up yet to see her gobble them down. She pinched her stomach through her nightgown and felt a ripple of fat. *Nee,* she would not eat one cookie over the entire Christmas season. Maybe she could give some to Melvin as a little thank you for making the clock for such a *goot* price.

Fannie got a mug and went over to the cook stove to grab the blue speckle ware coffee pot, glad that her *daed,* already out in the barn, had left half a pot full. The aroma seemed to slap her awake, as she sipped it black. With her *mamm* not feeling well, again, she'd be making breakfast alone.

Again, her mind fell on Melvin. Why was he so smitten with Lizzie? Yes, he called off their courtship and was free to find love somewhere else, but who wanted to live in Lizzie's shadow? Through the Amish grapevine she'd heard he liked her since he was a *kinner.* She poured herself some coffee….and grabbed a handful of gingerbread cookies.

~*~

Ella squeezed Zach's hand as he knocked on the front

door of Lavina's house. It seemed so formal to knock on a front door and not just go around to the side, but Ella followed Zach's lead. She thanked God for her husband, knowing he loved her, barren or not, and how supportive he was to adopt, sight unseen, a baby he never saw.

The wind whipped up her skirt and she snuggled up against Zach. Was anyone home? Zach knocked again, still no answer. She looked back at Suzy, waiting in the driveway, and wished she was in the warm van. Ella heard a creaking sound and the door slowly opened. A short Amish man with beady black eyes and a long gray beard asked them to step inside.

"*Danki,*" Zach said. "Awfully cold out."

The man said nothing, but yelled upstairs for his daughter to come down and meet the new parents. His tone sent a shiver down Ella's spine; this man sure wanted to get rid of his grandson. She heard a girl's voice screaming upstairs and her heart sank; it was Lavina, the piercing cry of a *mamm* who loved her *boppli*. She bowed her head and prayed for this poor girl, who shared her heart so freely in her letters. Lavina had never known the love and acceptance of a man, any man, not even her father. She looked for that love in other men, even men she barely knew. Her kneel down confession in front of so many in her church, told her that Lavina was brave, and Ella was determined to raise this little boy to be brave, too, like his natural *mamm*.

Ella heard another scream and grabbed Zach around the middle and buried her head in his chest. This was not what she'd expected. She'd hoped Lavina would greet them and happily hand over the child. This was a bad dream. Were they doing the right thing by taking her baby? She felt Zach's body jerk and looked up to see he was crying. She turned to see a woman coming down the stairs, a baby peeking out at her from a white knit blanket. Joy welled in her and she started to laugh and cry at the same time. It shocked her that she felt love for a child she'd never seen; a love that would die for this little infant. This must be a *mamm's* heart, she thought. The woman handed her the baby and she nestled his cheek against hers. She turned to Zach who was openly weeping and handed him their son. Ella nodded to the woman, who must be the *oma*. She saw that tears were in her eyes, but she lifted up a finger, telling them to wait while she fetched the other *boppli*…his twin?

~*~

Lizzie looked at Fannie, Melvin, and Roman from across the store counter. "Any questions?"

Fannie grinned. "Lizzie, you'll only be gone for a week, *jah*? I think we can manage."

Melvin smiled at Fannie. "*Jah*, your *Daed* will be here if we have questions."

Lizzie looked at Roman, who seemed so somber. "Roman, any questions?"

"*Jah*, are you only staying a week?"

Lizzie didn't know what to say, since she wasn't sure how long she needed to be gone. What if the counselor said she needed to stay for a month? She'd have to. Why she never thought of going to counseling before was a mystery, but when Luke was told he needed it, it seemed as plain as day she needed it, too. Or maybe she was now willing to talk about her secret, since it affected others. When Melvin called off their courtship, she knew she'd stay the same as the old rusted out water pump back in the cornfield if she didn't get some kind of healing oil.

"Lizzie, will you be back in a week?" Roman repeated.

"I, ah, might visit other relatives…"

Fannie tilted her head. "I thought you only had one cousin out there."

"Well, there's a distant relative I should meet, and cousin Lydia wanted me to meet some of her friends." Her eyes met Roman's and she felt her mouth grow dry. Why was it she felt Roman could see right through her? Because he was the only other person who knew her secret, yet threw her away like an old dish rag. She felt a knot in her stomach and grabbed at her middle.

"Are you okay?" Fannie asked.

Lizzie let out nervous laughter. "Maybe I have low blood sugar like Maryann. I do feel a little dizzy." She plopped down on the stool behind her. "Just need a glass of water."

She was surprised to see Roman run to the door leading to the house. What a mystery he is. No one had caused her as much joy and sorrow at the same time. He soon emerged with a glass of orange juice.

"Drink this. It'll make your sugars go up."

Lizzie lifted a shaky hand. "Roman… I don't have a sugar problem." She took the juice and sipped it. "Most likely fatigue from packing and all the excitement is all." She saw her *daed* emerge from the house, making his way to her on his crutches.

"You worry about this store too much. We'll be fine here. Go to Lancaster and have fun. You'll meet lots of young folk out there, and not be trapped in a store with your *Daed*."

Lizzie reached her arms out and embraced her *daed*. "I don't feel trapped here...honestly."

"Well, we need to get going," Fannie said, as she smiled at Melvin. "Have to pick up a clock for *Mamm*."

Lizzie noticed Melvin lit up when Fannie looked at him....and she didn't care.

~*~

Melvin helped Fannie into her buggy. "I'll follow you down the road, and then we can ride in one buggy over to my shop."

Fannie pulled the scarf Granny gave her around her neck, feeling timid. Melvin looked at her, his brown shaggy bangs almost hiding his green eyes. Was it her imagination, or was he looking at her in that special way? He was nine years older and probably only thought of her as a little sister, like Roman did. All men looked at her as a sister...

She pulled onto the road and remembered what Granny had said about reconditioning her mind ... and rolled her eyes. Granny had gone so far as to tell her to keep a "compliment journal." The very thought of it seemed vain, but she started one anyway. She knew Granny struggled with feeling unattractive at her age. She started a list of compliments on a piece of paper. Fannie's best friend, Hannah, said she heard someone say she was as cute as a button, so she wrote it on this list and kept it hidden in the top drawer of her bedroom dresser. It was a twelve year old boy who said it, but it was a compliment. She wrote what Jonas Miller told her at the store: Her beautiful green eyes were bound to catch her a husband soon. Two things on her list, but it was a start.

Fannie pulled her buggy past the Black Angus cows that dotted the snowy white pasture, and sure enough, they started heading her way. Birds of a feather flock together, she thought, as usual, but caught herself. She sat up straight and spoke out loud the scripture Granny made her memorize. *"I will praise thee; for I am fearfully and wonderfully made: marvelous are thy works; and that my soul knoweth right well. Psalm 139:14."* She took a deep breath and noticed that feelings of inferiority and self-pity hadn't swallowed her up like they usually did. Granny sure was wise.

Fannie pulled the horse into its stall attached to their barn, and was surprised that Melvin had pulled up the driveway and was right next to her, ready to help her into his buggy. She could have easily walked to the road, but he said he was afraid she'd fall. Did she hear him right? Did he say fall and scratch that pretty face of hers? She felt like running over in the snow and making a snow angel. Pretty?

"Fannie, are you alright?" Melvin asked.

"Jah, I sure am," Fannie said, as she took Melvin's hand as he helped her into his buggy.

When they got out to the road, Melvin stopped the buggy to let a car pass. "I have a confession to make," he said. "I deliver clocks to customers, but wanted to take you out on a buggy ride...to talk."

Fannie put her head down, preparing herself to put on the "happy sister" show. Good old Fannie, ready to listen to everybody's problems. Of course, he wanted to talk about Lizzie. She turned to him. "So, how can I help you?"

Melvin pulled out onto the road and brought the horse to a slow walk. "By just being yourself. You're so easy to talk to. I like that."

"So you need advice about Lizzie, and you can talk to me, right?"

Melvin furrowed his bushy brown eyebrows. "*Nee,* I don't want to talk about Lizzie. Not at all." He took her hand. "I'm too old to go to Sunday night singings and ask a girl out on a buggy ride. So I got you to come this way."

Fannie felt Melvin squeeze her hand, but she felt too shy to talk. Could it be true? Melvin cared for her?

"I'm glad you've been stopping over at the shop to check on the clock these past few weeks. Like I said, I can talk to you. Never knew that."

"You, ah, sure got over Lizzie quick-like. Rumor has it you've cared only for her since you were a *kinner,*" Fannie managed to say.

Melvin grinned. "Gossip has a way of growing something seed small to a bumper crop. I've liked Lizzie for a while, *jah,* but I've courted other girls. *Nee,* my affections haven't been on Lizzie for the past month." He pulled the buggy over on the side of the road, and took her by the shoulders. "Don't you know what a peach of a girl you are?"

Peach? Was she dreaming?

Melvin took a little white package from his coat pocket. "I made you something for Christmas. Open it."

Fannie looked at Melvin's kind eyes, and her fear started to slip away. She opened the box to find an intricately carved little wooden box. She opened it up to find neatly cut little pieces of paper with handwriting on each one. She picked up one and read, *He will rejoice over you with singing. Zephaniah 3:17.*

Fannie felt anger deep within. She remembered the cruel joke that was played on her in eighth grade, when Samuel Yoder gave her a gift in front of his friends, only to find it was a joke. She heard their mocking laughter ring through her mind and then the image of Lottie, little skinny Lottie. She came over and took the gift, saying Samuel had given it to the wrong girl and it was for her.

She looked into Melvin's eyes. Was this a joke, too? She put the little box on the buggy seat, and blurted out, "Melvin, I'm not a fool! Give it to Lizzie!"

"Why would I do that? It's you I have my eye on."

Fannie put her head in her hands and tried to stop, but just couldn't and let out a sob. Years of pain came out in a river of tears. She felt Melvin's arm around her, sometimes stroking her back. Embarrassed, she started to get out of the buggy and slipped, but Melvin caught her and pulled her to himself and held her head to his shoulder. "You're a beautiful young woman, you need to see that."

"How?" Fannie gasped, leaning her head on his

shoulder.

He cupped her face in his hands and kissed her on the cheek, and then on the lips. He took a handkerchief out of his pocket and wiped the tears from her cheeks and then picked up the wooden box. He opened it and started to read the Bible verses he wrote on little pieces of paper. He wanted her to carry a few around with her, so when she felt unloved, or unlovable, she could pull a verse from her apron pocket and see how much God loved her.

Fannie leaned her head on his shoulder and looked over at the cows that came closer to their buggy, and was surprised that she started to laugh.

~*~

Granny poured hot tea into two mugs and placed them on her oak table. "Won't be quiet here for a while. Let's enjoy it." She took up her needle and string and poked another cranberry and slid it down to her ever growing chain. "Ach, the birds will eat these berries up faster than we can string them."

Jeb sipped his tea. "Well, it's a tradition I want to keep up. And it's nice to have some peace and quiet over here."

She grinned. "Well, I'm used to it being quieter, too. Nathan and his bunch are rowdy over at Romans. Sure nice to have him and Beth home for Christmas though, although I sure do wish all my boys could be here."

Jeb leaned his elbow on the table. "*Jah,* me too. But Montana is far away."

Granny knew how her Jeb missed the boys at Christmas, and she looked to change the subject. "Can you believe that Ella and Zach have twins, a boy and girl each? Ach, those two will make the best parents."

Jeb pulled at his long gray beard. "Zach won't let Luke over until he sees the doctor. Ella's afraid that Luke's not right in the head. ."

"She's not the only one." Granny sighed. "You said Luke's leaning toward quitting that worldly job and living in the *dawdyhaus*?"

"*Jah,* told me this morning. But Ruth says she doesn't want him back. She's talking nonsense."

"She's awful upset, and rightly so," Granny said. "What a kettle of fish. And Ruth's family's supposed to hold church at their place on Christmas. So much stress on all of them."

"So much stress on the Bishop and elders, but we'll get through this." Jeb picked up an oatmeal whoopie pie from the plate that sat on the table and took a bite. "I could live on these..."

They both sat in silence, listening to the tick-tock of the pendulum clock. The wind beat against the windows at a steady pace, and Granny thought of all the shawls they'd made so far for the tornado victims, and the thought warmed her heart.

She was startled when Jeb sprang up and ran from the kitchen and out the door. What on earth? Is he so upset about Luke and Ruth he needs to take one of his walks? She got up and looked outside but saw nothing, it being pitch black. You'll kill yourself on that ice....old man. She went to her white cookie jar, needing a sugar cookie. They were gone? The grandkids had raided her jar again?

She huffed and put her hands on her hips, but then chuckled. They didn't realize just how many cookies she had hidden in containers all over the house. Granny heard the door open and felt a blast of cold air. She turned to see Jeb, riddled with snowflakes all over his black clothes, and saw that he held a large box.

"I just couldn't wait." Jeb walked over and gave her a kiss. "Here's your Christmas present."

She hugged him, even if his coat was freezing cold. "*Danki*, Love." Jeb placed the box, wrapped in brown paper, on the table. She sure loved presents and ripped it open in no time. "Ach, Jeb, I love it."

"When we were stringing the cranberries, it got harder and harder not to give it to you. Made it myself."

Granny's eyes misted as she saw the all-white gourd birdhouse. Jeb had grown extra gourds this year and she always wondered why.

"It's a purple martin feeder," Jeb said. "They can get in on all four sides." He picked up the large feeder and pointed to the opening on all four gourds that were attached to make a circle.

Granny looked at Jeb and wondered what she did to get such a loving husband. He hung on her every word. She'd mentioned last summer she'd always wanted a gourd feeder. She loved the feeder, but the fact that Jeb remembered what she'd said ... She squeezed Jeb again. "I love you...old man."

"I love you, too, Love. " He bent down and kissed her. "I have another present. Suzy ordered it for me." He ran into the living room and took a small package out of the desk and ran back, handing it to her.

"Amazon? Suzy ordered something from South America? Must have cost a fortune!"

Jeb grabbed the package and stared at it. "*Nee,* it says *$3.25* and doesn't have any foreign stamps. Must be some company called that in America, I suppose." Jeb scratched his head. "We'll have to ask Suzy."

Granny waved her hand. "I'm sorry. I'm spoiling your surprise." She ripped open the package and saw a red book with a lady surrounded by younger women. It was called Little Women.

"The lady in that there book had four *dochders*…you have five." He pulled her close to him. "Deborah, I know you've always wanted girls, and I think the Lord has answered your prayer. I've watched you with your knitting circle. They look at you like a *mamm.*

Granny scrunched her mouth to make her chin not quiver. Was it true? Did the girls think of her as a *mamm*?

"And the woman who wrote that book never got married, so never had *dochder* or a husband. When you read it, be happy you…have me?"

Granny went on her tiptoes to tenderly kiss her dear husband. "*Jah,* I sure am. Merry Christmas…Love."

~*~

Luke sat between Zach and Jeb and looked around the doctor's office. Christmas wreathes hung around the room and there was a little tree on a table with a nativity set under it. Joseph looking at his adopted son, Jesus. He thought of Zach's love for his adopted twins, a boy and a girl, and his joy at being a father. Luke couldn't wait to see his new nephew and niece, but Ella said he couldn't see them until he got professional help….from a psychologist. How humiliating it all was, but he'd agreed to take all the steps the bishop had asked him to take. He was touched that the church leaders really cared. The bishop had stepped in not only as his spiritual leader, but as a father figure, and that, along with the help of his brother, made him able to talk about his troubled childhood with Uncle Otis…

When the nurse came into the waiting room and asked him to come back, he was surprised Jeb and Zach got up, too. The nurse told them all about confidentiality and how they should remain seated. Jeb put his arm around him and told the nurse they were all in this together. Was it his imagination? Was the nurse getting tears in her eyes? Why?

~*~

The one-room schoolhouse was packed as usual. Granny stewed inside to think that Jeb would miss this Christmas Eve program, but she knew the doctor in Blairsville had made a special appointment just for Luke, and Jeb wanted to be there for support. Maybe Jenny, Millie, and Tillie would see how caring a man their *opa* was and not miss his presence too much.

She took a deep breath and closed her eyes. The greenery that the children had decorated the schoolhouse with was pungent and memories flooded her mind of when her boys where in this same place years ago, reading their poems and singing Christmas carols. She thought of her sons who she barely saw, but was grateful they wrote faithfully…and she had her "knitting *dochders*," as Jeb called them.

Granny was glad to see Maryann was looking better, color back in her cheeks and no more dizzy spells. She looked over at Ella who had her twins. Praise be. A boy and a girl. She saw Ruth sitting next to Ella, holding one of the twins. She closed her eyes and quickly said a "casting off prayer" so fear concerning Ruth and Luke's marriage wouldn't overtake her. She prayed for Luke, admitting to the Lord how hard it was to pray for someone you wanted to slap over the side of the head. After all, the Lord already knew her thoughts…

She saw Fannie walk in just before the program was ready. She was glowing like the candles in the windows. Granny braced herself when she saw that Melvin followed her and then sat down right next to her. Amen! This is the best Christmas present ever! It was clear that Melvin and Fannie really were a couple. Granny wanted to stand up and clap, but only started to giggle. She felt Roman's hand on her shoulder, asking her if she was alright. Then her son Nathan looked concerned. They thought she was losing her mind. This made her giggle all the more.

~*~

Lizzie sat in the one-room schoolhouse next to her cousin, Lydia. The decorations were the same as the ones back home and this comforted her. She didn't want to be away from home on Christmas, but when Lydia said she needed help in her bed and breakfast, she knew it was the perfect excuse to leave. It was time to finally dig up her buried pain. When Melvin told her he felt an icehouse wall between them, she knew she needed help.

Lizzie watched as the children filed into the front of the room and sat on benches facing their audience. One of the little girls got up to start the program.

"I'm glad it isn't size and weight
And age that counts today,
'Cause then I might not have the chance
To stand up here and say...
MERRY CHRISTMAS!"

Then several students got up to recite proverbs in unison:

"Sometimes the gifts you make bring more happiness than anything you can buy."

"Giving and making others happy is the best part of Christmas."

"The best gift you can give is simply called love."

One of the older students motioned for everyone to rise and sing God Rest Ye Merry Gentlemen and other Christmas carols. Lizzie was surprised when they sang songs that weren't strictly religious, such as Jingle Bells, but knew that all Amish differed a little. After several songs the children sat down and soon recited the Christmas Bee. Lizzie always loved to see the little ones pretend to be bees as they said their lines.

"Bees can sting, oh, this is true,
But bees can make good honey, too,
And that's the kind we have for you.
Be REVERENT in spirit low, at the manger lowly;

And catch anew the vision fair of the Christ Child holy.

Be GENEROUS, *give all you can, then give a little more;*
Be sure to give more largely now than you ever gave before.
Be THOUGHTFUL *of the people who are lonely, old, or sad;*
Be thoughtful of the children, too, and help to make them glad.
Be READY *quickly to respond to Christmastime appeals;*
Be quick to give to friends afar or for the needy's meals.
Be UNSELFISH --- *all self-seeking with abandon cast aside;*
Be unselfish --- that's the keynote of the happy Christmastide.
Be HOPEFUL *for the best in life, for hope has wondrous worth;*
It was to bring hope unto men that Christ came down to earth.
Be APPRECIATIVE *for great riches of Christ and of His love,*
And of all the blessings from our Father up above.
Oh, may these 'bees' with you abide,
All sweeten well your Christmastide."

Lizzie felt like the Lord was nudging her on the shoulder when they spoke the line about hope. It was for this reason Christ came to earth. Even though she dreaded the upcoming appointment at the counseling center, she could rejoice on this Christmas Eve, just like everyone else, because Christ came for her...to give her hope, and she needed Him more now than ever.

~*~

Luke got up earlier than usual for Christmas. He was determined to finish the wooden blocks he'd made for Mica. He also needed to think of something to give to Ruth. But everything was closed, even the English stores. Well, he could write her a letter.

He poured the boiling water into the coffee pot and got some paper out of the desk drawer to write as the coffee brewed.

Dear Ruth,

First of all, I need to say I'm sorry for my behavior. I love you and know you deserve better. I've done everything the elders and Bishop have asked, even seen a "head doctor". I hope in your heart you'll be able to accept me when you find out I need to take medicine for my brain. The doctor said I have a chemical imbalance. He called it Generalized Anxiety Disorder. I just get anxious and worry too much and my mind races. I've lost my temper with you because deep down, I know you're a strong person and I wanted you to fix me. I know now you can't, but this medicine is supposed to balance all the chemicals in my brain to make me normal. It may be my imagination, but I feel calmer since I started taking it yesterday.

I'm so afraid you'll think less of me for not being stronger. The doctor said it's like having diabetes: a diabetic needs insulin and I need certain hormones and things in my brain to be boosted. He'd like to have you go with me to my appointment next week, and I hope we can both be leaving from your parents' dawdyhaus. I'm ready to move in once you tell me it's okay.

I've already confessed looking at girly magazines, but Ruth, you need to know I see it as sinful and disgusting now. I forgive my uncle for exposing me at such an early age. Jeb's little book he wrote on how to love your wife has made me see what a real man is. I hope you'll give me a chance to show you.

I love you,
Luke

~*~

Granny closed her eyes as she lifted her voice in unison with other church members to sing the *Loblied*. Although this twenty minute song was sung each church service, Granny sang with a more fervent heart, as the song reminded them of God's provision: God had sent his son to earth to provide a bridge back to Himself. What better time was there to sing the song than on Christmas morning?

When the song was over Granny looked up front to see that Jeb came out with the other ministers and sat down. She thanked God the lot to preach hadn't fallen on Jeb today; he was exhausted with trying to spend time with family and help Luke.

She looked over at Fannie and she noticed the girl was still smiling. Praise be. Granny stifled a giggle as she recalled Fannie's visit early the next morning to tell her about their love. It was a secret and she was touched that Fannie would tell her before her own *mamm*. Well, like Jeb said, the knitting circle girls were her little women.

She glanced over at Ruth and the dark lines under her eyes told her she got little sleep. She was most likely helping her *mamm* get the house ready for the church service and deciding what she would do. Deep down, Granny didn't blame Ruth one bit for wanting lots of distance away from Luke, but she knew to be Amish and divorced was not allowed.

Ruth's safety was Jeb's concern and he felt confident if the couple lived in the little *dawdyhaus* beside Ruth's parents, there would be protection. He also felt it was mighty big of Luke to confess before the leadership and

Ruth his sin of looking at pornography. She shivered. If Jeb ever looked at one of those magazines, it would wound her heart so much....she'd wound him over the top the head with her cast iron skillet out of pure hurt. Granny prayed for Ruth to be able in time to forgive Luke...if he was sorry for his sin, and not sorry he got caught....

~*~

After the church service, Ruth quickly went into the kitchen to help bring the prepared food out to the men who were arranging the benches up against the walls in the large living room. She avoided eye contact with Luke as she handed him a little bag of Christmas cookies, but he put something in her hand...a letter.

She felt like throwing it at him. No apology could heal her broken heart. There was no excuse for his behavior, and Ruth was ready to leave the Amish altogether if need be. She would not be married another day to a man with no morals and no self-control. She shoved the letter in her pocket and continued to pass out cookies.

Ruth looked over at her *Daed* talking to his friends. Would this be their last Christmas together? His eyes caught hers in a questioning way. He motioned for her to come to him, so she laid down the empty tray and joined him. He asked her to get her cape and take a walk outside. She grabbed her wraps and met him on the front porch.

"Ruth, you know how precious you and Mica are to me and your *mamm, jah*?"

She felt his hand on her shoulder, lending his strength." *Jah*, I know that, *Daed*."

"So you'll be living next door again, like you did when you first got married?"

Ruth put her head down and willed herself not to cry. "I don't know yet."

She felt her *Daed* wrap both arms around her. "Ruthy. We can face this together."

She stiffened. Together? She had to live with Luke...be his wife. "*Daed*, I was thinking of going to Ohio. I wrote to cousin Emma and she thinks I need to leave Luke for *goot*."

"She's not Amish...what are you saying?"

She put her hand in her pocket and fidgeted with the letter Luke gave her. "*Daed*, I can't live with Luke as his wife. And I can't be Amish and divorced at the same time."

"Divorce? *Nee*, this can't be. Ruth, don't' be so headstrong. Luke repented and talked to me because –"

"He talked to you? What for? To show you his sweet side and turn you against me?"

Her *daed* put his hand on her shoulder. "Did you get the letter and read that Luke's an ill man?"

Ruth froze and fear gripped her. She knew cancer ran in Luke's family. She looked at the seriousness in her *Daed's* eyes. Luke was sick, most likely really sick for her *Daed* to mention it. And of course, Luke would tell her that in a letter since he could speak better on paper. She put her hand on her heart. "How long? Did they say how long?"

"You ask yourself this. If Luke only had today to live, what would you do?"

"I'd help him, of course."

"Ruthy, your husband doesn't have any terminal illness, but an illness just the same. Depression and anxiety. He promised me, as your *Daed*, to take medicine that will make him well. Balance out the chemicals in his brain."

Ruth felt fatigue wash over her. It drained her to think Luke shriveling up by cancer, just like his *mamm*. But it shocked her that she cared. She thought there was not a drop of love in her towards him. Now he needed medicine because his brain was sick? She knew of a few others who really changed once they went to a doctor and were put on medication. Maybe there was some hope for them, even if it started out the size of a drop?

~*~

Roman put the girls down for a nap and went to his room for solitude. As he lay on his bed, he heard Nathan and his bunch talking downstairs as they put together a puzzle. Nathan and Beth's laughter made him miss Abigail. They always put a puzzle together on Christmas and talked about what they'd be doing for Second Christmas the next day. Roman always got together with his lifelong buddies, but Abigail was from Volant, over an hour away. She'd always longed for her friends back home, but they always spent Old Christmas with them. She used to count the days until January 6th since she loved Old Christmas best.

Now all the running around he'd do tomorrow was running with the girls, taking them to visit relatives they hadn't seen in a while. They'd begged to see Ella and

Zach's twins, and he suspected half of Smicksburg would be visiting them, people bringing presents and food. He remembered his *mamm* bringing over baby blankets she'd knit for their twins. Were they in the hope chest?

He wished Fannie was with him to help him go through the chest. He sighed and went over and lifted the oak chest top. It was nearly empty now, only some sheets and other linens at the bottom. Roman picked up the material and there were the girls' blankets at the bottom. He picked them up and gasped. There was writing on the bottom of the chest and it was Lizzie's. *Oak 11/5/1996.*

Roman sat down on the floor and ran his fingers through his hair. He'd never seen the message. He didn't want to look at the hope chest after Lizzie returned it. Abigail must have read the pen marked message, but would have thought it had to do with oak wood…but it was a special code he and Lizzie had when they needed to talk about something serious. *11/5/1996* was the date they started courting. Oak meant the Oak tree in Old Smicksburg Park. She'd stuck a message in the woodpecker hole….

"You rejected me… you had the final say…" her words echoed through his mind. He shook his head. Surely she wouldn't have put a letter saying she still wanted to marry him in a tree…or would she?

~*~

Granny put down her knitting needles and grabbed another cookie from the table near her rocker. She counted the number of Christmas cards she had hanging on a lone string across the top of the living room wall.

Over a hundred cards again, postmarked from ten states, but many from Lancaster. She laid her head back and thought of Lizzie, too far away on Christmas Day. She heard the front door open and saw Jeb.

"Did you and the *kinner* get that puzzle done?" she asked.

"*Nee,* it's a thousand pieces with no easy pattern. We'll have it out until Old Christmas." He walked over and sat in the chair next to her. "So, how we spending Second Christmas, tomorrow?"

"In bed," Granny said. "I'm plum exhausted…and want to fast."

Jeb leaned forward. "Fast? It's a time to celebrate. Why're you doing that for?"

Granny put her hand on her heart. "I just feel the Lord wants me to pray and fast for Lizzie. Can't shrug the feeling off. Something's not right…"

"You care too much…Old Woman. Take everything too much to heart. Maybe go to bed early so we can visit Ella and Zach's twins tomorrow?"

"*Nee,* I need to knit. You know it calms —"She jumped up. "Jeb, I forgot to give you your present. Ach, so sorry." She ran into the kitchen and opened the bottom door of her oak china closet and grabbed a white bag. Jeb followed. "Made it myself when you weren't looking." She kissed his cheek. "Merry Christmas…Love."

He encircled her with his arms. "You're all the present I need." He opened the bag and pulled out a black sweater with no arms. "*Danki.* What is it?"

"It's an undershirt to keep you warm."

"Are we allowed? I mean, I've never seen such a thing."

Granny smirked. "The *Gmay* hasn't made a ruling concerning our undergarments."

Jeb smiled and bent down to kiss her. "I remember those fancy socks you knit for our wedding night...black with red trimming on the top. I'm the only one to see them....."

Granny slapped her husband. "That was half a century ago." She grabbed the woolen undershirt from Jeb and held it up to him. "Will fit you just fine, and keep you warm."

"Very thoughtful. *Danki.*" He yawned. "I'm headed to bed. You too?"

"*Nee*, I need to knit...and pray a while.

~*~

Dear Lord,

I'm so glad you came into this world, because I'm so heart sick tonight and only you can comfort me. My heart aches for Ruth and Luke. Her refusing to let him come home today made this Christmas not so happy. And with Lizzie gone...well, she's never been gone for Christmas since she was born. I know something's mighty wrong, and my Roman knows it too. He acted so funny today when we talked about her opening a little hotel next to her house. His face got white and he looked ill, but said that he was fine. Lord, I wish I could do more for my 'Little Women' as Jeb calls them, but I can't. I'm saying my 'casting off prayers' to you, because I know you care.

In Jesus name,

Amen.

~*~

Here are several recipes for Christmas cookies my Amish friend wanted to share. Enjoy!

Lydia's Sugar Cookies with Cinnamon Frosting

3 c. Crisco

2 c. white sugar

2 c. brown sugar

5 eggs

3 c. whole milk

Vanilla to flavor (1 tsp.)

6 tsp. baking powder

3 tsp. baking soda

Pinch of salt

Enough flour to handle, not too much. About 9 cups.

Cream shortening with sugars. Add wet ingredients. Sift dry ingredients and slowly fold in. Mix well. Drop teaspoon full of batter on cookie sheet. Bake at 375 for 8-10 minutes.

Cinnamon Frosting

1 c. Crisco

3 c. powdered sugar

1 tsp. vanilla

Pinch salt

Milk to thin a bit

Flavor with cinnamon to your liking.

Ginger Cookie

1 c brown sugar
1 c. shortening (Crisco)
½ c. hot water
1 egg
2/3 molasses
1/3 c. corn syrup
1 T baking soda
1 T cinnamon
1 T Ginger
1 T vanilla
Pinch salt
1 T baking powder
Enough flour to make soft dough. Start with 4 cups to start. Add flour slowly until right consistency.

Sift flour with salt and spices. Cream shortening and sugar; add egg and beat until light. Add molasses, corn syrup and vanilla, then dry ingredients. Dissolve baking powder in hot water, and add to mix. Add flour, not to exceed 9 cups. Drop by teaspoons on greased cookie sheet. Bake for 10 minutes at 350 degrees.

Oatmeal Whoopie Pies

4 c. brown sugar
1 ½ c. Oleo (Crisco)
4 eggs
4 c. flour
4 c. oatmeal

2 t. cinnamon

2 t. baking powder

2 t. baking soda dissolved in 6 T boiling water

Cream together sugar, Oleo, and eggs. Add pinch of salt, flour, oatmeal, cinnamon, baking powder. Add soda water last. Beat and drop by teaspoon full on greased cookie sheet. Bake at 350 degrees. Take two cookies and spread with filling, holding them together.

Whoopie Pie Filling

2 egg whites

2 t vanilla

4 T flour

4 T milk

4 c. powdered sugar

1 c. Crisco

Beat egg whites until stiff. Add other ingredients. Spread between cookies and enjoy.

Chocolate Whoopie Pies

4 c. flour

2 c. sugar

2 t. soda

1 ½ salt

1 c. shortening (Crisco)

1 c. cocoa

2 eggs

2 t vanilla

1 c. sour milk from the cow (and for the rest of us…1 tablespoon of lemon juice or vinegar plus enough milk to make 1 cup ;)

1 c. cold water

Cream: sugar, salt, shortening, vanilla and eggs. Sift: flour, soda and cocoa. Mix ingredients together and slowly add sour milk and water until right consistency. Can add flour to mixture if too gooey. Drop by teaspoonful. Bake at 350. Put two cookies together with Whoopie Pie Filling recipe.

Christmas Butter Cookies

3 c. powdered sugar

½ c. white sugar

2 c. butter

2 tsp. vanilla

3 eggs, beaten

6 c. flour

Cream together butter and sugars, add vanilla and eggs. Mix well and add flour and baking powder. Roll thin and cut. Bake at 350 degrees. Top with frosting.

Basic Frosting

3 egg whites

½ tsp. cream of tartar

4 c. powdered sugar

Water

Beat egg whites and cream of tartar. Add powdered sugar and beat until stiff. Add enough water so that you can dip the cookies in the frosting.

Butterscotch Cookies

2 cups brown sugar

3 eggs

1 cup shortening or lard

4 cups flour

1 tsp. baking soda

1 tsp. cream of tartar

1 cup nuts

Mix all ingredients except nuts. Stir the nuts in by hand. Roll the dough into tubes 2 inches thick and cut in thin slices. Press with fork or potato masher to make design. Bake at 350 for 8-12 minutes.

☐

EPISODE 6

Old World Christmas

Granny heaped venison stew into two bowls and placed them on her oak table. She took Jeb's hand and bowed her head for silent prayer, thanking God for the hot food on such a bitter cold January day. She thought of the shawls being knit for tornado victims in Missouri and hoped they warmed the hearts of the women who received them.

She looked over at Jeb, hunched over his bowl, looking too worn out. "You're worried about Ruth and Luke, *jah*?"

"She's not listening to our advice. She'll be safe living next to her parents and Luke is much better on medicine. She should have been to the doctors with him, not me."

Granny poked at her stew. "She's a woman, Jeb. She's hurt. Feels betrayed and needs time."

"But the bishop said they need to be under one roof by Old Christmas or we'll need to give her a warning."

Granny huffed. "Well, you men all agreed to that…"

Jeb's head shot up. "What're you saying? Women aren't involved with church leadership."

Granny didn't say anything because there was nothing

to say. All men were on the church ministerial team and how could they understand Ruth? Her heart was broken by verbal battery and then finding her husband was looking at pornography…. Yes, Luke was sorry and seeing a doctor, and for him, all was in the past. But for Ruth, damage had been done and no medicine but time and real love from her husband could heal it.

"You'll talk to Ruth tonight?" Jeb asked. "When your 'little women' come over to knit?"

Granny reached over for Jeb's hand. "What can I say? You've been *goot* to me, Love. I can only imagine her pain, but not really understand it."

She felt him squeeze her hand and look at her fondly. "You're easy to love."

Granny withdrew her hand. "Are you saying Ruth isn't?"

"Well, she's been awful critical of Luke."

"No excuse for him to treat her so –"

"I'm not making excuses, Deborah. There's no excuse for how poorly he's treated Ruth. Don't get your dander up. I was trying to tell you that you've always supported me…"

She got up and hugged Jeb around the neck. "I'm sorry…old man. My nerves are shot over Ruth." She went over to get her silver teapot and poured more Meadow Tea into their mugs. "Roman's talking nonsense, too. Trying to find an old letter from Lizzie in a woodpecker hole, of all things. Why not just ask her what she wrote?"

"I'm thinkin' maybe Lizzie met a fellow out there in

Lancaster. Maybe talking about wedding plans."

Granny froze, her mug almost up to her lips. "Never thought of that. Maybe she's been writing to someone and that's why she and Melvin aren't courting."

"I think Fannie had everything to do with that. She's just a burst of sunshine, and the Lord, the real matchmaker, opened Melvin's eyes to notice her. Was hoping Roman and Fannie would be a pair, but…"

"Won't you please talk to Roman? He's acting so foolish, looking in all the oak trees he and Lizzie hid letters in a decade ago."

"I did. Told him to write to Lizzie and ask her what the letter said and he did. No reply." Jeb pulled at his beard. "I never thought he'd react this way to an old letter. One he never read."

"He's reacting out of love. Look at how someone reacts. That's their real feelings. He still loves her. I know it."

Jeb groaned. "You and your Jane Austen books…."

~*~

Granny welcomed the women into the knitting circle one by one, and couldn't help notice all the different emotions each woman brought to her home. Fannie was love-struck, Ella tired but happy, Ruth depressed, and Maryann somber. "There's Meadow Tea warming on the stove to warm *yinz* up, but let's get to knitting now and not linger. We need to get more shawls done. Downright freezing out there."

"Well, I was warm in the buggy," Fannie giggled. "Snuggled up against Melvin."

Granny beamed. "*Yinz* look *goot* together."

"*Jah*, you sure do," Ella said. "Glad to see you not only found love, but you haven't made one joke about yourself since you've been courting."

Fannie threw a ball of black yarn up in the air and caught it. "He's *goot* medicine. Helping me transform my mind; he really thinks I'm pretty, but not just on the outside."

"Transform?" Ruth asked.

"*Jah*. He showed me in the Bible we need to take our thoughts captive and transform them. So when I think I'm fat, I catch the thought and take out one of the nice things Melvin's said about me from the little carved box he made."

"I thought it was filled with Bible verses," Granny said.

Fannie sighed and grinned. "Oh, he made me another box. Didn't I tell *yinz*? One for scripture and one for compliments. He's so sweet."

"And it works?" Ruth asked, head down, intent on knitting.

"*Jah*. Kind words can bring healing in a mighty way."

Maryann looked over at Ruth. "If it worked for Fannie, it'll work for you. You need Luke to come home."

Granny cringed at Maryann's bluntness and lack of empathy. Maryann had a kind husband and had no idea what Ruth had gone through. "Let the Lord be the one who leads, Maryann. She still has a few days to make up her mind."

"But to be Amish is to listen to instruction. To heed what the Good Book says. We are not to separate."

Ella put her hand on Ruth's shoulder and glared at Maryann. "We're all believing Ruth will make the right decision —"

"I heard from Lizzie," Fannie interrupted. "Well, I read the letter she sent to her *daed*. She loved the Moravian stars in Lititz and is learning how to run a bed and breakfast. Problem is, there's an offer on the house they want to buy. Melvin found out. So they might not get it. Wonder why she'd stay longer if they knew there was no house to be had?"

"Could find another house," Granny said. "But it's almost two weeks now. When's she coming home?"

"That's another thing." Fannie sighed. "Jonas got a letter saying she won't be home for at least two more weeks."

"What?" Granny asked. "Isn't she needed at the store? Roman can't keep spending time there. I'm plumb worn out watching the girls."

"*Jah*, she is missed. It's only Melvin, Roman, and me that volunteer. Roman said the other day Lizzie is sorely missed."

Ella looked over at the pendulum clock on the wall. "I wonder how little Moses and Vina are?" She turned to Maryann. "You say Becca has lots of experience with babies?"

Maryann nodded. "She and Zach will be fine."

"I love the names you gave the twins," Fannie said. "Moses was adopted in the Bible, like you said, but I've never heard of Vina. Most unusual, although it's pretty. Is it a family name?"

Ella pulled cream yarn from her ball. "Jah."

"Who's side? Yours or Zach's?" Granny asked.

"Neither. We decided to name the girl after her *mamm.*"

Maryann clucked her tongue. "Now why would you do that? And her *mamm* wasn't a moral woman."

"Wasn't, a moral woman, but is one now," Ella snapped. "We've been writing and I know more about her; she needs lots of love and help."

"And you plan to do that?" Maryann asked. Her face was set like flint on Ella. "Help her? How?"

Granny cleared her throat. "Maryann, raise your *kinner* as you see fit and let Ella and Zach do the same." She shifted in her rocker. "So we're going to the doctors tomorrow, Maryann? Just you and me with Lizzie gone."

"*Jah*, if you insist, but I still think it's a waste of time."

"You have time since Christmas dinners are over and just need to prepare your heart for Old Christmas," Ella sighed. "I love that sacred day, the last of the twelve days of Christmas when kings came and worshipped Jesus. Something so…sacred. I think it's the fasting and focus on God."

Granny's eyes glistened. Ella was the one girl she felt appreciated her Amish heritage the most. Many fasted, but to Ella, it was a true act of worship from a heart who cherished her Amish upbringing. Granny had no fear that Moses and Vina would learn of their heritage, observing all religious holidays the People held dear. "Ella, I do believe you'll be reading the Martyrs Mirror to the twins as wee ones. Your heritage means so much to you."

Ella looked around the circle. "I think we all do, *jah*? Or we wouldn't have been baptized."

"*Jah*, you're right," Granny said, not wanting to embarrass Ella with her praise.

Again the circle was quiet and only tapping of sleet on the windows could be heard.

"*Yinz* don't take my baptismal vows seriously, *jah*?" Ruth asked, face red.

Granny gasped. "Ach, we didn't mean anything of the sort. Not at all, Ruth."

Fannie chimed in. "Ruth, we're all praying for you. Lots of casting off prayers I've been doing at night. We all love you, you know that, right?"

Ruth looked at Fannie and her chin quivered. "*Danki*, Fannie. If you say words can heal, you seem to be proof of it. Maybe Luke needs a compliment box, too."

Fannie beamed. "How about I ask Melvin to make him one? Tell him to fill it with genuine words of love before he comes home."

"I only have two days."

"I think Melvin has some at the store. Sells all sorts of things."

Granny put her yarn in her lap. "And I'll have Jeb deliver it. Jeb wrote him a little book on how a *goot* man should treat his wife. Luke says he reads it. Maybe along with the box, it will all work out."

A tear trickled down Ruth's cheek. "I want to believe it. I'd like to have the man I courted back, but at times I feel so hopeless."

Granny got out of her rocker and went to embrace Ruth. "Hope deferred makes the heart sick, but when the desire comes, it is a tree of life. That's in proverbs." She held Ruth by the shoulders and looked into her eyes. "Your heart is sick by disappointments and lots of painful words. How about you give Luke a trial period to heal it...to make it like a tree of life?"

"He might make it worse, Granny. I'm so afraid."

Fannie got up. "But you're not alone, Ruth. If you let Luke back in, if he says or does another cruel thing...I'll sit on him."

Ella moaned. "Fannie, no more jokes about your weight!"

"It was a joke. Just trying to cheer Ruth up and let her know she's not alone..."

Granny watched as one by one the girls got up to embrace Ruth and encourage her. No, Ruth would not be alone if she had to live with Luke again. Her "Knit Pickin" friends would be with her, as Luke used to call them.

~*~

Roman looked out the windows to his parents' *dawdyhaus*. The warm glow of the oil lamps was in sharp contrast to his pain. Lizzie didn't write back and he still couldn't find the letter she'd written years ago. Did he miss something? Another clue?

He took the oil lamp over to the hope chest and looked at the bottom again. *Oak 11/5/1996*. He put the lamp closer, but there was nothing else written. He closed his eyes, trying to think of which tree she could possibly mean? Better yet, why did he care so much?

He thought of his first buggy ride with Lizzie. She was so light and carefree. She laughed openly and her smile came from her heart. She never flickered either, until their wedding day approached; three years of bright light from her eyes were snuffed out somehow.

All he thought about was himself back then. When she called the wedding off so coldly, he cowered, feeling so rejected; he was afraid to ask why the sudden change in her countenance. If the pride of a young man hadn't been wounded, he might have seen a wounded fiancé.

Something caused Lizzie to change abruptly. She took delight in every piece of furniture he could make. She'd brought catalogs over showing him pictures of the carved headboard she wanted. She wanted a double Amish rocker, too, so they could sit together and rock on the porch, and then when she had *kinner*, she could hold a baby and have another one right next to her. So she had dreams of a future with him.

He turned down the wick on the oil lamp, snuffing out the light. Something had snuffed Lizzie's light and he'd find out, even if he had to go to Lancaster. He only had a few more trees to look in, and he'd do it as soon as the girls left for school.

~*~

Suzy told Granny and Maryann she'd pick them up in an hour, having some shopping to do in Indiana. Granny gripped Maryann's hand and they walked into the radiology center of the hospital. After filling out paperwork, they took seats in the waiting room.

Granny looked up at the television that was mounted on the wall. Images of women with perfect bodies, with hardly any clothes on, made her blood boil. She looked around at the people in the room, all transfixed on the television, no one talking to each other. She looked back to the television and to her horror, saw a woman taking her clothes off, showing her naked from the back. She shot out of her chair. "What on earth?"

"That's what I say," a large woman with flaming red hair said. "The soap operas shouldn't be shown in the daytime. Little kids could be watching."

Another woman with skin-tight jeans turned toward Granny. "We're not Amish. We do watch television."

"I don't," a young man said. "Waste of time. And it's gotten so immoral."

"Who's for you to judge what's moral and what's not?" the girl in tight jeans asked.

Granny put her hand on her heart, and muttered. "I thank God I'm Amish."

The lady with red hair walked over and sat across from Granny. "I admire how you live off the grid."

Maryann leaned forward. "Off the what?"

"Off the grid. Off electricity. Live more simply."

Granny looked into the woman's green eyes. She was sincere. "Well, I have a friend who's not Amish, but has adopted some of our ways. She has electricity, but no television. Seems like she has it harder than we Amish though, because she has so many choices. She started to cut back when she moved up our way. Said she'd never seen how fussy her life was until she started to get to know some of us."

"So the Amish will talk to people who aren't?"

Granny snickered. "I'm talking to you."

The woman tilted her head. "I live here in Indiana. Could I visit you? See the inside of an Amish house?"

"Just don't go stealing all my jewels." Granny winked. She took a piece of paper and pen and wrote down her address. "Come and visit any time. I can show you a string of Amish houses."

The woman clasped her hands. "Thank you so much. My name is Marge."

"I'm Deborah…"

~*~

Granny wrung her hand and sat next to Marge in a different waiting room. Why was she in one and Maryann in another? She turned to Marge. "I'm concerned. When the nurse said Maryann needed a test to see everything more clear-like, what did she mean? Didn't they get a *goot* picture to begin with?"

Marge scrunched her lips. "Not sure, but that happened to me once. I had a cyst. It was benign, thank God."

"*Jah*, thank God. So you think they're checking Maryann for something unusual? Can they see cancer?"

"Well, I'm not a doctor, but I am an LPN…licensed practical nurse. Work here part-time. They can see if a tumor or cyst looks suspicious."

Granny couldn't remember when she wrung her hands. Suspicious? Cancer?

She felt Marge's hand on her shoulder. "Is she your daughter?"

"*Nee*, but like one to me. She has eight *kinner*. She can't be sick…"

"Did she breastfeed her kids?"

Granny never understood why the English bought milk for a baby when an ample amount was provided by the *goot* Lord. "'Course she did. Still nurses the baby."

"Then her chances are better. When you nurse, your chance of cancer goes down. I'm sure your friend's alright. They're very thorough here. Good hospital."

A nurse came in and told Marge she was free to go and that she could schedule an appointment for next year. She looked at Granny and told her the same. They could get dressed and were free to leave.

"How's my friend, Maryann?" Granny asked.

"She'll be out in a second."

Marge shook Granny's hand. "So nice meeting you. We have each other's addresses and can write. When the roads clear, maybe I'll venture out into the country. Got a GPS for Christmas."

"What's that?"

"How about I come visit and show you. It's hard to describe, but it's a map that's fun to watch. Promise you'll write?"

"Well, I can't promise, but I will try," Granny said.

As Marge was leaving, Granny saw Maryann come into the special waiting room. She was pale and her eyes looked dazed. "What's wrong?" Granny asked.

Maryann sat next to Granny and took her hand. "I

need to come back. They found a mass…some lumps. Need to do a biopsy."

Granny squeezed her hand. "When?"

"In a few days. They have an opening on Saturday, January 7th."

Granny felt her throat tighten. Could this be happening? She thought of Old Christmas, a day to fast, pray, and reflect. She'd be doing a complete fast all day…for Maryann.

~*~

Roman dropped the girls off at the one-room schoolhouse and was glad to see Tillie walked with her head up, despite the fact that she wasn't confident about the spelling bee. His little Tillie, timid yet tender. So much like her *daed,* at least the timid part. Too timid to open his mouth when he saw someone who was wounded.

The memories of Lizzie haunted him all night; he even dreamed of their happy courtship. Why all these memories were so fresh baffled him. Maybe when he learned about the lost letter, he remembered how they exchanged letters all the time, stuck in secret places. Lizzie loved a mystery and he tried to make each search a challenge. He could usually find out from hints where her letters were, why not this one?

He thought of the hope chest. The writing was on the top, in the right corner. Did that mean anything? He slowed his horse to a walk and thought. Could it be a direction? Did it mean northeast? Did she mean Old Smicksburg Park then? So many happy walks down Trillium Trail and wading across Little Mahoning Creek in the summer when it was shallow. Could it be in the massive oak at the far northeast corner?

He turned his buggy around and headed northeast.

~*~

Lizzie looked at the pictures of trains on the far wall of the Iron Horse Inn Restaurant, to avoid the eyes of Amos Miller, heavy upon her. How her cousin got her to agree to go out to eat with this lonely widower was a mystery to her. Maybe it was Amos' four little ones. He surely needed a wife and it felt good to be needed for something besides filling up bag after bag of dry goods.

"So, how far is Smicksburg from here by bus?" Amos asked. "Have never been to the western part of the state."

Lizzie fidgeted with the end of the white table cloth near her lap. "Four hours. And the bus service is very nice. They changed my ticket to a later date at no charge."

"So when are you going home?"

"My *daed* needs me in the store, so no more than two more weeks. We have friends helping run it now. They won't accept pay, saying my *daed's* company is all the pay they need." She smiled. "He's *goot* at checkers and Dutch Blitz. They have lots of fun…the store isn't so busy in the winter."

"And your *daed* has MS? Is it the slow moving kind?"

Lizzie didn't want to talk about Smicksburg; she was already too homesick for a grown woman and it shamed her she missed her *daed* only being away for two weeks. She missed the knitting circle and seeing Roman, to her surprise. "My *daed's* on an experimental drug for MS. He took a great risk in taking it, but it seems to be stopping the disease dead in its tracks. No further damage and we're mighty thankful."

"*Ach*, that's *wunderbar*. Your *daed* taking a new drug shows how brave he is. Maybe the *goot* Lord allowed him to get the disease so others could be helped?"

Lizzie furrowed her brows. "I never thought of it like that. I guess everything works out together for the *goot*, *jah*?"

She saw empathy pour out of Amos' brown eyes. "There were no other medicines for my wife or she would have taken them. She was brave too." He put both elbows on the table and rested his chin in his fists. "But, we move on. It's been two years."

Lizzie looked at the snow slapping the window; she wished she could open it and let some cold air in to help her blushing. Two years was the usual time that an Amish person remarried. Her mind turned to Roman again. It was three and a half years now that he was a widower. Why he hadn't found anyone else was another mystery. Her life was turning up mysteries everywhere.

The counseling sessions and the help of her cousin were the only sure course of action she was positive she'd taken. Keeping her secret, her shame, for so long had only made it grow larger, towering over her every day and she lived in its shadows. No more though. She was not a little bird trapped in a cage with no hope. There was always hope when you let others share your burden. If she'd only not been too independent and confided in one person, her life would have been so different.

But she did confide in someone: Roman. She told him

to go to the big oak, the one in Old Smicksburg Park, a few days after she returned the hope chest, but he acted like he didn't hear her. Ignoring eye-contact with her and pretending she wasn't there. But surely he heard and saw the letter, and he rejected her. Now that her cousin and the counselor knew, she realized it was cruel of him. He'd never truly loved her, even though she had all the confidence in the world while they were engaged. But like Granny said, she watched how people reacted; that was the true person, and Roman reacted with silence and anger. She looked over at Amos, and his mellow eyes seemed to help draw her out of the cocoon spun around her. What would the next two weeks hold?

Ruth put little Mica down for his afternoon nap and walked down the little hall to the living room. A little house was easier to clean; having no man track mud through her freshly washed floors was also a relief. She sat in her rocker and looked out at the birds that flew from feeder to feeder. She looked at the cardinals through her binoculars; the males were vibrant red and the females' light brownish-red. She looked at the females more clearly. They had a beauty of their own; their feathers appeared softer and their orange beaks were more noticeable than the males'. The females' eyes always seemed more attentive, too.

A black image blocked her view, and she saw it was a buggy, with Luke in it. Ruth quickly put down the binoculars, remembering all the times Luke chided her for watching birds and not cleaning the house, and ran to the little kitchen sink to wet a rag and started to wipe down the counter.

When she heard a knock, she felt weak. She did not want to open that door, but she couldn't hide forever. So she opened it and a knot formed in her stomach. He held a present in his hand, and in the past, all his little bouquets of flowers or boxes of chocolates were only traps made to get her to trust him again. She did not want the little present in his hand; she wanted a new man.

"Can I come in?" Luke asked. "It's freezing out here."

Ruth pointed to the rubber mat she'd placed, inside the house, by the door. "Take off your boots first."

Luke stepped in on the rag rug and obliged her. "Where do you want my coat?"

"Are you staying long? I have things to do."

Luke leaned toward her and took her hands. She noticed his breath smelt of peppermint and he had no under arm odor. His hygiene improved but she backed away. "Luke, we can talk, but don't even try to come near me."

"I understand," Luke said, head down.

"Do you? Or is this a show like the children's Christmas play? They all pretend to be something else for a day. Is that what you're doing?"

Luke held up a little box gift-wrapped in white paper with a red ribbon. "Take this. You know I can write things better than say them."

Ruth reluctantly took the little package and opened it. A carved wooden box. Fannie didn't waste any time in getting one from Melvin. She opened it up and was surprised it was full to the top with neatly cut papers that fit flat in the box. The top one read, "Your tenacity. I love that about you." It was what he'd said to her the first time he told her he loved her. She thought back to the buggy ride when she first bent over to kiss him. He was too shy to kiss her, so she not only had to ask him to go on a ride, but she took the initiative to kiss him first. Almost unheard of in an Amish woman.

But was it healthy? Looking at their marriage, she assumed not. She thought of the softness of the female cardinal; there was something so lovely about a woman with a gentle nature. The male birds all pursued the females also, even fighting off rivals. Why did she feel like the male bird in their marriage? She wanted to be a female with soft feathers.

Ruth read the paper in the box now on top. "Your dark eyes pierce my soul." Was this a compliment? She bore holes through his head with her glares, most likely. Then she thought of all the times he'd try to tell her about his upbringing and he'd said her eyes pierced his soul. When he'd said that in the past, she thought he meant to stop staring, but was he saying her eyes poked holes in his soul? Holes into his heart only she could see and was he asking for help? She remembered once when he tried to tell her about what was in Uncle Otis' barn, but when he'd said how she stared, she'd changed the subject. He was trying to confess years ago.

But he left bruises on her arms and all the name-calling pierced her heart. She didn't know of a balm that could heal it. "*Danki* for the present, Luke. But like I said,

I'm busy. You need to go."

"Ruth, it's January 5th. We need to be together by tomorrow or you'll get a warning."

"And I have six weeks to repent, if I do," she snapped. She looked into Luke's hurt blue eyes. He looked more like his brother, Zach, someone who was the embodiment of kindness. She always wanted him to be more like his brother, and now she saw softness in his eyes, not wild and mean like they'd been. He seemed relaxed and not anxious. Was the medicine really working?

He walked near her and took her hands. "Give me a chance to show you I'm a changed man. I'm calmer and Jeb's little book he wrote about marriage is goot. I've been trying to snuff you out Ruth. Jeb told me that. He said Granny's spunk is her God-given personality, and your strong, take-charge personality is from Him, too. I'm so sorry I didn't see that, and compared you to women who weren't opinionated, like Ella." He took her hand and kissed it. "I don't want anyone but you, and I mean it."

She froze with her hands in his. She didn't want him touching her if he came home, for a long while. If he liked her opinionated self, she'd have to make that clear. "If I let you come live here, you'll be in Mica's room, in a twin bed, understand?" She withdrew her hands. "I don't want you touching me."

"Never again?" he asked softly.

Ruth was shocked he didn't fly off the handle, but she saw remorse in his eyes, or was it love? She thought back to their first nights together and how sweet they were, but she wouldn't let memories of the past blind her to the fact that she was married to a man who'd made her feel so unclean in the marriage bed. "Never…maybe. But I'm not even sure I want you back. I'm fasting on Old Christmas and will let you know my decision tomorrow night."

Luke turned and got on his boots. She turned toward the sink and could hear he was crying, as if totally broken, and her first reaction was to run and comfort him. But she didn't and let him walk out the door. She didn't know why, but she ran to the door and opened it, but saw her *daed* out by the buggy talking to Luke. He showed no sympathy toward him, only admonishing him that he'd better be treating his daughter right. With her parents next door, and a man who appeared to be changing, maybe things could work out for her to remain Amish, the life she loved so much.

~*~

Roman said a prayer for Luke as they passed on the road. It appeared he was crying. Maybe his daed was right; Luke was a changed man and Ruth needed to give him a chance to prove it. He thought of his mamm mentioning her prayers for Lizzie, her casting off nightly prayers. He knew he was always included and lately, he wondered if her prayers were softening his heart to remember the Lizzie before all the pain she caused him. Bitterness had blinded him to the girl who was warm and loving. How could he be such a fool? Something hurt her and he was determined to find out what it was.

He pulled into Old Smicksburg Park and tied the horses' reins to the post, and started down the path that led to the old oak tree. He was glad she hadn't put it in a white pine or maple tree. Since they grew quickly, the woodpecker hole would be closed from new growth. No, the oak grew slowly and surely he could reach the old hole, still open.

As he walked down the path, he remembered the many times he chased Lizzie around the park. How fun-loving she was, even wanting to play Hide-N-Seek like a child. He loved sneaking up on her and catching her, nestling her in his arms. A yearning to hold her again overwhelmed him. Feelings he hadn't felt in over a decade were as fresh as if they'd happened yesterday.

He picked up the pace to warm up but also to get to the tree. When he reached it, he spied for any holes. Roman looked at eye-height but didn't see anything. The tree was massive, at least four feet wide. He circled it again, scanning the tree higher, and then he saw it; a woodpecker hole, but too high up to reach. Roman turned to find something to step up on, but there was nothing. He trudged through the woods off the beaten path and found nothing. Without thinking he started to run, run the whole way back to his buggy. He couldn't get the buggy down the narrow path, but he could get is horse. He unhitched it and jumped up on the horse, riding it bareback.

Roman soon got to the tree and could see into the hole. He reached in and felt... leather? He pulled out a leather pouch and groaned. Was someone hiding their chewing tobacco in this hole? Most likely. He opened it up, and his heart raced when he found there was a note wrapped up in a plastic bag. Lizzie must have taken great care to make sure the letter wasn't damaged.

He ripped it open to read:

Love,

I can't look in your eyes. I can't speak. The path you told me not to take, I took. A man saw my hair... and other things. A hunter saved me so, I'm still a virgin. R, a man saw the hair I saved for you. The breasts no one has ever seen. My arms are badly bruised, but my heart is broken, and filled with shame and fear. Please forgive me for bringing this on myself. I returned the hope chest last week in haste.

If you forgive me, bring wildflowers to my house like you used to? Please, R, don't reject me.

Roman read the letter twice and put his head down against his horse's mane and sobbed. You rejected me... Now he understood. She thought he'd seen the letter. Never! I'd never reject Lizzie...my Love. He wailed and cried, until he could barely move. *Ach*, Lizzie, it wasn't your fault. He looked at the letter again, and remembered how he brought her wildflowers wrapped in ribbons. How she'd run into his arms every time he brought them to her. She always loved the purple ones best. His tears dripped against the letter. I would never reject you...

~*~

Granny flew out of her door, exasperated. How could Roman forget to pick the girls up on such a frigid day?

176

The poor girls had to be picked up by another Amish family, as if they were stray kittens. She had both hands on her hips, her shawl flapping in the wind, as she saw Roman's buggy slowly move up the driveway. Had the horse lost its shoe? He was moving so slow.

When she could make out his face, she put her hand on her heart. An accident. Something horrible had happened. "Roman, what is it? Is someone hurt?"

She'd never seen her son cry so uncontrollably. It reminded her of when he was a child and skinned his knees. How he'd wail. Not wanting the girls to see their *daed* in such a state, she told the girls to stay in her place. Jeb came outside, flew down the stairs and ran to the buggy, demanding Roman to tell him who got hurt. But Roman only sobbed. "Is someone hurt?" Jeb yelled, pulling Roman from the buggy. "Tell us. Who got hurt?"

"I…" Roman gasped.

Jeb looked up at her, puzzled, but Granny knew that something had finally broken in her son's heart. A heart that started to harden when Lizzie called off their wedding; God had heard her casting off prayers and honored her fast on Second Christmas. God was healing Roman's heart; some tears a woman knew were just for cleansing and healing.

~*~

Ella rocked Moses while Zach fed Vina. The twins had kept them up most of the night, but what greater gift to have than two healthy, beautiful babies? She couldn't help but wonder about the father. The twins were so young and their eye color could change, but for now they both had green eyes and reddish peach fuzz hair. Half Irish perhaps? She picked up little Moses and kissed his cheek.

She thought back to all the years of hopelessness. Thinking she was pregnant time and time again, but never could conceive. She looked out the window into the twilight morning and thanked God that he really knew her deep down; that these two *kinner* were gifts from Him and she and Zach had a special carved out place in their hearts that only the twins could fill.

Ella noticed an unfamiliar car moving slowly down the road, as if lost. There appeared to be an Amish woman in it, maybe someone visiting relatives for Old Christmas. She was glad the church leaders agreed to not have church since Old Christmas fell on a Friday, so close to Sunday. She and Zach would have a quiet day to fast and rest.

She thought of the meaning of Old Christmas; the last of the Twelve Days of Christmas, when the kings arrived to bring gifts for the Christ Child. Why the English started shopping and baking in the autumn, to only have Christmas for one day, she'd never understand. No, the Amish held fast to their old German ways, and celebrated and reflected much longer.

The white car came back down the road and pulled into their drive-way. Most likely someone lost and in need of directions. Zach put Vina in her playpen and went to greet the visitors. She heard concern in his voice, and then fear. Was something wrong? She clenched Moses tight and didn't move. She seldom heard Zach talk in such a confused tone. She got up and walked across the living room back to the kitchen, and saw Lavina. What was she doing here?

The teenage girl ran to Ella, hugging both her and Moses. She wants the *kinner* back?

Ella pulled away and stepped back. "Lavina, the twins are ours now. We agreed, *jah*?"

Lavina stared at her with empty eyes. "Ella, I don't want the babies back. I just can't live in Troutville anymore. You're the only person who doesn't judge me…"

Zach put his arm around Ella's waist. "I don't judge you either, but what can we do?"

Ella saw Lavina search her eyes for an answer…an invitation. But surely, she couldn't live with them. Anger started to fester in her; today was Old Christmas, one of her favorite days, a sacred day of peace to reflect, and now it was ruined. "Lavina, you can't stay here. You understand that, *jah*? We can't have the *kinner* confused as to who the *mamm* is."

"I told the driver to drop me off. I thought *yinz* would understand. From your letters, you seemed so loving."

Ella's throat grew tight, choking the words she wanted to say. I do care about you, but these are my babies. Mine!

Zach asked Lavina to sit down and asked her if she wanted a cup of Meadow Tea. Ella spun on her heals and went into the living room to check on Vina. Her Vina. She'd waited so long for children and it was hard to soak it all in; she needed Old Christmas to reflect, but not with Lavina here. How could Zach ask her if she wanted tea? May as well get a spare room ready!

She never had her emotions change to rage so suddenly before. Was this a *mamm's* heart protecting her young? Ella sat on her rocker, feeling exhausted. Up most of the night, and now having the biological *mamm* show up on her favorite day was too much. She put her head against Moses' and cried. She let the tears flow freely, as she nuzzled his cheek against hers. How she loved the twins; they were little angels from above that descended on their home, and no one was taking them. And little Vina would grow up to be a good, moral Amish woman, like her. Writing to Lavina was one thing, but having her in her life another.

She looked up and noticed that Zach was sitting in his rocker, holding Vina tight. "Is she leaving? After her tea?"

"Ella, I'm as dumbfounded as you, but let's calm down to think straight. It's Old Christmas. What is the Lord trying to show us?"

"Nothing," Ella snapped. "It a coincidence."

Zach gawked at her. "You're exhausted or you wouldn't be acting so unkind."

"*Jah*, I would. I'm the *mamm*. She wants the twins back and she can't have them."

Zach put Vina back in the playpen. "We need advice. I'm getting Jeb."

~*~

Jeb looked across the kitchen table in disbelief. "Son, you can't just pick up your bags and go to Lancaster. We're not spring chickens anymore. Your *mamm's* exhausted watching the girls while you volunteer at the store. She's still over at the house in bed."

"But Lizzie's not answering my letter. I need to talk to her; what if she did meet someone out there and is planning a wedding?"

Jeb heard the girls playing upstairs and was glad they couldn't hear their *daed* talk so foolishly about his old fiancé, as if Abigail never existed. He pulled at his beard. "We're just too worn out from Christmas to watch the girls for a week."

"What if I hire a helper? Maybe Becca?"

"*Nee,* not Becca. Maryann has a doctor's appointment tomorrow and will need her help. Just don't know."

"*Daed*, you think I'm being hasty, don't you?"

Jeb sipped his tea. "Well, your situation is unique; haven't really counseled on such a matter before…"

"There's counselors in Lancaster…"

Jeb sighed. "Since when do we need to hire a professional counselor to make decisions?"

"Since there's no clear cut answer."

Jeb cocked up one eyebrow. "Regrets over yesterday and fear of tomorrow are twin thieves that rob us of the moment." He leaned forward. "Son, rest in God today. It's Old Christmas, a day to rest and reflect. Read your Bible and God will lead, but not in a haphazard way like this." He noticed a buggy coming down the driveway, the horse kicking up snow. "Why's everybody in a rush today?"

Roman groaned and put his head on the table. Jeb went out on the porch to see Zach and waved for him to come into Roman's house, so Deborah could rest. Something was wrong. Really wrong. "Zach, what's the matter?"

"I need your help…"

~*~

Ruth looked up from her knitting. "*Mamm*, I'm afraid to let him back. I'm starting to heal and he might crush me again." She lowered her head, knitting furiously.

"But you had your *daed* come over here to put up a twin bed in Mica's room for a reason. You're letting him back, *jah*?"

"I don't have much choice, do I?" she snapped. Her *mamm* didn't understand at all. Her *daed* was a loving man; he'd warned her about Luke but she was headstrong and didn't heed his advice. She had choices in the past, but made wrong decisions. Now she was trapped. "I made a mistake in marrying Luke. Should have listened to *Daed*."

"We live in the present, *jah*?" her *mamm* asked. She went over to the woodstove to put another log in and then took the little hand broom to sweep up the ashes on the floor. She slowly turned her head toward Ruth. "He gives us beauty for ashes…"

Ruth stared at the ashes in the metal dust pan. He gives us beauty for ashes…one of her favorite Bible verses. But was it true? He gives…the Lord would have to do the work…give her love for Luke…give her mercy to forget…give her peace in her home. How would she know if He could do this for her unless she let Luke come home?

Her heart beat slower and she felt the tension in her arms ease. She couldn't trust Luke, but she could trust the Lord to do the impossible…give her beauty for ashes.

~*~

Jeb always felt peaceful in Ella and Zach's home; so the tension was foreign to him. Ella in the living room, clinging to the babies, both in her arms, fear in her eyes. Lavina sitting at the kitchen table, hovering over a cup of tea, looking mighty lost. He thought of his remark to Roman about not needing professional counselors. He wished he had one now. The world was getting so complicated.

He put his hand on Lavina's shoulder. "I'm Jeb. A friend to Zach and Ella and an elder in the church." He pulled out an oak chair and sat by the girl, the biological *mamm* of the twins. "Why are you here? Can you tell me?"

Her fear filled eyes met his. "I repented, you know. I knelt down in front of my whole church, but there's still talk. I'll always be seen as an immoral woman."

"Did you say you didn't know who the *daed* was when you knelt and confessed?"

"*Jah,* 'cause I wanted to be honest."

"And no church elder or bishop helped you choose your words? There are ways of confessing that you acted immoral."

"Well, my *daed* was in a rage. He told me to confess details; even though the bishop tried to stop me, I just kept on going or I'd hear it at home."

Jeb's heart sank. He never had a daughter, but he loved Jenny, Millie and Tillie with all his heart. How'd a little girl grow up to find herself in so many fellows' arms? Who taught his girl what love was? His mind wandered to Roman; despite the pain of losing Abigail, he was selfless and his girls knew they were the apple of their *daed's* eye. Jeb had an awful hunch that Lavina never knew the love of a *daed*.

"I hear you want to live in Smicksburg. We have a spare room open for a week, and then we'll see what we can do…"

He watched in pity as the girl put her head on the table and sobbed. He tried to comfort her, but he remembered Deborah tell him that some tears cleansed the body, so maybe she needed to get all the hurt out somehow. He got up and went into the living room and looked into Ella's bewildered eyes.

"I'm taking her to my place. For a week, so things can settle down."

Ella pursed her lips and her face was beet red. "Why?"

"Why not? We're supposed to celebrate the arrival of the kings today, *jah*? The kings who brought gifts to the Christ child?"

"And?" Zach probed. "What's that got to do with Lavina?"

"Well, when I think of the whole scene there in Bethlehem, there're shepherds, too. And they were looked down on as the lowest of the low back then. But they stood alongside kings. You understand?"

He noticed Ella's eyes soften and then a flicker of light shone. "I see. Ach, I was afraid of her being a bad influence on the *kinner*. I was looking down on her…"

"I was too…" Zach said. "She did repent and gave up the babies. That would be hard since I'm attached to them already."

Ella walked out of the room and Jeb soon heard her talking to Lavina, trying to sooth the girl, insisting she stay with Jeb.

~*~

Maryann and Michael held hands as they snuggled on the bench turned toward the windows, and looked up at the full moon. Its light bathed a deer grazing in the field and she thought of the light of Christ. His light took away all her fear long ago when she almost lost a child. Could He take away her fears now, too? Life was so fragile and she was afraid the result of the testing tomorrow would shatter her, shatter Michael. What if she did have cancer and needed surgery? What if she lost her whole breast?

She leaned her head on Michael's shoulder, feeling secure in his love. He'd told her today he only wanted her healthy, no matter the cost, the loss. She knew he meant it, but how would she feel if she had a mastectomy? Like half a woman?

As if sensing the noise in her mind, Michael turned and kissed the top of her hair, now flowing down over her. "Maryann, you'll always be the most beautiful woman in the world to me. Do you know why?"

She gasped for air, as if drowning. "Why?"

"You have a beauty that never dies, on the inside. It's so beautiful." He stroked her long brown hair and tilted her lips toward his and kissed her gently. "I want to see that beauty for a long while and grow old with it. I need it…do you understand?"

She understood. If she had cancer and needed the most radical surgery, he wanted her to get it, so she would live… She reached up and clung to his neck. "I'm so afraid." She put her head on his chest as he cradled her and rocked her back and forth. With Michael by her she could face tomorrow…she was not alone. Oddly, her thoughts turned to Ruth, and how alone she must feel, having a husband she couldn't talk to. Maryann closed her eyes and prayed a casting off prayer for her knitting friend.

~*~

Granny sat in her rocker knitting furiously. Jeb should have asked her first if Lavina could stay with them for a week, but she knew her old man. He picked up stray animals, kittens along the road, and found them homes. What did she expect with a wounded girl?

She thought of Lavina and all they'd talked about. Maybe some time away from Troutville would be good for her. She needed to recondition her mind, too. To see that she was forgiven, and made clean by a God who loved her. She'd confessed, and all was in the past.

She thought of Ruth's decision to let Luke back home tonight. Married to an elder could be a curse at times, since she knew more than most people when Jeb needed to unload. So Ruth felt God would give her beauty for ashes. Granny sighed deeply and put down her knitting loom in her lap. She had seen such a change in Luke, but fear that Ruth would get hurt again made her sick with worry at times.

And Roman, what he'd told her in confidence about Lizzie. She grabbed for her middle. Such a terrible thing, but like Roman said, it could have been much worse. Just thinking of it made her ill; if the hunter hadn't come by…but she caught herself. A hunter did come by! Maybe an angel! And she would not allow her mind to think of what might have happened.

She knew when she was overwhelmed, to just bow her head and pray:

Dear Sweet Jesus,

Oh, I'm so thankful you came into this sick and fallen world to make things right. I'm trusting you to lead all those close to me. I know your Word says they're in the palm of your hand and I shouldn't fret so, but I'm human and I do.

Help Maryann tomorrow as she and Michael go for further testing. Danki for friends who made us go to the doctors in the first place; some of my little women spun us around to see our need to go. Danki.

Lord, help Ruth. We are all holding our breath over how her marriage will turn out, but if she's asking for beauty, give it to her.

And Lord, Lavina, she's broken and though I don't know her at all, she pulls at my heart. Is it you pulling my heart toward her to help?

And as usual, Lord, I lift up Lizzie and Roman. If it be your will, I'd be so happy to see them finally be wed, in your goot time.

In Jesus Name,

Amen

~*~

Here is a recipe for Meadow Tea. It's a popular tea among the Amish and country folk alike. It's easy to grow your own mint patch, even if you live in the city. It's a good plant to cultivate in a container, either indoor or outside.

If you grow a patch in your garden, to harvest simply take the long stalks in bunches, tie with string and hang upside down to dry. Then pull all leaves off the stalks and store in an airtight container. Mint has much medicinal value; good for colds and helps calm the nerves.

Meadow Tea

1 cups water
1 tbsp. mint leaves
1 tsp. honey

Heat water to boiling. Put leaves in an infuser and add to water. Let simmer for a few minutes. Add honey to taste. If you don't have a metal infuser, you can put leaves into the water and then strain tea threw cheesecloth. For a quart of tea, the size of many teapots, simply add four times the amount of ingredients. You can serve hot or cold. Enjoy!

EPISODE 7

Beauty for Ashes

Maryann held her baby tight and rocked back and forth, forcing herself to hum the *Loblied,* the second song at church that was never rushed, but sung slow intentionally. To focus on the words and the fact that God would be their provision. She needed His provision more than ever.

She willed herself to be thankful for things she'd overlooked, despite her diagnosis. The cancer was contained, and if she hadn't been in the company of such dear women at her knitting circle who forced her to get a mammogram, her condition might be terminal. She was sure they would be praying for her tonight and it was a comfort.

She was going to go to the knitting circle but craved solitude, and real food. Granny always had goodies to eat, and only Michael knew she'd been to Dan Miller's herb shop and was on a fruit and vegetable cleanse. Dan said he'd seen tumors shrink over time, and hoped hers would be smaller; small enough to only do a lumpectomy, only losing part of her breast.

She hummed louder at the thought of being away

from her *kinner*. Looking at them now, doing school work at the long oak table after supper, warmed her heart. Why hadn't she noticed this beautiful scene before? Michael always sat down at the table to help with any math problems, having a keen mind for figures. She never thanked him....she never took the time...

Time was what she wanted more than anything. The doctor had told her the cancer was most likely contained, and that gnawed at her soul. "Most likely", wasn't a definite answer. What if she didn't make it? Who would raise her *kinner*?

She leaned back and hummed the hymn more slowly until she calmed down. In the multitude of my thoughts within me Thy comforts delight my soul. She thought of this verse, her motherhood verse. How anxious she was at times over such little things concerning her kinner, and God always comforted her. Now her problems seemed so petty, facing this mountain she'd have to climb.

But she wasn't alone. She had her church family and Michael by her side. Her eyes quickly darted to Michael. What if he didn't love her, being half a woman, with one breast? He'd never say it or even show it, but what if deep down he was appalled by her? At having a disfigured wife? She hoped that the tumor shrunk so she wouldn't lose her whole breast. Better yet, Dan had said he had customers that had a tumor disappear with proper cleanses and change in diet.

Her mind rapidly shifted to Luke. Is this what it's like to have a mind filled with anxiety? She'd never felt her mind flap about like the clothes on the clothesline. What a torture to live like this every day. She saw more peace in Luke, and she thanked God for helping him.

She bowed her head to confess her harsh judgment of Ruth, separating for a time from her husband. Of how she'd treated Lavina, the unwed *mamm* of the twins, like she was so superior to her. She gave Ella a tongue lashing for naming her Vina after her natural *mamm*, her immoral *mamm*. She always had the answers in the past and easily gave them, even when not welcome. She prayed for Lavina, the young girl who seemed awful resistant to go home with her *daed*. She asked God to forgive her actions, and then got up and handed Michael the baby.

She was going to sit down and write that girl a letter of apology, telling her she was welcome to come spend time with her family anytime she liked. And then she'd write letters to everyone in her knitting circle, just how Granny wrote each one of them a letter, inviting them when she started it. Yes, she needed to write out words of gratitude and love, or anger about her condition would consume her. She'd get them in the mail by tomorrow and they'd all have them by Friday, and hopefully they'd come visit and talk on Saturday...a few days before her surgery. How she needed her friends.

~*~

Fannie let Melvin tuck her under the buggy robe and then steal a kiss. "*Danki?*"

"You don't have to thank me for a kiss," Melvin said, smirking. "I enjoy taking you over to the knitting circle, but we need to pick up Lizzie, now that she's back."

Lizzie? Would she win Melvin's heart back? "I don't

know why she can't get a ride from Ella…"

"It's out of Ella's way." He put his arm around her tight. "What's wrong?"

"Nothing."

"*Nee*, there's something wrong. What is it?"

Even though February was right around the corner, the coldest of all months, she felt sweat form on her forehead. "Okay, I'm afraid."

Melvin slowed the horse to a slow walk. "Are you afraid of me seeing Lizzie?"

"*Jah*, I am. She had your heart before, and could get it back." Ice crystals blew into the buggy from across the field, and she leaned into Melvin.

He took her by the chin and looked at her, green eyes puzzled. "I've already seen Lizzie in the store a week ago. I go there all the time for supplies. And I can say, I don't have a love for her like you."

Fannie let the word love roll over in her mind, not able to absorb it. He loved her, but she was not a beauty like Lizzie. But Melvin said she was, so maybe this was her old unconditioned mind dragging her down. No, she was fearfully and wonderfully made, like the Good Book said. But why was she so afraid?

She let Melvin steal another kiss, and then pulled the buggy over to the side of the road, where a huge oak would shield them from the wind. He pulled a little heart -shaped carved box out of his coat pocket and gave it to her, his hand lingering on hers. She knew Melvin sold these little trinket boxes to the English for Valentine's Day, but never expected to get one. He told her to open it, and when she did, there was a little white piece of paper on the bottom that read, Marry me this spring.

Marry me? In the spring? The shock of it all made her freeze stiff like all the icicles hanging from the split rail fence. They'd only been courting for two months. She could see out of the corner of her eye, Melvin's head lower, and then turned to see him looking dejected.

"I suppose that's a no," he said. "Maybe I was hasty."

She slid her hand through his arm. "I do want to marry you, Melvin. I'm just a little surprised. Are you sure you want to marry me? And why the rush? Why not a November wedding?"

He put both arms around her and drew her close. "I want a parcel of *kinner* with you. A house full. I'm thirty and want to start a family."

She rested her head on his chest. "I want the same thing, but couldn't we wait until November? So much preparation…and you'll know for sure about your feeling for Lizzie."

She felt Melvin sigh as his chest went up and down. "If we wed in November it'll be so you'll know about my feeling for Lizzie, *jah*?"

She looked up at Melvin sheepishly. "I do feel inferior to her, you know that."

He bent down and kissed her. "Need to make more things to put in that compliment box I made you. But, can you at least give me an answer? Will you marry me?"

Fannie looked into the eyes that said she was the best thing since ice cream. "*Jah*, I will." She flung her arms around him and laughed. "I will, for sure." She looked across the field and through the twilight saw a farmhouse that had black smoke gently swirling upward from the chimney. The ashes in her life were being blown away too.

~*~

Granny whirled around her kitchen, making tea and muffins. The girls would be mighty cold when they got to the knitting circle. She turned when she heard Jeb stomping the snow off his boots outside, but didn't expect the concern on his face. "What's wrong, Love?"

Jeb took off his boots and put them on the black rubber mat, and slowly walked to the table, head down. "Long talk with Roman, and I'm plumb worn out."

"Does he agree with you or me? "

Jeb took off his wool hat. "With you of course. It's the easy road…"

"Jebediah Weaver! When have I ever been known to take the easy road?"

He ran his fingers through his gray hair. "You know what I'm saying, Deborah. The natural way, the hasty way, is what I'm talking about."

"Well, he obviously agrees with you. I told him to take a bouquet of purple flowers to Lizzie as soon as she got home, but he didn't. I remember those bouquets he used to take her –"

"Deborah, have you forgotten there are three pairs of eyes watching this? The girls may get the impression Roman never loved their *mamm*."

"The girls don't know that they used to court. He's been a widower for over three years and I say let him set things right with her. She never married because she only ever loved Roman."

Jeb moaned. "*Persuasion*. *Ach,* Deborah, you're thinking about love all wrong from those novels you read. That lady almost ruined her life waiting for a sailor. Seven or eight years? I think she needed counseling."

Granny sighed. "How do you know the story? Been reading my Jane Austen books again?"

"*Nee*, just the back cover. All you need to be reading too. Just don't know if her notion of love is right. It's not some feeling you can't shake. It's a commitment for life."

"Well, we're not going to agree on this because I have a woman's heart," she said. "Thank God," she mumbled under her breath when she opened the oven to take out muffins.

"I heard that," Jeb chuckled. "But Roman's a man and need a man's advice, *jah*? From a man's heart?"

She turned and smiled at him. "I've always trusted your advice...old man. I'll be trusting you on this. But, when will Roman tell Lizzie he knows about the note?"

"That's something that needs bathed in prayer. Dunked in prayer. A note written eleven years ago about such a sensitive matter..."

"Hard to believe it could happen here in Smicksburg." Granny put her hand on her stomach. Pain shot through her middle every time she thought that Lizzie was sexually assaulted, and wouldn't be a virgin if the hunter, or angel, as she called him, hadn't come along and saved her. To think Lizzie carried that burden for years, breaking her engagement off to Roman. Granny always thought all along Lizzie's dad's MS diagnosis was at the heart of her sudden change in behavior. Tears pooled in her eyes and she felt dizzy and sat down.

"Love, it was in the past. We move forward, *jah*? "Jeb put his hand on hers.

But obviously a woman's heart didn't move forward, or Lizzie would have spoken up. Being an elder's wife, she felt hurt Lizzie couldn't confide in her all those years ago. Now, Jeb was asking her to not tell anyone, not even Lizzie…that she knew she really went to Lancaster for counseling. She closed her eyes tight, so tears wouldn't spill out, but it didn't work. She let them flow freely, for the girl who was twenty-one, who was supposed to marry her son, if some scoundrel hadn't made her feel unclean, and bruised not only her arms badly, but her heart.

Then her thoughts turned to Maryann, and her upcoming surgery. A full mastectomy of one breast? Her whole body shook as she sobbed. She hadn't cried like this except at funerals. What was wrong with her? Lack of faith? Not trusting in the sovereignty of God?

"Cleansing tears," Jeb said. "Remember you told me some tears are for cleansing? Let them flow Deborah, let them flow."

~*~

Ruth watched in shock as Luke shoveled ashes in front of the buggy wheels, helping dislodge them from the snow. She always did it herself the many times she couldn't make the buggy budge. He took the horse by the bridle and soon the buggy was free. She started to walk out on the icy driveway, but Luke slid over to take her hand, so she wouldn't slip.

She'd let him home on Old Christmas, and over the past three weeks, his behavior was good. Almost too good? But was it the real Luke, the anti-anxiety medicine setting the real man free, like the psychologist said? She looked down at the ashes on the ground. He gives us beauty for ashes, the oil of joy for mourning, the garment of praise for the spirit of heaviness...Isaiah 61:3. But could he do it for her? Her heart was in pieces. How could a woman get over the fact that her husband looked at pornography? That wasn't part of his anxiety problem. Yes, his temper hadn't flared, and she was grateful, but she couldn't help but be disgusted by the sin of lust.

She let him help her into the buggy, and felt warmth coming up from the buggy robe. Luke had heated up a brick to keep her warm? Maybe it was something Jeb did for Granny and wrote it in his little book on how to treat your wife right, and she couldn't help but smile. "*Danki*, Luke."

"Now be careful on those roads. Don't go making up for lost time. Ella will understand the buggy was stuck."

Was she dreaming? He was actually thinking of her safety? After all the rules she'd laid down, even not letting him babysit little Mica, which she knew broke his heart, she was surprised. He looked up at her with those blue eyes, with tenderness. At times she just wanted to run into his arms and forget all he'd put her through. She forgave, the Amish way, she knew for certain, but the feelings would have to follow. She nodded her head and urged the horse to move forward.

~*~

Lizzie pulled her black cape tight around her. Sitting in the back seat of the buggy, being shielded from the wind by Fannie and Melvin helped ease the chill. She liked the buggies in Lancaster much better, being enclosed with glass. Her shock over seeing a battery operated windshield wiper made Amos laugh.

She dreaded running into Roman again and hoped he didn't come over to the knitting circle. He kept stopping over at the store, and each time, her anger only got worse. Was this part of the grieving process the counselor told her about? But she didn't expect this much anger, crying, or sometimes thinking she was over reacting. Her mind seemed to sway like the wind, but she did feel clean inside again, and no one could take that away. She even was able to forgive her assailant and pray for him. He had no more control over her. Forgiveness really was a healing balm; the nasty man that tried to assault her was the real prisoner, a prisoner to lust and rage.

She breathed in the crisp air, feeling refreshed, as the buggy passed a grove of pines. She loved watching Fannie and Melvin together, her head on his shoulder. They really seemed to be in love. Who would have thought?

As they approached Granny's house, a sharp pain jabbed at her stomach and she felt nauseated. Seeing Roman was so bittersweet. She loved him and totally despised him at the same time. He was the only one who knew about the attempted assault years ago, yet did nothing. She thought back to her trip to Lancaster and

Amos Miller. Such a fine man and four beautiful *kinner*. He knew about her former trial and why she went to counseling. The crying spells and anger she felt after each counseling session, she couldn't hide, and she blurted it out. Amos took her hand and lent strength to her. She needed a man like that. Someone not self-centered like Roman. The letters Amos sent were encouraging, and he was a part of her healing. Would he be a part of her life?

She let Melvin help her up the icy steps, and was glad Roman was nowhere in sight. But when she saw Granny, she was taken back. She'd been sobbing. Most likely distraught over Maryann's diagnosis and surgery. She went over to Granny and hugged her tight. "We're all grieved for Maryann, but we'll get through this together?" But Granny didn't recompose herself, but tore herself away and ran to her bedroom.

Fannie's mouth gaped open and turned to Jeb, sitting at the kitchen table. "What happened?"

Jeb sighed. "Cleansing tears. She just needs a good cleaning out. She'll be out in a few minutes. You girls want some tea and muffins?"

"*Jah*," Lizzie said.

"Well, I'll pass," Melvin said, as he turned to Fannie, eyes glowing. "I'll be over at Roman's."

Roman...just the name made Lizzie squirm. How long would this last? She tried to turn her attention to something else. "Jeb, how's the *mamm* of the twins? Have you heard from her?"

"*Nee,* and that's another thing weighing on Deborah's heart. She got real attached to that precious girl, and isn't too sure her *daed* is sincere in wanting her back. She was forced to be baptized when she was fifteen, of all things. She said she'd made the vow without really meaning it."

"She said that out loud?" Fannie asked, hand over her mouth.

"Well, I probed her pretty hard. Anyhow, what fifteen year old knows their own mind? Best wait until at least eighteen."

"No *rumspringa* either, I suppose," Lizzie added.

"*Nee,* the *daed* squeezed her too tight. Deborah loves her red roses, as *yinz* know. They climb up over the porch rails in the summer. When the girls pick them she always warns them to not squeeze them too tight, or they'll die. She gives them mason jars filled with water so they can take them home and enjoy them. Lavina was crushed, like those roses, and needed water."

"Sounds like something Granny would say," Fannie said.

Jeb winked. "Some words of wisdom that come out of my mouth, I've learned from my wife."

The door opened, blowing in a brisk chill. Lizzie jumped, thinking it was Roman, but it was Ella and Ruth. "My buggy was snowed in or we'd be here sooner." Ruth looked around. "What's wrong?"

"Nothing some knitting can't help," Granny said as she walked into the living room. "You girls all get some muffins and tea and come over here and join me. Awfully cold and our shawls are needed in Missouri."

Lizzie went over and sat next to Granny. "Lavina will be alright, and Maryann too. It's a blessing she went to the doctors, *jah?*"

Granny put her head down and started to knit. "You're right. The doctor said it could have spread to her lymph nodes but appears it's contained."

Lizzie took up her bag of yarn and shawl that was almost done. "Knitting is so *goot* for the nerves."

"*Jah*, it sure is," Ruth said, as she took a seat. "I've been knitting more than I ever have."

"Me too," Ella chimed in. "But I must admit, I'm not always making shawls. I'm working on prayer blankets for the twins."

"Prayer blankets? What's that?" Fannie asked, as she took up her knitting.

"Well, you may think it's silly, but I made up the name myself. It's just what I call them. When I knit, I pray for my twins so I call them prayer blankets."

Fannie put her yarn in her lap. "That is so sweet. And I like the confidence in your voice, when you say *my twins*. You and Lavina got everything worked out, *jah?*"

"Well, I don't know. I wrote but haven't gotten a letter back. I did tell her she could visit every once in a while, but just let us know first."

Granny pursed her lips. "That *daed* of hers…well….he frightens me. But I keep saying 'Regrets over yesterday and the fear of tomorrow are twin thieves that rob us of the moment'." She looked up. "You girls know that proverb, *jah?*"

"*Nee*," Ruth said. "Is it in the Bible?"

"It's a saying passed down in my family, I suppose. But if you think about it, we can't change what's in the past so it only robs us of joy. And fear can cripple us worse than arthritis, robbing us from moving on."

Ella beamed. "Granny you are so wise."

"My *mamm* was wise. She engrained that in me since I was a *kinner*." She looked over at Ruth. "And now I'm meditating on beauty for ashes. Really turning the whole thing over and over in my mind. It's a promise from the Good Book. Ruth, your *mamm* was wise to instill that in you, *jah*?"

Ruth shifted. "*Jah*, but it's not easy when you smell ashes all around you, like a little spark could make them ignite again."

Lizzie thought about all that was being said about regrets, fear of the future, and now beauty for ashes. She felt her throat constrict and the uncontrollable urge to cry overtook her again. She put her hands to her face and let the tears flow freely.

"Lizzie, are you upset about me and Melvin?" Fannie asked.

Granny put down her yarn and put her arm around Lizzie. "Cleansing tears?"

Lizzie looked around the room at the baffled women. "I'm sorry. I have a lot on my mind. I miss Lancaster…"

"And Amos Miller?" Fannie asked.

Lizzie felt like she was suffocating and gasped for air. "*Jah*, I do actually. He's a *wunderbar goot* man, with four dear *kinner*. Lydia thought we'd make a *goot* match. But, we'll see."

"We'll see what?" Granny asked.

"Well, we're writing for now. I get a letter almost every

other day." She turned to Granny. "Where do you get your pretty stationary? Punxsy-Mart?"

Granny knit furiously. "Some of it, *jah*. But I won't be going up there anytime soon; Groundhog Day in Punxsutawney is something I avoid. So much traffic."

"But Suzy's a *goot* driver. I think it would be fun to go up and watch. I don't think there's anything wrong with it, is there?" Fannie asked.

"I think with Maryann's surgery scheduled for Monday, we need to stay put and help with the *kinner*," Ruth said. "I'm making a meal chart, making sure there's meals taken over for a long while."

Granny looked up at Ruth. "I see it already in you Ruth. Beauty. You're spreading beauty around even from your ashes. "Granny got up and embraced Ruth. "Lord bless you child."

Maryann remembered what Fannie had asked, Are you upset about me and Melvin? What an odd thing to ask. "Fannie, what you said about you and Melvin and me being upset...what did you mean? Why would I be upset?"

Fannie lips spread and her eyes lit up. "It's a secret."

Ella clapped her hands. "And we know what's kept a secret."

Granny froze. "You and Melvin have a secret? We all know what that means."

Fannie put her hand over her mouth. "Weddings are kept a secret, but other things are too. Melvin and I have only been courting for a few months. Why would you think we had plans for a wedding? If you think that you're

_"

Granny laughed. "You're trying so hard to pull the wool over our eyes. We're not daft."

Lizzie looked at all the animated faces, and she was so happy for Fannie. She thought there was more of a tenderness in the buggy between Fannie and Melvin than usual. Her mind wandered to Amos, of all things. Would she have a secret to keep some day? Would she see beauty for ashes?

~*~

Roman crossed his arms and slouched in his rocker, unable to speak. The flame of the oil lamp didn't compare the glow on Melvin's face. He was engaged to Fannie?

"Look here, Melvin, I'm not prying, but it does seem hasty. You've only courted for two months, is it?"

Melvin looked keenly at a bird he was whittling for Fannie. "She's the one. I know it."

Roman didn't want to bring up his courting Lizzie just last year, although it was a short spell, but after the talk with his *daed* about being hasty, he felt obligated. "Adopt the pace of nature; her secret is patience. You've heard that, *jah?*"

He leaned forward. "Roman, I'm thirty and never been married. Don't you think I've been patient enough?"

"But you were courting Lizzie not long ago."

Melvin took the tip of his pocket knife and poked the wood to form the bird's eyes. "When I got to know Fannie... Well, how can I put it? It's like someone gave me an apple pie and a rhubarb pie. Now I know how seldom a rhubarb pie comes along. It takes three years to get a decent crop, but apples are everywhere. Fannie's a rhubarb pie, understand?"

Roman shrugged his shoulders. "I suppose, but Lizzie is no common apple though."

"Well compared to Fannie she is, at least how I see it."

"To me, Lizzie's rhubarb..." Roman mumbled as he got up to throw a log in the woodstove.

"I heard that. I knew it. You care for Lizzie and it's most likely why she'd never warmed up to another man; she cares for you."

Roman felt a headache coming on. Lizzie couldn't get close to a man all these years because she was a wounded bird.

"I've notice how she looks at you, Roman. Part of the reason I called off the courtship."

"I don't understand. Seems like she doesn't care to be around me."

"Well, maybe it's because she's nervous. Women are hard to understand, but I know how much Fannie hid her emotions. All the hurt and pain she carried was pitiful. Thinking she was fat and all. But she said it all started to change when your girls compared her to a pretty snowflake. *Ain't* that something?"

Roman grinned. His girls were like a healing salve to a wound. Their child-like faith so trusting...so hopeful. Maybe they could help Lizzie trust too. When Melvin started to whistle, he looked up, realizing he'd never heard him whistle, hum or sing. "Melvin, can I ask you something in confidence?"

"*Jah*, sure. Would be glad to help."

"I'd like to marry Lizzie but –"

"You aren't even courting yet."

Roman sighed. "Okay, I want to court Lizzie again. But I have my girls, and they'll know someday I was engaged to Lizzie before their *mamm*. Over time, through the Amish Grapevine, they'll know for sure. My *daed* fears they'll think I never loved their *mamm*."

"Why?"

"Because after Abigail died, I married an old girlfriend."

Melvin shook his head as if trying to release something. "Roman, it was ages ago you and Lizzie courted. You and Lizzie have both changed. Both seen tragedy so maybe you see things the same. Look at Lizzie with losing her *mamm*, the house fire and now Jonas' MS. You had a wife you loved killed in a buggy accident. You're not the same people. If the girls ever question, tell them that people are like meandering rivers, never looking the same."

Roman couldn't help but stare at Melvin. "How'd you get to be so wise?"

Melvin laughed. "Well, I'm not. But I do want to see you happy again."

Roman scratched his beard. He went over to the woodstove and poked the fire with a metal pole, allowing the air to circulate around the logs, and soon the fire grew bright. What if Lizzie needed more space? What if he smothered her too fast? He put down the metal rod and swept up the ashes that fell out. He'd heard his *mamm* encourage Lavina over the dinner table, telling her God would give her beauty for ashes. He'd have to trust that in time, his relationship with Lizzie would be something honoring to God and his late wife. A story his girls would find beautiful. Maybe a story his girls could be a part of; a part of Lizzie's healing.

~*~

Roman pulled into Miller's Variety the next morning, after dropping his girls off at school, and visiting Smicksburg Florist; they had lots of purple flowers to pick from, Lizzie's favorite color. A purple ribbon was tied around them, like he'd always done when they were courting.

In her letter she'd put in the woodpecker hole eleven years ago, she'd said to come to her with wildflowers tied in a ribbon if he forgave her...and didn't reject her. He bowed his head in silent prayer before entering the store, asking for God's strength. When he opened the door he was relieved that the store was empty; most likely people were doing their morning chores. He saw Lizzie measuring out spices into little bags by the scale and Jonas was nowhere in sight.

She looked up at him, eyes more timid than Tillie in a crowd. Was he doing the right thing?

"Morning, Lizzie," he said. "Can I talk to you private like?"

She looked more intently at her spices. "Something wrong?"

"*Nee*, but it's serious."

Lizzie nodded and motioned for him to come into the house. He followed and when entering the kitchen the smell of pastries wafted from the stove. "Want some muffins? They should be done."

Roman cleared his throat and took the bouquet of flowers from behind him. "Lizzie, these are for you."

A puzzled look spread across her face. "*Danki*, so unexpected. Flowers in winter."

He noticed she wouldn't make eye contact with him as she took the flowers. He sat at the table. "Muffins sound *goot*."

"Do you want coffee?"

"*Nee...*"

"So, what do you want to talk about?"

Roman lowered his head and clenched the fists he had on the table. "Lizzie, can you ever forgive me?"

"For what?"

He looked over and searched her face. The flowers obviously didn't bring back any memories to her; of their courtship or the letter. "Lizzie, sit down."

She sat across from him and he reached for her hands. They were as cold as ice and stiff. "Years ago, when you broke off our engagement, I was a proud man. I thought only of myself, and couldn't see your pain."

He noticed the color drain from her face. "Roman, what are you saying?"

He tightened his grip on her. "I found the letter in the oak tree when you were in Lancaster."

"What letter? I don't know what you're talking about."

Roman studied her face. She didn't remember writing the note? He had it in his pocket. Should he show it to her? The bewildered look on her face told him that he should. He placed the letter in her hand, and watched in horror as her face became contorted as she read it. She shook her head and crumbled up the letter, and then ran to the sink, holding her stomach.

He got up and spotted her from the back, afraid she'd collapse. He put his hands on her shoulders and felt her tremble, and caught her in time, as she fell backwards, fainting in his arms. He picked her up and carried her to the padded bench and propped her head up with a pillow. Maybe his *daed* was right! He needed to move in pace with nature…

He ran to the icebox and saw there was orange juice. He poured a glass and raised her head, trying to wake her up. Her eyes opened, wild looking, and he put the glass to her lips. She took a sip and he encouraged her to drink the juice, and she did.

She sat up and he took her hand, sitting next to her. "Lizzie, it wasn't your fault."

"R-Roman, you never knew until now?"

"*Jah…*"

She held her middle again and pain was etched on her face. He rubbed her back and she moved away. "Roman, this is hard…"

"I'm so sorry. If I'd known I-"

"Jacob waited for seven years for Rachael…"

"I know…"

"You couldn't wait a few months." She turned to him. "Roman, I was in counseling in Lancaster. I've come to realize you never really loved me…"

"That's not true. I was selfish and immature. When

you acted so cold toward me, I thought you found someone else. My pride was hurt, and like I said, was blind to see you were really hurting." He reached for her, yearning to hold her, but she pushed him away.

"Lizzie, I'm asking you to forgive me and give me another chance."

She looked at him, eyes hollow. "Roman, I forgive you. *Jah*, I do."

"So we can court again?"

Her eyes grew round. "Court?"

Roman took her hand. "*Jah*, I never stopped caring for you Lizzie. And we're different people now. I've seen tragedy and so have you. We're more mature…"

"I'm going through quite a lot. Since I talked about my secret to a counselor in Lancaster, I'm going through what they call the grieving process. Grieving over all I've lost because of the assault. One minute I'm fine, the next in tears or angry. It's going to be a long journey…"

"And I can be there to walk beside you." He pulled the card the girls made Lizzie out of his coat pocket. "The girls and I would like to have you over for dinner. Here's their invitation."

Lizzie took the homemade card and nodded her head. "I'd like to come…"

~*~

Dear Granny,

Sorry I haven't written. I've been so busy taking care of the little ones. The flu hit our house something awful, and my mamm was in bed for several days.

It was hard saying good-bye after spending a week with you. My daed says he's trying to forgive me of my immoral ways, but still treats me like I'm Mary Magdalene, the prostitute in the Bible. My mamm's a comfort though, always saying she believes me.

I hope to come to Smicksburg soon. I love talking to you and Jeb. He's a wunderbar man. I wished he was my daed.

I like what you wrote to me, that God can give me beauty for ashes. But it does seem impossible. My name is so tainted by sin here in Troutville, and now people in Smicksburg know I'm the unwed mamm of the twins.

How are Moses and Vina? Ella touched my heart in naming the girl after me. She said I can visit, only if I make arrangements first, and have a place to stay. She and Zach don't want the kinner confused as to who the real mamm is, and the real mamm is Ella, for sure.

Well, I hope to visit soon, and if there's anything I can do for you, just write.

Lavina

Granny grinned. She knew exactly what Lavina could do for her and Maryann. She heard Jack barking and soon saw a small red car coming down her driveway, kicking up snow behind it. The English are always in a hurry.

When the car pulled up to the house, she saw a lady with bright red hair and remembered Marge's letter. She'd said she'd stop by to visit, wanting to see the inside of an Amish house. When she met her in the waiting room at the hospital, she was amused at the woman's desire to live like the Amish, as if their lives were simple; if she only knew how complicated life in the Amish world really could be.

She met Marge at the door and tried to keep a straight face. The animated woman was almost jumping for joy that she was going to be in an Amish house.

"Come in Marge. *Goot* to see you again."

Marge rushed at her and took her hands. "I'm going to see an Amish house. I can't believe it." She slowly looked around, taking in her surroundings. She looked over at the pendulum clock and sighed. "It's so quiet in here, and so clean."

"I scrubbed the floors the other day," Granny said.

"*Nee*, I mean it's not cluttered. Do you only put clocks on the walls? No pictures?"

"We put up calendars and shelves for things we need. But washing walls is easier with little on them."

"And these wooden floors are so gorgeous. Wide planked and all."

"Well, my sons built this house and got a goot price from the sawmill. I picked oak because it shines real nice when polished."

"I love it. I feel like I need to go home and throw out half my house. I have too much." She looked over at the black wood burning stove. "So, you cook in this and it heats the house too?"

"*Nee*, that one's for heat. Just full of logs burning." She walked over to her stove in the kitchen and Marge followed. She opened the black door to show some muffins that were baking. "This is my stove. It's propane powered. We changed the *Ordnung*."

"The what?"

"Ach, I'm sorry. It's German for rules or order. Our church has one and we vote on new things every year, around Easter. Last year we were allowed propane powered stoves and refrigerators. " She walked over to her icebox and fondly touched the wooden front. "I won't part with my icebox though. It was my *mamm's* and Jeb likes cutting ice too much."

Marge gawked at Granny. "Cut ice? What do you mean?"

"He's doing it now. The men dam up a creek to make a pond and the men cut it into blocks. Then we haul the ice to our icehouse." Granny pulled Marge to a window facing the back of the house. "See that little white building? It's full of ice, some of it's a few years old."

Marge shook her head. "So much work. I'd get a propane refrigerator if I were you."

"Well, like I said, my husband enjoys cutting the ice. He's been doing it with the same group of men for years, and it gets him closer to his fish."

"His fish?"

"*Jah*, the men ice fish for a while and then cut up ice. He got two fish yesterday."

Marge grinned. "I knew I wouldn't be disappointed. You Amish know how to really live. I never knew you ice fished. Do the Amish hunt too?"

Granny furrowed her brow. "Of course. Most English men hunt, *jah*?"

"*Nee*, not really. I know my husband would love to, but we don't have land."

"You should buy the farm down the road. Herds of

deer in the fields and you'd have venison year round."

"Could I see it? The house for sale?"

"After you show me that moving map in your car. I'm curious about that."

"The GPS still amazes me still."

"Well, sit down and have some muffins and tea before we go. Mighty cold outside."

~*~

Ella sat in her rocker holding Vina while she gently rocked the cradle floor with her foot. She looked down at Moses and then the cradle. Zach started making it the night he found out about the possible adoption. If he'd known they were getting twins, he probably would have finished the second one the next day. But the twins were a surprise, and he hadn't had any free time to make another cradle. He didn't have time for her...

She willed back tears. They'd fought bitterly after she returned from the knitting circle. Harsh words were spoken so quickly, but now, two days later, she still hadn't recovered. How could Zach yell at her is such a tone? About dinner being burnt of all things. She'd improved her cooking skills over their seven years of marriage, but Zach used to laugh over a roast that turned out like charcoal.

Yes, he had his brother on his mind too, but Luke was acting calmer that Zach now. She took a deep breath and blew out air slowly. She'd have to forgive Zach and forget his cross words. She heard the door open downstairs and then someone stomping snow off boots. Zach was home. A knot formed in her stomach and her heart lunged into throat. Was it already four o'clock? She thought it was two at the latest. She quickly read the letter of encouragement Maryann sent her:

Dear Ella,

When you think you might lose your life, the people in it seem all the more precious. I want you to know how sorry I am for being judgmental toward you. How you've treated Lavina is how I should have. You were kind and I was not. Ella, I admire you for your kindness. It's one of those fruits of the spirit I need to water. Your love and patience are a great source of strength to me.

Please be kind to yourself as a new mother. It's a big adjustment having kinner. It's exhausting and Michael and I have had spats just for that reason. Rest and take care of yourself so you have something to offer your family. Sit down and knit sometime or bake your favorite pie.

Please try to stop by and visit on Saturday or Sunday. I need to see my friends before surgery.

Your Loving Friend,

Maryann

She heard Zach come up the steps, taking two at a time. When he entered their bedroom, she could tell he was irritated with her again.

"Ella, no dinner again? We had leftovers last night."

"Why don't we go to the Country Junction?"

He took off his black wool hat and flicked off snow that was on the brim. "It's too cold to take the twins out."

"*Nee.* We can put a hot brick under the buggy robe and it's such a short drive."

"You need to get more organized, Ella. Think about what you're going to make in the morning, like my *mamm* used to."

Ella bit her lower lip and handed Maryann's letter to him. He grabbed it and skimmed over the words. "Zach, I think we need to take Maryann's advice since she has eight *kinner*. We need more rest. We don't even rest on the Sabbath anymore."

She was glad to see peace settle in in Zach's eyes. He'd been so unnerved by Lavina showing up on Old Christmas, and then living with Jeb and Granny. Fear had gripped them that she'd want the twins back. Lavina went back to Troutville two weeks ago, but had an invitation to come to Granny's anytime.

"Zach, are you afraid. Afraid we'll lose the twins?"

"I don't trust Lavina's *daed*. He seems squirrely to me." He sat in the rocker near her. "I guess I am. My nerves have taken a beating and I took it out on you. I'm so sorry."

She reached for his hand, thinking of how Maryann said her kindness gave her strength. "You need more rest."

"Jeb said we need to treat ourselves like we'd like to be treated."

Ella shook her head. "What?"

"We're supposed to treat ourselves *goot.* Not be too hard on ourselves or each other."

Ella lifted up Vina and kissed her cheek. "So then let's treat ourselves to a dinner at the Country Junction."

Zach grimed. "Okay, and then I'll treat myself to a dessert or two. I miss your pies."

~*~

Granny didn't realize she was holding her breath until Marge pulled the car into the driveway of the farm for sale. She gasped for air. "You English drive too fast."

Marge frowned. "I was going the speed limit. I was going slow for you."

"*Ach*, must be my age. Tend to slow down in all ways once you're ready to turn seventy."

When do you turn the big 7-0?"

"February 14th. Jeb always says I was born on Valentine's Day for a reason. I'm always trying to match people up. I love to see people in love get married."

"That is so sweet. Do the Amish celebrate Valentine's Day?"

"Well, not really. Jeb gets me a heart full of candy from the store though."

"So you're allowed to celebrate if you want to?"

Granny wasn't sure what Marge was asking. Did she think the Amish needed permission to buy chocolates on Valentine's Day? "When I told you we had a set of rules, they're there to make sure we aren't distracted from our plain way of living. You see how we live off the grind, like you call it."

"You mean grid….you live off the grid."

"*Jah*, we don't have heating or electric bills. We don't want be dependent on anyone. Now, using a propane stove doesn't give us a monthly bill."

"So you don't have to pay the English anything?"

"*Jah*, taxes on our property. We pay school tax too, even though our *kinner* don't use the English schools, and that's hard to swallow sometimes, because we pay for our Amish schools and their teacher." She turned to Marge. "Still want to look at this house?"

"Yes, I sure do. It's bigger than I thought though. I wanted something the size of yours."

"My house is a *dawdyhaus*. We lived in Roman's house while raising the boys, but we don't need all that room now. There's one in back of this here farm, but it's so small for a family."

"Joe and I don't want kids, so a smaller house would be better. "

Granny thought she was hearing things. "Did you say you don't want *kinner*?"

"We have dogs. They're like kids. Kids are expensive and the world's so messed up, I don't want to bring any into it. Anyhow, since you shared your age, I'll share mine. I'm thirty-eight and I think it's too late for kids."

"It's not too late, and *kinner* are a blessing from the Lord. How can a dog be like a kid?"

Marge put her head down. "Well, we don't make much money, and feel we can't afford kids to be totally honest. But, I told Joe, if we live off the grid, we might be able to afford one. Once I hit forty, I think it's too risky having kids."

"So you want a small house so you can have *kinner*?" Granny asked.

Marge looked at Granny fondly. "I don't know why I told you that. It's hard to share my feelings, but I feel like I've known you a long time. "She took the car keys out of the ignition. "Yes, I do want a child and if I can show Joe we can afford it, I know he'd want one too."

A smile spread across Granny's face. "I love to be a matchmaker and save money. I find it's like a game, to see how thrifty I can be. You'd be surprised at how little it takes to raise a family if you pinch pennies." She put her hand on Marge's shoulder. "Let's go see the *dawdyhaus* then. You'll need to pull the car further down the driveway since it's in the back."

Marge started the car back up and pulled down alongside the house to where the *dawdyhaus* stood. "See, it's real close to the main house but much smaller."

Marge put her hands on her cheeks and squealed. "It is so cute. I love it. And there's so much land," she said, turning to look at the vast amount of land in back of the house.

"There's sixty acres...plenty of land to raise turkeys."

"Turkeys?"

"*Jah*, the people who lived her raised organic turkeys and couldn't keep up with the orders. The English put their orders in for Thanksgiving in September."

"Really? But we don't know anything about raising turkeys."

"Jeb does and I'm sure he'd be happy to help. In the winter, you can raise rabbits."

"For pets?"

Granny giggled. "*Nee*, for eating. You can sell them at

the auction in Dayton. People come up from Pittsburgh to buy them."

"Do you eat bunnies?" Marge put her hand over her heart and gasped.

"*Jah*, it makes *goot* stew."

Marge shook her head. "You Amish live like Little House on the Prairie."

Granny raised her eyebrows. "Well, you'd have a little house and lots of land."

Marge roared. "Let's go see the house."

Granny was surprised at how Marge quickly got out of the car and opened her door, trying to help her out of the car. "*Danki*. I'm sixty-nine, but I can still walk." Granny winked at Marge.

"I know. Just don't want you to slip. There's ice over here."

"I'm sorry. Maybe more sensitive about turning seventy. Hard to believe." She saw the ice and was grateful for Marge's assistance. She held on to her for the short walk to the little house.

When she opened the front door, Marge clucked her tongue. "Someone forgot to lock the door."

"We don't have locks on our doors."

"Are you kidding? No locks? Is it against your rules?"

"*Nee*, just don't see the need I suppose. Not much to take if someone wants to rob us. And if someone's that needy, they're welcome to take our food."

Marge shook her head and pursed her lips. "Well, I'll get a lock if we buy this. Someone might take our flat screen."

"What's that?"

"Our TV."

"Are you going to run it off a generator?"

"I guess living off the grid means no TV. Oh well, I'd survive. Nothing good on anyhow." She walked into the house and her eyes lit up. She slowly moved her head, trying to take in all that she saw. "It's charming. Just what I imagined." She walked over to the black wood burning stove. "We can heat the whole house with this?"

"*Jah,* and you'll be nice and toasty. You have a few acres of woods out back to chop your own wood too."

Marge went over to the kitchen. "No appliances. But you said I could get a propane powered ones, right?"

"*Jah,* we have a catalog at home. I can show you."

"Marge walked into the living room and reached out her hands and spun around. "I love it. I feel like Goldilocks and the Three Bears."

Granny found it tiresome to understand what the English were talking about, so she didn't ask what she meant, but assumed Marge liked the house. "There's two bedrooms upstairs. Let's go take a look."

They made their way up the steps to the landing where two doors stood opposite each other. "The rooms are both the same size." She opened one door and let Marge in.

Again Marge squealed with delight. "It's a Cape Cod. Oh my. I love how the walls are slanted and the dormers stick out." She walked over to the window. "The view is magnificent. The barn looks much bigger from here."

"It's medium sized. Big enough to raise a cow, some

chickens, a pig. Things you need to live off the land. And there's an orchard out back, full of fruit trees and berries. Do you know how to make jam?"

"Oh, I could never do that. Looks too hard."

"It's so easy, my *grandkinner* can do it. We make it and sell it to the English. There's lots of little ways to make money."

"Could you teach me? I'd love to learn."

"*Jah*, I'd be happy to. Ach, and you could be an Amish driver. We really need someone now with Maryann's surgery in Pittsburgh." Granny said.

"Oh, I could help drive, and remember, I'm an LPN. I do home visits and could check in on Maryann."

"Really? Praise be." Granny said. "I know we didn't meet by accident in the hospital. Maryann will need checking on, but the roads get so bad in the winter, but we could hire you to drive up and help her."

"I hate to say this, but I work for an agency that isn't cheap. Could Maryann afford help with eight children?"

"Our *Gmay* has money set aside. We just didn't know any English who was a nurse."

"What's a *Gmay*?"

"It's German again. I'm sorry. It means community. It's what we call our church."

"And your church will actually pay for nursing care? I can't believe it." She rubbed her hands together. "I can't wait to share all this with Joe. He could be a driver and I could be assigned cases up here in Smicksburg." She took Granny hands and jumped up and down. "I'm so excited."

~*~

Dear Lizzie,

I've enjoyed your letters, but miss talking to you. When you told me how much cheaper land is in Western PA, I started thinking. I should head out on the bus and take a look at some of those farms for sale. And I could visit with you too. I don't have any kinner to stay with though. Are there hotels nearby? Or maybe an Amish family with a spare room I could stay with for a few days.

I know you have restaurants, because you told me how much you enjoy the Country Junction. I'd like to take you out for dinner again. I think I could come in a few weeks. Let me know in your next letter if you'd like my company.

Amos Miller

Lizzie held the letter to her heart and was surprised at how much she wanted to see Amos again. Yes, she'd be going to the special dinner Roman and his precious girls were making her next week, but she needed to move slowly, looking for those special people the counselor said God would put in her life to help her heal. And it wouldn't be an overnight process. Was Amos Miller one of those people God was putting in her life? Roman and the girls too? Well, if He was, it would all work out and she wasn't going to fret. She'd cast her cares on God who was leading her down a path of redemption, a path that would give her beauty for ashes.

~*~

Later that night, Granny was still chuckling over her new animated friend. Marge was a bundle of energy and she had no doubt that she and her husband could live in the little house and have *kinner*. It made her feel good to help out the English, especially ones that seemed not to be making it. When Marge told her how her husband lost his job, being self-sufficient seemed to be a wise decision.

She looked up into the dark night, not a star in sight, all hid by thick clouds.

Lord, I'm thankful that you hear my prayers even though I can't see you, or feel your sweet presence sometimes. I confess my mind is troubled with the cares of this world, and it's choking me. I cast off Maryann to you Lord. I'm beside myself with worry. Take care of her body and mind. She needs your to help her emotionally, to feel like a whole person. I pray you help the *kinner* and Michael over the next month as she heals. *Danki* for Ruth caring so much to organize meals.

Lord,

I see Lizzie's cleansing tears and I'm so thankful you're giving her beauty for ashes. I hope she gives Roman another chance. The girls are so excited to help make a special meal for her. Lord, use the girls again, like you did for Fannie. Help Lizzie to trust again...to be as trusting as a child...and let her trust Roman. I know she's writing to an Amish man, but Lord, please, open her eyes to Roman. Help her forget the past and move forward.

And Lord, I give Lavina to you. She said she wished Jeb was her daed. Something's not right with her own daed for her to say such a thing. It's so unusual for see such a mean Amish man. Help Lavina's daed forgive her. Soften his heart to see what a treasure

Lavina is.

I ask all this in Jesus name…Amen

Granny put her hand on her heart. Peace flooded her soul and she had to fight back tears. Why she felt she could carry all these burdens herself, and not take more time to cast them on the Lord throughout the day, was a mystery. She needed to stop and pray three times a day, like Daniel in the Bible. She remembered when all five boys were home and she'd stop after each meal and pray, and the strength she felt. Why did she stop? Well, starting tomorrow, she'd say her casting off prayers three times a day. The more burdens she had to carry, the more often she'd need to stop and unload.

~*~

Here are a few Amish muffin recipes. Enjoy!

Blueberry Muffins

1½ c. flour

¾ c. sugar

½ tsp. salt

2 tsp. baking powder

1/3 c. vegetable oil

1 egg

1/3 c. mill

1 c. blueberries

Mix ingredients and place in muffin cups. Bake at 400 degrees for 20 minutes.

Oatmeal Muffins

1 c. rolled oats

1 c. milk

1/3 c. shortening

½ c. brown sugar

1 egg

1 c. flour

½ tsp. baking soda

1 tsp. baking powder

1 tsp. salt

Mix oats and milk together. Add remaining ingredients and place in muffin cups. Bake at 400 degrees for 15-18 minutes.

Apple Butter Muffins

1 ¾ c. flour

½ c. sugar

2 tsp. baking powder

½ tsp. cinnamon

¼ tsp. salt

¼ tsp. nutmeg

Pinch of ginger

Pinch of allspice

1 egg, lightly beaten

¾ c milk

¼ c. oil

½ c. apple butter

Combine first 8 ingredients. Add egg, milk and oil until moistened. Fill greased or paper-lined muffin cups with rounded tablespoon of batter. You can add a teaspoon of apple butter on top of each muffin for added flavor.

Bake at 400 degrees for 15-18 minutes.

EPISODE 8

Wings to Fly

Roman watched as his girls eagerly set the table, and thanked God they were so excited to have Lizzie over again this week for dinner. Their trusting nature seemed to be rubbing off on Lizzie's wounded heart and maybe his *mamm* was right. They're just what she's needed all along, a living example of total childlike trust.

Last week, when Lizzie came over before the knitting circle, he'd had Millie and Tillie jump off the steps, playing their little game of "Catch Me". They went up to the third step and yelled "Catch me," and he did. Then they'd go up to the fourth step, on up to the fifth. As much as Millie begged to go higher, Roman knew he couldn't risk her getting hurt. He hoped Lizzie learned from his girls just how trusting they were; they risked getting hurt but knew that he'd catch them. They trusted him and hoped Lizzie could learn to do the same. To trust her Heavenly Father to catch and carry as she went through her time of healing.

When she mentioned Amos Miller was coming to visit, right around Valentine's Day of all things, he panicked. She did think so highly of this widower from Lancaster, saying how much he wrote. So Roman wrote her letters too and went to the store more than usual. And these little dinners with his girls seemed to be opening up Lizzie like the sun does flowers. But what if it opened her heart to Amos Miller when he came tomorrow?

He went over to the stove and stirred the rabbit stew he'd prepared, and said a silent prayer. His *mamm* had told him about her "casting off" prayers, now doing them three times a day, like Daniel in the Bible. He aimed to do the same.

~*~

Maryann lay on the living room couch and looked over at Lavina, rocking her *boppli*. "I'm so glad you're here to help with the *kinner*. I'm so thankful."

Lavina patted the baby's back. "I'm glad to be here in Smicksburg, but don't think Ella and Zach want me here."

"Well, the Lord needs to soften their heart towards you. He softened mine." She put her head down and fidgeted with her wool shawl. "I'm so sorry I treated you like Mary Magdalene…"

"All's forgiven, Maryann. We've talked about this before."

"Just the same, I'm still working on my judgmental attitude. It creeps up in other places at times."

"Well, you need to work on getting better too. You have another radiation treatment tomorrow."

Maryann clenched her hands and willed fear to go away. "I'm thankful too that I only had a lumpectomy and didn't lose my whole breast. Radiation therapy came with that choice. Doctors said I wouldn't need it if I got a full mastectomy, but I'm not regretting my decision." Maryann turned to look out the window and saw a red car pull up the driveway. "Marge is here, right on time. Granny says she's an angel that fell from heaven."

Lavina grinned. "She's looking at the house down the road from Granny's. Wants to live like the Amish. I was almost ready to leave for the fancy world until I met Granny…and you."

Maryann thanked God Lavina had learned so much about a loving family by seeing hers interact over the past few days. She mentioned several times how she never knew love could be so strong in a marriage, and hoped to find a man like Michael someday. But would most Amish men judge her in their heart, knowing she had twins out of wedlock?

~*~

Ruth hadn't let Luke get so close to her in over a month, but they were both looking out the same narrow window to watch birds. The Audubon bird count was something she looked forward to every year, as did most people in the settlement. It broke up February with its thick clouds and gloominess. She looked up at the new white gourd feeder Luke made her, something she still couldn't believe. He'd always criticized her birding in the past, but was now doing it with her.

She kept thinking of how sorry Luke said he was about looking at pornography on English cell phones at work. Having quit his job and working with her *daed*, she knew he had no access to them, but what if he did? Would he have to look at other women to see beauty, not being satisfied with her? Yes, he was still sleeping in a twin bed in Mica's room, and this couldn't go on forever, but she just couldn't let him back in her bed...in her heart.

She felt the warmth of Luke's peppermint breath when he spoke. "God said He'll give us wings to fly again, Ruth."

"What?"

"Jeb showed me in the Bible. If we wait on the Lord, He'll renew our strength and mount up with wings like an eagle's."

Ruth looked more intently at the birds through her binoculars and felt Luke's arm on her back.

"Just want you to know I'm waiting on God and waiting on you, too. Waiting until you can let me in that heart of yours."

She had that urge again to run into Luke's arms, to forget all the pain. She put down her binoculars and looked at him, his mellow blue eyes piercing her heart. His eyes got closer and she felt his lips rub against hers. She yearned to be with him again, but an image of a lady, nude, raced through her mind and she turned her head.

~*~

Lizzie took her long brown hair and wrapped it up in a bun, then put on her prayer *kapp*. She looked in the little mirror on her bedroom wall. Amos told her she was beautiful and he seemed to really mean it. Actually, everything Amos said she believed came from his heart. Why couldn't she believe Roman like that? Had too many things happened between them?

She heard buggy wheels on snow and looked out the

window, down to the driveway. Roman had come to pick her up for another special meal. She didn't want to go because she felt nervous around Roman, but the girls were so insistent, making cards inviting her. Their love touched her...after church on Sunday they practically begged her to come to dinner before knitting circle. Amish *kinner* were taught not to plead, but she couldn't help but say yes to the three smiling girls.

She heard a knock at the side door and ran down the steps to answer it, letting her *daed* rest. Since the weather was harsh, fewer people came to the store, and seeing him relax, reading a book by the woodstove, was a calming sight. His MS seemed to have stopped in its tracks by the experimental drugs he started taking, but the doctors said he needed less stress.

She opened the door to see Roman, and as usual, she felt uneasy. Why? She felt at ease with Amos. "Come in, Roman. You can talk to my *daed* while I get my cape and bonnet."

"I'd like that," Roman said, eyes heavy on her.

She went to get her black bonnet and cape off their pegs by the front door, and heard her *daed* warmly greet Roman. He was happy she was going to dinner at Roman's house, and she could tell by the tone in his voice he hoped they'd be a couple again. But it was ages ago that they dated...a wife ago for Roman. He met Abigail during their short break-up and quickly forgot her. So, he never really loved her.

When she entered the living room, she was surprised her *daed* was talking about Lancaster, as if he wanted to live there. Amos had told her in letters how much more progressive they were, adopting things into their *Ordnung* that would never be allowed in Smicksburg. An enclosed buggy her *daed* would like; he got out so little in the winter, but if he had a warm buggy, he'd be out and about. It was also warmer in Lancaster, usually by ten degrees. Her *daed's* joints might do better there.

"Their buggies have turn signals like the English?" Roman asked. "Why?"

"Well, Lizzie's friend says that there's so much traffic, cars need to know when to slow down. I'd say that's too much traffic to pay attention, if you ask me," Jonas said, leaning forward. "I can see why Amos wants to find land out here. Prices are cheaper and we live more rural-like."

Lizzie looked at Roman's red face. When her *daed* mentioned Amos by name it seemed to turn the color of tomatoes. Why was her *daed* talking about Amos right in front of Roman? Was he trying to judge his reaction? Did he want to see if Roman really cared for her?

"Yep, that Amos really seems like a nice man. And not one of those widowers who wants to find a housecleaner and wife, all wrapped up in one," Jonas said.

Lizzie put her hand on her heart. Why was her *daed* egging Roman on so?

Roman cleared his throat. "I don't see how any widower could marry a woman he didn't love. He could easily get help within the community for his *kinner*." He looked over to Lizzie. "Does Amos have a *mamm* to help with his *kinner*, like I do?"

"*Jah*, I believe so, but she doesn't live by him, like your *mamm* does you."

Roman nodded to Jonas. "Well, I best get Lizzie over to my place. My *mamm's* watching the girls now."

He opened the side door and took Lizzie's hand. "The driveway's icy. Best hold on to me."

Lizzie took his hand, a hand she hadn't held in a decade. Memories of their courting days rushed through her mind. As she stepped out on the driveway, she had to cling to Roman's arm, and more memories flooded her mind. How he used to hold her...

She was relieved when she was settled in the buggy, glad he had a hot brick under the buggy robe. As the wind wisped snow into her face, she thought again of the enclosed buggies she saw in Lancaster. Maybe bring up having enclosed buggies when the *Gmay* votes on the *Ordnung?*

Roman got under the buggy robe and she felt the warmth of his body next to her. She tried not to think of the times they'd snuggled on winter rides, but her mind seemed to be traveling through time, as if it were yesterday.

"The girls are awfully excited to have you over," Roman said, looking over at her. "You have snowflakes on your eyelashes."

He told her to close her eyes, and took his thumb and swiped the snow off her eyes. More memories....more desire to want to hold Roman. She turned her head. "I'm fine, really."

He took her hand under the buggy robe and steered the horse with one hand. "So, when's your friend coming?"

"Tomorrow."

"Will he stay at your house?"

"*Nee*, Melvin offered to let him stay with him. Amos doesn't want to give the appearance of evil."

He tightened his grip on her hand and for some reason she didn't pull away. "Lizzie, you aren't seriously thinking of courting this Amos, are you?"

What could she say? The truth. Yes, Roman needed to hear the truth. "*Jah*, I am. He's a *goot* man."

He slowed the buggy to a walk. "And how do you feel about courting me?"

What was wrong with her? She felt like kissing Roman. He put his hand on her cheek and she turned to him, eyes locking. "Roman, when I'm with you, well, the past gets mixed up with the present. Are we living in the past?"

"I don't understand. What do you mean?"

She couldn't tell him of the emotions she was feeling. Emotions she thought were dead, but were now being resurrected, much to her surprise. "Remember our buggy rides in the snow...down deserted back roads? Such happy times. Memories from the past can trick us though..."

Roman drew closer. "I thought that once, but since I found the letter you hid, my feelings for you came back and won't go away."

Lizzie remembered what the counselor said about forgiveness and how it releases happy memories. How bitterness blinds us to them. It dawned on her that anytime a man got too close, memories of her attacker came, but not this time. She felt joy rise up from within her. "Roman, I think I'm free."

"What do you mean?"

"Y-You know about me being... attacked. Since that day, when any man took my hand, or got too close, memories of the assault would come back." She grabbed his hand with both of hers. "See, I can hold your hand and feel clean...not ashamed."

Roman's eyes moistened and then a tear slid down his cheek, and then he encircled her in his arms. "I'm so sorry for not helping you."

She remembered something about Roman she'd forgotten, too. How tender and compassionate he was. Why did she hide that letter years ago and not just give it to him? It wasn't one of their silly love letters to hide in a woodpecker hole, but serious. "Roman, it wasn't your fault. I should have handed you the letter. So silly of me. You're a *goot* man and I should have trusted you."

Roman gasped for air and his whole body shook. She'd never heard a man cry like this before. "Lizzie, don't leave me..."

"Leave you? "

"Don't see Amos."

The sun peaked through the overcast sky. Live each short hour with God and the long years will take care of themselves. "My *daed* says when he fears his MS might be getting worse, he gives each hour to God, and doesn't worry about the future. Let's live for God and see where He takes us...slowly..."

"And you'll do the same with Amos?"

She remembered how insecure Roman was as a teen. Always afraid she might find someone else. She couldn't help but smile. The teenage boy in him was just below the surface. The Roman she always knew was still there, but she hadn't seen him in a long while. Not until she forgave her assailant.

He released her and made the buggy move faster. "Since you didn't answer, I take it you'll be giving Amos a chance, even though you hardly know him."

Lizzie sighed. "He has his ticket bought and it's all arranged. Like I said, let's just give each hour to God and wait for His direction. I don't want to move too hastily."

~*~

Granny adjusted her binoculars to see the red-tailed hawk in detail. "Jeb, write down five red-tailed hawks. This one is different than the others."

"Are you sure? We need this count to be accurate."

"I've been counting birds for Audubon for how many years? I'm sure."

"Don't have to get your dander up, Deborah. Need to watch yourself."

Granny put her binoculars in her lap. "What are you trying to say...old man?"

Jeb sat down in the rocker next to her. "Well, the bishop's getting concerned. You're being seen in that little red car too much, and not out of necessity."

"Marge and Joe are looking at farms. You know that. And you're in the car half the time too, helping Joe see what needs fixed."

"But you're with her more..."

"Ach, she picks me up before going to check on Maryann. Remember, we're paying for her nursing skills."

"Well it's not the only thing the bishop's concerned about."

"Jebediah Weaver. Spill the beans."

"The bishop thinks your Jane Austen books aren't *goot*. Wants to take up a vote to ban them. Asked us to go over Friday to his place for a chat."

"His wife reads Jane Austen, too. Did he actually say that?" Granny put her head back on the rocker, trying to calm herself.

"*Jah.* He wants his wife to get rid of hers, too. Says Austen has romance all wrong, like I say. It's not a feeling, but a commitment."

"How about Pennsylvania Field and Stream?

"What about it?"

"Well, you're addicted to it. Isn't that wrong, too? If Jane Austen is banned, then fishing magazines should be too."

Jeb let out a chuckle. "It won't happen."

Granny tried not to say what she was thinking, and bit her lower lip. The bishop reads fishing magazines too, so of course they wouldn't be banned. "I could bring it up for the vote. I'm sure lots of women would vote against those fishing and hunting magazines."

Jeb put his hand on his heart. "You'd do that to me? Deborah, what would I read all winter?"

Granny heard Jack bark and saw a buggy coming down the driveway. It was Roman with Lizzie and she was glad for the distraction, being upset with Jeb and needing to cool off. The girls ran to the window and squealed with delight. They were so proud of the roast they helped their *daed* cook. The cards they made for Lizzie, filled with words of love and encouragement, would surely help Lizzie heal.

"*Oma*, can we go over to our house now? We want to see Lizzie," Jenny asked.

Granny wanted Roman and Lizzie to have more time alone. "You girls need to clean up after making a craft. The oak table needs scrubbed down."

"But we were careful," Millie said. "No glue got on the table."

Granny felt Tillie's hand slip into hers. "*Oma*, I'll help you clean."

Granny bent down to hug the sweet girl. "Ach, what am I thinking. You laid down newspapers and the table's spotless. Just make sure you put all your things away in the craft drawer before you go home."

Jack barked with a fury and darted down the driveway out of sight. Soon a red car could be seen and Granny clenched her fists. Marge drove too fast, and the way Jack chased cars, he might get hit. When the car slid to a stop, she saw that Marge wasn't the only one in the car. She'd brought Lavina over. Wasn't Lavina supposed to stay with Maryann?"

She watched as Lavina got out of the car and ran up the steps. Jeb met her on the porch and embraced her. Despite her being irritated with Jeb, Granny couldn't help but melt over the affection her husband showed this dear girl who was starving for love. Give her wings again…give her wings like an eagle, Lord.

Marge charged through the door and came to embrace Granny. "We made an offer on the farm down the road, and Jacob accepted it." She jumped up and down with Granny in her arms. "I am so excited!"

"I knew that farm was the one for you. So Jacob agreed on a price?"

"*Jah*, I mean yes," Marge giggled. "I'm starting to sound Amish already. And he'll hold a land contract with no interest. He insisted, even though Joe didn't think it was fair, with the cost of living going up."

"Well, some Amish don't believe in charging interest. And we try to give fair prices, too."

"I showed Lavina the farm. Jacob said it was alright to just walk inside. She's a nice girl. Said she dreams of having a family and living on a farm someday." Marge turned to look out the window. "She's still out there talking to your Jeb. She's real attached to him, huh? "

"*Jah*, she can talk to Jeb. He's like a *daed* to her."

"When's she going home? She told me about her *daed* and I'm concerned."

"About what?"

"He seems too mean. Maybe it needs to be reported."

"To who?"

"Child Protective Services, of course."

"We don't let the government get involved in our problems. We solve them ourselves."

Marge froze with her mouth gaping. "What?"

"We solve our problems within the community."

"But what if there's abuse and a child needs taken out

of the home."

"Lavina isn't a *boppli*. A baby. She can leave if she wants to."

"But she's still a minor."

"A minor what?"

Marge sat down at the kitchen table. "She's under eighteen. Her *daed* can demand she stay at home, I think."

"Well, we don't believe in that either. When a teen wants to leave at sixteen, they can. They're grown up by then."

Marge shook her head. "Well, I'm not Amish, and if that girl tells me one more thing about her father, I'm reporting it."

~*~

Granny made twice as many pies last Saturday, knowing she needed a few to take to Maryann's and to serve at the knitting circle. She touched the pies to see if they'd defrosted. Keeping them outside in a cooler doubled as a second icebox. Satisfied they were thawed, she placed them in the oven to warm up. She heard the side door open, and Jeb appeared.

"Deborah. I don't want you fretting over going to see the bishop on Friday."

"I'm not. I have nothing to hide or be ashamed of."

"I'm just afraid I worried you. I'm sure it's nothing."

"Me too. Did you have a *goot* talk with Lavina?"

Jeb walked over to the kitchen table and collapsed on a chair. "She's real special. Those little freckles on her nose are sure to catch her a man."

"She's a pretty thing. Maybe the twins got their red

hair from her."

"She has brown hair."

Granny shook her head. "It's called auburn, dark red, almost brown. But she's pretty on the inside and that's what counts all the more."

"I asked her to come to your knitting circle. She's over at Romans."

"She didn't leave with Marge?"

Jeb shifted. "I said I'd take her over to Maryann's after you're all done knitting. I'm telling you, she opening up about her *daed*, and I feel I need to get to the bottom of what's wrong. If I have to go up to Troutville and talk to their bishop, I will." Jeb pounded the table with his fist.

Granny spun around. "Jeb, we need to cast her on God. He cares for her more than you." She sat across from him. "I don't know how Ella will act around Lavina."

Jeb patted her hand. "Don't worry. We're talking about Ella. She's a *goot* Christian woman."

Granny went over to her birding journal. "Birding is *goot* for the nerves. I look forward to these four days all year. So cold out that the birds have to come to the feeders, and we have over twenty-seven different types of birds. Can you believe it?"

"And we're not done yet." Jeb scratched the back of his neck. "If you try to ban fishing and hunting magazines, someone might want to ban birding ones too."

Granny got up and hugged Jeb around the neck. "old man, you're the one fretting. Ach, I would never try to ban your magazines. I was just upset."

Jeb grabbed her and she sat on his lap. The side door opened and Lizzie and Roman appeared. Granny noticed Lizzie had a glow about her, like she had in her youth…when she was in love with Roman. Praise be.

Roman put his hand over his eyes, laughing. "We'll come back later."

Jeb squeezed Granny tighter. "Son, life's short, so I aim to get as many hugs from your *mamm* as possible."

Roman looked at Lizzie. "He's right, *jah*?"

Lizzie nodded. "My *daed* wishes he'd spent more time with my *mamm*, and not out in the barn."

The door opened again, blowing in a cold chill. Ella and Becca stepped in. "Ach, it's so cold."

Granny went over to collect their capes and bonnets. "Where's Ruth, and Becca, aren't you needed at home?"

"Ruth insisted on taking care of Maryann tonight, and Becca's been too cooped up," Ella said, putting her arm around Becca. "Anyhow, she's fifteen today and needs a birthday treat."

Granny hugged Becca. "Happy Birthday. I'm so glad you came. Just worried about your *mamm*. How's she feeling?"

"Nervous about getting radiation therapy tomorrow, but she has lots of ginger on hand for nausea. Dan Miller said it helps."

"Well, I'm sure he's right. Best herbalist in town."

Granny spied Lavina come to the door and shot up a casting off prayer. How would Ella feel around the biological *mamm* of her twins? How she reacted would tell her a lot. Granny went to Lavina and asked for her wraps. She looked over at Ella, the color in her cheeks fading. Ella darted into the living room and immediately started to knit.

"Ella, want to have some pie first?" Granny asked.

"*Nee*, no appetite."

Fannie appeared in the doorway. "Hi everyone." She looked over at Lizzie. "You look mighty happy. How was your dinner?"

Lizzie put her hands on her cheeks to hide her blushing. "*Wunderbar goot.* The girls made a roast, of all things. They went on and on about peeling carrots and potatoes and putting it all in the oven with the meat." Lizzie patted her stomach. "I think I gained some weight."

Fannie wagged her finger at Lizzie. "Now don't go sounding like me. I mean, the way I used to talk about my weight and being fat. No more."

Lavina stared at Fannie. "You're not even overweight."

"I know it now, but I used to think all kinds of ugly thoughts about myself."

Lavina looked down. "Maybe you could teach me how…"

Granny tightened her grip on Lavina. "Let's go sit down and have some pie."

"I'm stuffed," Lizzie said.

"Okay, if you girls want pie later, it's in the oven. Let's knit."

Lavina went to sit by Ella. "How are the twins?"

Ella looked as stiff as a poker. "My twins are doing fine. Know their *mamm* and *daed* love them."

Lavina put her hand on Ella's shoulder. "I'm glad they have a happy home. It was my prayer."

Ella said nothing, but knit faster than usual. Silence settled over the room, and only the wind could be heard outside along with the ticking of the pendulum clock. Granny cast a prayer up, getting used to doing this several times a day now, and found more peace in her soul. Yes, she fretted about her Jane Austen books being banned, but cast her care off on God, and noticed she hadn't thought much about it.

"What's everybody thinking about? So quiet tonight," Becca said.

Fannie beamed. "Well, I'm thinking about my secret."

"Are you and Melvin getting married in the spring or fall? No secret around here. We all know *yinz* plan to wed."

"*Jah*, and we need time to make a wedding ring quilt," Lizzie said.

Fannie looked up from her loom. "Maybe *yinz* need to make two. One for Lizzie, too. But Lizzie's a mystery. Will she wed Roman or Amos?"

Granny groaned. "Fannie, don't tease about such serious matter." She looked at Lizzie. "When does this man from Lancaster get in tomorrow?"

"At noon. He wants to see the farm down the road. He wrote to Jacob and has an appointment in the afternoon."

"Well, just tell him not to bother. My English friend

and her husband bought it."

"Marge?" Becca chimed in. "I just love her. She makes my *mamm* laugh with all her questions about the Amish. She reminds me of the wind-up toys my *brieder* play with. They start out real fast and then fall over, as if tired."

"Ach, that isn't nice," Ella snapped.

Becca flinched, as if Ella's words hit her hard. "I mean it as a compliment. Marge has lots of energy and gets things done real quick-like, then seems too tired to talk. She has tea and gets wound up again."

Granny saw the hurt look on Becca's face, and turned to Ella. "I remember when my *boppli* kept me up half the night. I was sleep deprived and snapped at people a lot."

More silence and Granny saw that everyone was intent on knitting. Wasn't that what they were there for? But why knit together if you're not going to talk; just knit at home. She feared Lavina would take the silence as rejection of her being in the circle. "Are any of you counting birds?" Granny asked.

"I am," Lavina said. "Maryann's teaching me so much about birds."

"Like what?" Granny asked.

"Well, we haven't seen an eagle yet, but Maryann said they fly higher than any bird. She said you can't see them without binoculars sometimes because they fly so high. And when they're way up high, they don't flap their wings, only glide, riding the wind. She said the closer we get to God we don't need to flap so much. She said God carries us." Lavina looked over at Granny. "I'm not real sure what that means, but I think I do."

"Well, in the Bible it says they that wait on the Lord will renew their strength, they'll mount up with wings like an eagle, they'll run and not get weary....can't remember exactly, but something like that. Well, it means when we wait on God we'll have wings like an eagles'."

"But how do you wait on God? What does that mean?" Becca asked.

"Well, we're waiting for spring now, *jah*? Are we afraid it won't come?"

"*Nee*, it always comes."

"Isn't God more dependable than the weather? If we wait, He'll come, too. He'll come to our side to help us in every situation." Granny looked around the room. "Seems like all we need to do is put out our wings and let him carry us."

"That's a beautiful thought," Lizzie said. "So we don't worry then? Just wait and see which way God takes us?"

"That's how I see it," Granny said.

Ella put her knitting down. "I'm not feeling too *goot*. I think I'll head home."

"Would you like to lie down on my bed? You just got here. And it's Becca's birthday."

"I can go home with Lavina," Becca said.

Ella shot a glare at Lavina. "Fine, go home with her then."

Granny put her arm around Ella's waist, leading her to the utility room where she hung up everyone's capes and bonnets. After shutting the door, she counted to ten mentally. She wanted to chide Ella for treating Lavina so cruelly. "Ella, explain to me why you were so mean to

Lavina."

"Explain? Me explain? Maybe you need to explain why she's here. "

"Do you need a warning? So you can prepare how you're going to act?"

"*Jah*, I do. To compose myself. All sorts of emotions come over me when I see Lavina. Fear she might take the twins back. Anger that I couldn't have *kinner* myself. And then guilt that I'm angry and frustrated. Then Lavina preaches about eagles to me? It all made me sick. And now I really do have a stomach ache."

Granny reached out to take Ella's hands. "I'm sorry, Ella. I guess I don't know how you're feeling."

Tears started to spill down Ella's cheeks. She clung on to Granny. "Unless you're barren like me, you wouldn't know. Zach and I are afraid. I don't want Lavina in Smicksburg."

Granny patted Ella's back, not knowing what to say, but she knew what to do…another casting off prayer.

~*~

Ruth sat in the chair next to Maryann's bed. She held up the shawl she'd almost completed. "What do you think?"

Maryann took the edge of the shawl. "*Ach*, you knit so *goot*. Such close, even stitches."

"I knit more than ever, and watch birds. Helps my nerves." As soon as Ruth said this she regretted it. Here was Maryann facing radiation tomorrow and she was talking about herself.

"Want to talk about it? One married woman to

another?" Maryann asked.

"*Nee*, you need rest."

"*Nee*, I need a diversion. Helping you will take my mind off my problems."

Ruth looked down at her knitting loom. "Feelings for Luke are coming back, but I'm afraid."

"Why?"

"What if it's just a show? He's had *goot* behavior ever since he took medicine for anxiety. No screaming at all. But I'm afraid if I'm too nice, he'll just start up again."

"So you think you're controlling his behavior?"

"*Jah,* maybe. Me putting my foot down forced him to change."

"I agree. And bringing in church discipline was the right thing, for sure. But Luke has repented and made such hard changes, giving up his job with the English, moving into the *dawdyhaus* by your parents."

"I know. He doesn't complain about it either. Just seems sad."

Maryann grabbed the Bible on her bed and flipped the pages. "When I discipline my kids I make sure they don't have sadness that lingers, or a broken spirit. Remember the story about the man who was living immorally in Corinthians? How Paul told the church to shun him?"

"*Jah,* we all know that story. It shows shunning is right."

"But in Paul's second letter to the Corinthians it says that the man repented so now let him back in so he won't be overcome by sorrow. Here, I'll read it:

"…You ought rather to forgive and comfort him, lest

perhaps such a one be swallowed up with too much sorrow. Therefore I urge you to reaffirm your love to him."

The words pierced Ruth's heart, as much as she tried to guard it. The Bible also said to guard your heart.

Maryann kissed her Bible. "This Bible has become like a best friend over the past few months. Such comfort and strength. Do you read yours Ruth?"

"*Jah*, sometimes."

"Sometimes? I'm working on not being judgmental, but Ruth, it sounds like you hardly read it at all. Is that true?"

"Well, we learn about it in church and I think about what's said."

Maryann moaned. "Ruth, didn't you and Luke have nightly Bible reading?"

"*Nee*. Luke just started reading his Bible."

"*Ach*, Ruth, the Bible is changing him, along with the medicine. You both need to read it out loud together. Just like your body needs food, your spirit does, too, and Jesus said He was the bread of life."

Ruth stopped fidgeting with the yarn. "I'd like to let Luke back in…to our bedroom."

Maryann reached for Ruth's hand. "When a couple prays together and reads the Bible, they're drawn closer to each other. Why not do that first, and see what happens naturally."

Ruth couldn't believe how simple, yet profound this advice was. Granny had told her that marriage had three members in the union: husband, wife, and God. She said

God held the couple together. So if they both got closer to God they'd get closer to each other? Reading the Bible could create a bond?

"You're a wounded bird on the mend. Look how much time it's taking for me to recover from surgery. It's painful but I know the outcome is *goot* and I'm thankful."

Ruth squeezed Maryann's hand. "*Danki.*"

~*~

Ella rocked Moses, patting his back, trying to make him stop crying. A colicky baby sure could unravel a person's nerves and she yearned for control. She needed to knit. That was something that calmed her and she had control over.

The past few days she'd missed out on the bird count, something she grew up doing. But Zach had time. He did work hard all day for the English, and then did his farm chores, but why did he get to leave the house, while she stayed home, shielding the twins from cold air? Guilt over resenting staying at home and not running as she pleased came like an avalanche. She loved the twins but being so tied to the house was like being on a leash.

In the early morning light, she saw a red car pull into their driveway and up to the side door. Who could be here at 7:00 a.m.? She went to the window and saw Lavina get out of the car. She gripped Moses tight. She would not take him or Vina.

Lavina knocked, and Ella was tempted to not answer the door, but found herself walking to it, like in slow motion. She opened the door to see Lavina, eyes red and puffy. "Can I talk to you Ella?"

Ella froze. This scene was in one of her nightmares. Lavina coming to her door, asking for the twins back. It replayed in her mind throughout the day. She opened the door to let the girl in. She needed to face her fears. "Do you want something, Lavina?"

Lavina took a handkerchief from her cape pocket and put it to her eyes. "I'm going back to Troutville, and won't be coming back to Smicksburg. I wanted you to know that."

Ella felt light headed and went to sit at the kitchen table. "Why do you say you're never coming back?"

"Because I see how much pain it gives you to see me. How nervous you are. I want the twins being raised by a peaceful *mamm*." She gasped for air. "I saw the tire swing coming up the driveway. I always wanted a family with a tire swing, and knowing the twins will be raised her by their *mamm* makes me happy, even though I'm crying right now."

Ella saw something in Lavina. Not a teenager, but a woman who was willing to sacrifice her own happiness for the twins' good. And here she was wrangled that she had to stay home so often. But her mind quickly turned to Granny. Had she told Lavina about their private talk at the knitting circle?

"Lavina, whose idea was it for you to leave? Aren't you helping Maryann?"

"I was helping her, but I had a long talk with Jeb, telling him how I thought I was hurting the twins by being in town."

"And did he agree?"

"*Nee,* he wants me to stay," she said, head down.

"What else did he say?"

"He had five sons and said how having a new baby turns the house upside down and it takes time for things to get normal again."

Ella let out a loud sigh. "So, how I'm feeling is normal? *Ach,* I've been so emotional. Lavina; it's not *goot* to have our feelings run our lives, and I fear my feelings are running you out of town. Am I right?"

"Well, you're a nervous *mamm* with me here. But I don't know why."

Ella raised Moses' cheek up to hers. "I'm afraid you'll want the twins back."

"*Nee,* I don't. What makes you think that?"

"I heard you scream when you had to give them up."

"It hurt, that's why. But I knew it was best for the twins."

Ella looked evenly at Lavina. "So you never came to Smicksburg to try to be around the twins to get them back?"

"I don't like being with my family. Now that I know there's love in homes, like Granny and Jeb, it makes me want to never go back."

"It was that bad?"

"*Jah,* it still is. But I shouldn't be telling anyone."

"What?"

Fear contorted Lavina's face. "I can't say."

Ella got up and put her hand on Lavina's shoulder. "You can't go back. I can tell you're terrified of something, and you don't have to tell me, but —"

"*Danki,* Ella. *Danki.*"

"You best go tell Marge to take you over to Maryann's. She'll need your help after radiation today."

~*~

Lizzie pulled the buggy robe up to her chin, trying to shield herself against the chilly wind. She didn't dare move closer to Amos, hardly knowing him. She thought back to the conversation her *daed* had with Amos. Lancaster did have a little milder climate and enclosed buggies, better suited for her *daed.* Since he never talked about his MS, she didn't know how much pain he was in during the winter months.

"Lizzie, I remember when my *opa* drove a buggy with no windows."

The remark stung. It made her feel like he thought the Amish in Smicksburg were backwards. "We do have the vote this spring. I'm thinking of bringing it up, since my *daed* would get around better."

"*Jah,* that would be nice," Amos said with a warm smile. "It's beautiful out here with all the rolling hills, but cars can come up on you real quick-like, with so many blind curves."

"We stick to the back roads as much as possible. "

"It's nice you still have back roads. Too much development in Lancaster, like I said."

Lizzie saw the driveway to Roman's house and remembered Granny saying there were other farms for sale, since Jacob shook hands with Marge and Joe, selling his land. "Let's stop in and talk to Granny and Jeb. They know of other farms for sale."

"How about on the way back. I'd like to see this farm down the road as a comparable."

"*Goot* idea," Lizzie said. "

She looked down the driveway and saw Roman's house off in the distance. She wondered what he was doing. Why did she care? She pushed him out of her mind and focused on Amos. "So, how's your *kinner*?"

"Ach, they grow up so fast. Elma, my youngest, will be five. She looks so much like my late wife. Nice to look at her and remember Anna."

"Do you miss your wife a great deal?"

"At first it gnawed at me, like a hungry bear. But we need to move on and time has a way of healing the heart. *Nee*, I'm fine now, and look forward to the future."

She felt him reach for her hand under the buggy robe. Lizzie was glad the farm was now in sight; Amos was rushing things a tad, by taking her hand. They pulled into the driveway, and Amos soon jumped out of the buggy. "Do you know how much this farm sold for?"

"*Nee*, I don't know much about it, but Jacob lives across the street. It was his son's farm."

"Well, let's go talk to Jacob then." He steered the horse back onto the road and pulled into the long driveway leading to Jacob's. The many buggies that went down the driveway left deep grooves on each side of the dirt road. Amos mumbled. "Folks in Lancaster maintain their driveways a little better than this."

"We have more freezing and thawing than Lancaster, I'm thinking. You're always ten degrees warmer, jah?"

"*Jah.*"

"Well, the ice expands and breaks up our roads. With all the thawing and freezing, even the English roads have potholes." Lizzie snickered. "Some English call them craters."

"I just hope we don't get stuck."

"We'll be fine. We're almost there."

She looked at the trees that lined the driveway. She saw a woodpecker hole high in a maple, and thought of Roman again. Why was she thinking of him so much? They made a turn in the driveway and saw Jacob outside, shooting clay pigeons with some friends. "Jacob has company. Maybe we should come back later."

"I'm only here for three days." Amos continued toward the house, ignoring Lizzie's suggestion. He got out of the buggy.

Lizzie was relieved that Jacob welcomed them with a smile. She knew he cherished any free time with his friends. She gasped when Amos said he was interested in buying the farm. She made it clear that the farm was sold.

Jacob looked over at her. "You heard I sold the farm, *jah*, Lizzie?"

"*Jah.* Amos, I told you the farm is sold."

Amos shifted his black wool hat. "Are you happy with the offer?"

Jacob cocked one eyebrow. "My son was. He can buy more dairy cows in New York now."

"How much did you get?"

"Well, we came down to $150,000. It only has sixty acres. My son raised turkeys for a *goot* profit though. But he always dreamed of being a dairy farmer."

"Only $150,000? Are you serious?"

"*Jah*, I'm serious."

"Is the house in poor shape?"

"*Nee*, it's fine."

"Would you mind showing me the inside? Walk the property with me?"

Jacob looked over at his friends. "I have company and I don't see the point. It's sold."

"What if I offered more?"

Lizzie felt the shock that was on Jacob's face. "We shook on it. The farm is sold."

"No contract signed?"

Lizzie knew the Amish felt their word was better than a signed contract. Why was Amos asking such a question? He was in Lydia's church district and all the people she met in Lancaster seemed Amish to their core.

Jacob's eyes darkened. "My word is my contract. You're Amish. You should know that."

Amos spun around and got back into the buggy, obviously irritated. Lizzie said good-bye to Jacob and tried to smile. "Your Amish need to be more progressive," he blurted.

"Progressive has the root word of progress. I don't think it's progress to go back on your word. You should know that."

"What if this English couple doesn't honor a verbal agreement? So few of them are honest."

Lizzie sat up straight. "It's the principal that matters. Let your yes be yes the Bible says."

He slowed the buggy down and looked at her. "You're

the kind of Amish woman who could keep me in line."

~*~

When they got to Granny's driveway, Lizzie asked Amos to pull in. She'd told Granny she'd stop by and introduce Amos to her. She also was in a desperate need of tea. As they pulled down the dirt driveway, Amos complained again about all the ditches. Lizzie bit her lower lip, eager to get out of the buggy. When it came to a stop, she hopped out and headed straight to Granny's door and walked in, not waiting for Amos. She was shocked at some of his ideas, and needed a hug from Granny.

Granny was in her rocker, counting birds. When she saw Lizzie she stood up and Lizzie hugged her tight. "What's wrong, Lizzie?"

Lizzie turned to see Amos in the doorway. "Ach, I need some tea. I'm freezing."

"I'll put some water on then," Granny said, looking over at Amos. "You can come in after you take your muddy boots off. You can place them on the mat."

"Granny, I'm so sorry. I just walked right in, not thinking." Lizzie made her way over to the door and took off her black boots. "I'll mop up your floor before I leave."

Granny swatted at the air. "I can do it. Don't you worry."

"Where's Jeb?"

"Over at the Bylers, cutting ice."

Amos sat down at the table. "Why would men cut ice?"

Granny put her hands on her waist. "Don't pull my leg. You know why. Lancaster can't be that different."

"*Nee*, I'm not joking," Amos said, waiting for an answer.

"To get ice," Granny said.

"And you need lots of ice for a gathering of some sort? Is that it?"

Granny walked over to her icebox and opened the door. "This here icebox was my *mamm's*. We put blocks of ice in this here side." Granny opened the other door to show him where she kept her food. "Made of solid oak."

Amos put a hand over his mouth, as if hiding a grin. "Well, I've never seen one. We've been using gas refrigerators for ages."

Granny went over to get mugs. "Well, we voted on propane ones last year, and now they're allowed, but I won't part with my icebox. Besides, my husband loves to cut the ice."

"Now you're pulling my leg. He cuts ice from a pond?"

"After they ice fish. Jeb's been doing it with his buddies since he was a teen. He's out hauling ice today."

Amos grinned at Granny. "You're not joking; I can tell. Well, if I move out here I'll be getting a real refrigerator."

Lizzie didn't know if Amos realized how arrogant he was appearing. She was in Lancaster for almost a month, and knew there were some Amish who still adhered to the older ways, especially the elderly who saw no need for change. "Granny, I think it's *wunderbar* you treasure your icebox; it shows how much you cherish your *mamm's* memory."

Amos smiled at her. "I agree. It's inspiring really. And your husband is brave to go out on ice and cut it. I couldn't."

Granny put two mugs of tea on the table. "*Danki,*" Amos said.

Lizzie realized that Amos was most likely exhausted from his trip, and having such little time to look at farms, was a bit nervous. He'd also mentioned being away from his *kinner* made him uneasy. She remembered how odd she felt in Lancaster at first; she was sure Amos was just overwhelmed by his surroundings.

~*~

That night Amos took Lizzie out to watch the stars. She'd hardly ever looked at the stars in winter, always being too cold. But Amos brought his thermos on the bus, and now had it filled with hot chocolate.

He took out his binoculars. "These are for watching stars." He adjusted the binoculars as he looked up into the night sky. "I'll focus them, and then let you take a peek."

"So, any farms we saw today interest you?"

"I'd like to take another look at the one on Mahoning Road, by the Baptist church."

"*Ach*, you'd have such *goot* neighbors. Jerry and Janice came here years ago from down south."

"And you say they're *goot* friends?"

"*Jah*. They plan to open a house for homeless *mamms*."

"Where're their husbands?"

"They aren't married. Janice says it's the churches job to help those who can't help themselves."

"But doesn't that promote sin?"

"*Nee.* We have a girl who comes to our knitting circle now that gave birth to twins. She repented and now needs built up. Women like that will be coming to the Baptist for help."

Amos put down his binoculars. "Don't you think it will send a message to young Amish girls in this area, that if they're promiscuous, and say a simple 'I'm sorry', it'll make it easier for them to fall into temptation?"

"If you met Lavina, you'd know she's paid a heavy price for her sin, and she has lots of scars. Sin leaves scars, but the love of God can erase them. I think that's what Jerry and Janice are trying to do."

"Well, we're not bound to agree on this matter. Sin needs to be dealt with harshly."

"Amos, you're Amish. You know that if someone strays and kneels before the People and confesses their sin, all is forgiven, and forgotten."

"Well, I know a girl who gave birth to a *kinner* out of wedlock, got caught, and repented. She ended up leaving with her English boyfriend a few months later."

"I think we should do the Christian thing and forgive, always thinking the best of others."

Amos turned toward her. "You're a *goot* woman, Lizzie. So, you're saying we're to love others and there's healing in that?"

"*Jah.* I believe that."

"Well, it gives me something to think about. My

judgmental ways can blind me at times, so my bishop says."

~*~

Ruth looked at her bird tally for the first three days of the four-day count. More finches by far than the bickering blue jays and cardinals. She peered out the window at the cylinder finch feeder; they lived in harmony; was it a sign she and Luke would have peace in their home eventually?

"*Guder mariyer*, Ruth," Luke said.

"*Jah, guder mariyer*. I got up with the birds," Ruth said with nervous laughter. How much longer could she keep Luke sleeping in Mica's room? Why did she yearn to be held by him one minute and felt repulsed the next? "I can make some fresh coffee if you'd like. There's eggs and pancakes still warm in the oven."

Luke put his hand up. "I can make coffee. *Danki*. I was thinking we should have Bible reading together. Jeb said it's the best part of his and Granny's day."

"Maryann suggested the same thing…"

"Do you want to wait until after your bird count to start?"

Ruth looked out of the frosted window. A beautiful pattern of ice crystals formed across the edges of the pane. She noticed some thawing as ice streaks ran down into other clusters of frost. Could her heart melt too; was it already? "We can start today, Luke. That would be *goot*. Mica's still in bed."

Luke poured coffee into his blue speckle ware mug and sat in the rocker next to Ruth, Bible tucked under one arm. "I was thinking we read the Psalms first. They're light hearted."

"Okay," Ruth said, picking up the shawl she was knitting. "Do you mind if I knit while you read?"

"Can you pay attention?"

"Knitting calms me so I can hear better."

"Alright. Here we go with Psalm 1 and then I'll go on to chapter 2." Luke read slowly, stammering over words. How many times had he tried to read aloud like most Amish men, but she'd clucked her tongue or rolled her eyes as he stammered? Conviction washed over her. It was no excuse for his behavior, but she was hard on him, not respecting him, and she needed to apologize.

When he finished he put the Bible gently in his lap. "Ruth, I feel like the first verse of chapter one is good advice. I'm glad the elders and bishop live by this Bible."

"What do you mean?"

"Well, let me read it again:

Blessed is the man

Who walks not in the counsel of the ungodly,

Nor stands in the path of sinners,

Nor sits in the seat of the scornful;

"Zach doesn't seem to have a problem working for the English, and maybe it's the crowd he works with, but I was with a bad lot. Lots of cussing, dirty jokes, talking real bad about their wives. I was standing with sinners and sitting next to scoffers of God. It says here a man is blessed to not be living like I used to." He reached for her hand and she took it. "I'm blessed to be working with your *daed*. He's better company."

Ruth held his hand and good memories flooded back. Memories of their courting days before he worked for the English. When they bought the house, Luke was afraid of the mortgage and took the job. Was it really that hard on him? "*Jah*, you are blessed. My *daed's* as *goot* as men come."

"Ruth, I love you. Do you believe me?"

"I want to, but I've been damaged…in my heart. It won't seem to mend."

"But you seem more comfortable around me now. Do you think your heart's on the mend and just needs time?"

She didn't withdraw her hand as he stroked the top of it with his thumb. She looked down at her yarn, and thought of how a jumbled mess of yarn can make a beautiful design, once knitted. "Seems like our hearts need to be knit together by God. I'm willing."

"What are you saying, Ruth? I can come back into our marriage bed?"

Ruth froze. "*Nee*, not yet. God has more knitting to do before that happens." She expected Luke to explode, but he continued to stroke her hand. "We need to wait on God, like Jeb said, and soon we'll have wings to fly again."

She looked over at Luke and a smile spread across his face. "We'll just keep waiting then."

~*~

The smirk on Jeb's face made Granny wince. Was he taking delight in the Bishop having a word with her? Where was her normally supportive husband? Dinner at the bishop's meant something was awfully wrong;

breaking bread together sometimes meant smoothing over rough places, the meal being a place of communion, a place of unity.

Was it so awful she read Jane Austen? And she couldn't help it she had so many English friends. She had many more Amish to keep her on the straight and narrow. She pulled her black cape tighter around her as they pulled into the bishop's driveway. When she saw several buggies lined up behind the house, she panicked. The Bible clearly said if you had something against someone, to go to them in private.

"Jeb, what's going on?"

"Looks like the bishop has lots of customers today. Selling lots of furniture, I suppose."

"To Amish people? There are no cars here."

Jeb took her hand. "Maybe his son's having a meeting in the woodshop."

"At dinner time?"

"Deborah, don't be nervous. If the bishop thinks you need discipline, isn't it for your *goot*? He's a kind man and won't be harsh."

Granny shrugged her shoulders. "I have a clear conscience, Jeb. I'll just tell him I'm not tempted to do wrong in any way by the English or Jane Austen."

Jeb patted her hand. "That's my Deborah." He helped her out of the buggy and across the snowy driveway. "Watch your step...old woman."

When they got to the door, Jeb stood behind her with both hands on her waist, as if ready to catch her if she fainted. "I'm fine, old man. Really. Tougher than you think."

The door opened and she saw Sarah, the bishop's wife. She had the same smirk on her face as Jeb had. But she read Jane Austen, too. Wasn't she going to have a "talking to" also? This didn't make any sense. Sarah asked her to have a seat in the living room, which was also odd. They were having dinner and she wasn't too old to help in the kitchen.

When she walked into the next room, Jeb still had his hands on her waist. What's going on?

"SURPRISE!"

Granny stepped back in shock. One by one someone came up and hugged her, wishing her a happy seventieth birthday. All the women from her knitting circle were there, except Maryann. She turned to Jeb, who was doubled over laughing. "I'll get you back…old man." She turned to hug Jeb, and felt hot tears forming, so she buried her head in his chest to compose herself.

Jeb cradled her head. "Can you take another surprise or should we wait?"

Another surprise? "*Jah*, I'm okay. Little shaky, but I'm fine."

Jeb motioned with his hand to bring something forward. Granny saw a young man walk from the back of the room. He came up to her and gave her a kiss on the cheek. "Happy Birthday, *Oma*."

Granny studied his face. She didn't know who he was! Did seventy mean she'd lost her mind? Jeb whispered in her ear, "It's Nathan. Can't you tell?"

"*Ach*, Nathan!" Granny grabbed him by the neck. "It's

been so long I didn't recognize you." She put her hand on his face. "You've grown up to be so handsome. Blue eyes like your *daed*."

"I couldn't come down from Montana for Christmas. Had to watch the farm, and *daed* bought me a train ticket to visit for a while."

"Last time I saw you, you were twelve."

"Fifteen," Nathan said with a crooked grin. "Just turned twenty. Getting old."

Granny pulled him to her. "I've missed you so. All of you up there in Montana. Too far away." Granny heard the chatter of everyone, but wanted this moment to last a bit longer. Her Nathan was home. She had many *grandkinner*, but Nathan was so tenderhearted and always talked and visited with her the most. When the family moved to Montana, he wrote regularly, but then as his teen years came along, not so often. She wanted to keep him in Smicksburg forever.

"How long are you staying?"

"For a month…or longer."

Granny couldn't contain her emotions any longer and cried. "I've missed you." She held him tighter. "I'll make you lots of chocolate whoopie pies, your favorite."

She looked out at the crowd gathered in the living room. Lavina walked over to her. "Granny. Are you okay?"

"Happy. Just so happy. This is my Nathan, home from Montana."

Lavina and Nathan's eyes met and Granny couldn't help but notice they both seemed struck dumb. Their eyes held, but no one said anything. She shook her head. She was reading too many Jane Austen novels. The image of Jane Bennet being taken with Mr. Bingley flashed in front of her.

She felt a tap on her shoulder and a pull on her dress. She saw Roman with a broad grin and the girls. "We kept it a secret all week," Jenny said.

"And it was hard," Millie said. "It's hard not to talk about a party."

Tillie wrapped her arms around Granny. "I love you. Happy Birthday, *Oma*."

Granny bent down and held her tight. She looked over across the room at Lizzie and Amos. *Dear Lord, let Lizzie be this little one's mamm someday.* Her eyes met with Amos and he came over with Lizzie. "Happy Birthday. Were you surprised?"

"*Jah*, for sure."

"Sarah and I made a lemon cake," Lizzie said. "I can't wait for you to try it. Something spring-like in winter."

"*Danki*, Lizzie. So thoughtful."

"I need to say good-bye now.' Amos said. "I'm headed back to Lancaster."

"So soon? Did you find a farm?"

Amos turned to Lizzie. "We looked at several, but I think I need to go back and pray about it all for a spell. Have a driver out front waiting to take me to the bus stop." He nodded his head and turned to everyone. "*Goot* to meet *yinz*."

Granny looked at Lizzie, who didn't follow Amos out to the car, but looked over at Roman and smiled broadly.

Praise be... But Lizzie made her way over to the front window, waving at Amos as he left, her other hand on her heart. More casting off prayers, Granny moaned.

~*~

That night, Granny looked over the list of birds she'd spotted this year. She's never had thirty varieties of birds before. When Jeb spotted a golden eagle flying high above the trees behind the pond, she saw firsthand how they glided, just like she'd read. Not flapping their wings about like most birds. She wanted to be an eagle and soar effortlessly, not a flapping duck. But she couldn't soar unless she kept up her casting off prayers several times a day.

Her mind turned to Nathan, her dear grandson. Memories of them putting together puzzles when they all lived in the big house. Then Nathan moved to Montana, leaving the house to Roman. Having him home was such a treat, but the way he looked at Lavina bothered her, to her shame. And the way Lizzie waved rigorously out the window at Amos, upset her too. Surely Lizzie could see Roman was the one for her. Maryann got sicker than usual after radiation and she missed her at the party. She bowed her head in prayer.

Lord, here I am again, and I'm sure glad you don't get pestered by me. Your love never failed, new every morning, and night. Lord, I give Nathan to you. Bless his visit home. He's twenty and doesn't have a sweetheart back home in Montana. Not writing to a nice Amish girl either. I noticed how he looked at Lavina fondly and they talked forever at the party. Was it because they both didn't know many people? And Lord, I give Lizzie's heart to you. Turn it whichever way you want, even though I'd be so happy if you turned it away from Amos and toward Roman.

And Lord, it says in the Bible you never get tired or weary, and I'm thankful since sometimes I imagine I do wear you out.

I give my knitting friends to you. Ruth said she was trusting God to knit her heart together with Luke's but it would take lots of time. Help them. And I give my fretting to you about Maryann. It was hard to see her so sick, but she's so relieved to have a lumpectomy and said it was all worth it. But still Lord, it's hard to see a friend suffer. Help her Lord....I give all my loved ones to you. Help Ella feel like the real mamm of the twins and give her rest. I've known that girl since birth and she's always had a cheerful nature. Restore joy to her troubled heart.

Amen....for now.

~*~

Here is an Amish birthday cake recipe.

Amish Birthday Cake

2 ½ c. flour

2 ½ tsp. baking powder

¾ tsp. salt

2/3 c. oil

¾ c. milk

2 Tbsp. lemon juice

2 tsp. grated lemon peel

3 eggs

1 ½ c. sugar

Sift first three dry ingredients. Add oil, milk, lemon juice and peel. Beat until it forms a smooth batter. In a separate bowl, beat eggs until thick and foamy. Gradually add some sugar, continue beating until well blended. Fold in eggs and rest of sugar thoroughly into batter. Pour into two waxed paper-lined 9 inch round pans. Bake at 375 degrees for 25-30 minutes.

Amish Cream Cheese Icing

1 package cream cheese (8 oz.)

2/3rd c. sugar

1 tsp. vanilla

Pinch of salt

2 c. Cool Whip

Beat cream cheese, sugar, vanilla and salt until fluffy, and   then fold in Cool Whip.

EPISODE 9

Spun Together

Fannie gazed at the intricate carving on the new clock Melvin made, and then walked across the shop to the plainer, straight-cut ones. She no longer felt plain and fat, but like something beautiful that was designed by God. All the encouragement from the knitting circle and Melvin had made her see herself more clearly. The scriptures that were now deep in her heart were like a mirror, too, so she could see who she really was, fearfully and wonderfully made.

She heard footsteps and she turned to see Melvin come out of the workshop and into the little clock shop. But he didn't look too happy. "What's wrong?"

Melvin sat on the stool behind the counter, gazing straight ahead as if not hearing her.

"Melvin, are you sick? You look so pale."

He slowly turned to her. "We need to talk."

She looked into his eyes, and didn't see love. She knew it wouldn't last. He wanted to break off their engagement. She'd seen him go over to Lizzie's more than normal. He'd fallen for her again. How would she endure this? "Like I said, Melvin, what's wrong?" She slowly walked over to the counter to face her fate.

He cocked his head forward. "I don't know how to say

this?"

"I know. I can see it in your face. You proposed, but I want you happy, Melvin."

A slight grin pulled at one side of his mouth. "Fannie. Come back here and give me a hug. I wouldn't marry anyone but you."

Thank you Lord! She scurried around the counter and wrapped her arms around Melvin. "So what's the matter? Something is awfully wrong."

"*Daed* just told me something that will change everything. You know how the Coblenz's are moving up to Marathon, New York? *Daed's* been talking to them and is looking into moving up too. The farm next to theirs is for sale at a *goot* price."

Fannie dug her fingers into Melvin's black vest. "What did you say?"

"Nothing. Just walked out here. I'm shocked." He took her hands. "Could you see living in New York?"

Fannie wanted to burst into tears. She had so many nieces and nephews, and her sister was expecting. She always imagined her *kinner* playing with relatives...here in Smicksburg. She thought of Granny who was more of a *mamm* to her than her own, having the time to talk. But a wife was supposed to be supportive of her husband. She ran her fingers through Melvin's hair. "Wherever you go, I will follow. In the Bible, Ruth said that to Naomi. How much more should a wife say that to her future husband?"

Melvin put his hand on her cheek. "You're such a peach. But I love this clock shop. Wood is in my veins, not dairy farming. *Daed* will need to sell this house to move. "He got up and walked around the shop, hands in his pockets, looking at all the clocks. "I did say I could make clocks in New York."

"Would you have time? How many cows would you have? And would you hand milk them?"

"*Jah*, no diesel-fueled milking machines are allowed. Would give me so little time to carve."

Fannie knew Melvin's ability to carve was a gift from God and something he took pleasure in. His *Daed* did cut the wood, but it was Melvin who actually made the clocks. "When do you have to decide?"

"That's another thing that bothers me. *Daed* said as soon as our place sold, as if he had someone interested. It's not like him at all. He's so steady a man."

"He must really want the farm in New York, *jah*?"

Melvin sighed deeply. "*Jah*."

~*~

Ruth took Luke's hand from across the table, and bowed her head.

Our Father, which art in heaven,
Hallowed be thy Name.
Thy Kingdom come.
Thy will be done in earth,
As it is in heaven.
Give us this day our daily bread.
And forgive us our trespasses,
As we forgive them that trespass against us.
And lead us not into temptation,
But deliver us from evil.

For thine is the kingdom,
The power, and the glory,
For ever and ever.
Amen.

Luke held her hand tighter after the prayer, but she pulled away. They'd had daily reading of the Psalms and now saying the Lord's Prayer three times a day, but she still had a wounded heart. Luke still slept in Mica's room and no matter what he said, she felt like he was being deceitful. Would this ever change? Would she ever be able to trust him again?

"I keep thinking about the baptisms that took place on New Birth Sunday," Luke said as he shook salt on his mashed potatoes.

Yes, she knew! New Birth Sunday was the beginning of the annual five week cleansing time before Easter. Baptisms took place this past Sunday, then a week off to think about any unforgiveness. The third week was their committee meeting, where the *Ordnung* was reviewed and any changes came up for the vote and then another week off, before Easter.

How she loved Easter, when communion was celebrated and washing each other's feet, a sign that they were all servants to each other. But this year was different. She saw people having reconciliation dinners to extend forgiveness. Here she was eating with Luke every day with still only a drop of love and forgiveness. She poked the green beans with her fork. "Luke, I know the Easter season is a time of renewal, but my heart still feels old and worn out. I'm sorry, but I have to be honest."

He slowly looked up. "It's been over two months and you feel nothing for me?"

Ruth cringed. Was he going to lose his temper? Yell at her? She watched in astonishment as tears formed in his eyes, and he got up from the table and walked into the living room. She quickly got up and poured more milk into Mica's Sippy cup and put it on his highchair tray. "Now you eat while *Mamm* talks to *Daed*." She kissed the top of his head and made her way into the living room.

She was not prepared for what she witnessed; Luke was sobbing, head in his hands, bent over on the bench. She ran over and put her arm around him. "I'm sorry. I didn't mean to be harsh. Just honest."

He choked back tears. "I'm so stupid."

"What?"

"I should have never looked at my uncle's girly books." He clenched his fists and hit his knees.

"Luke, you were ten. Only three years older than Roman's Jenny." The thought pierced her heart. He was only three years older than Jenny when his uncle exposed him to pornography? Stacks of magazines hidden in the barn had planted thoughts in Luke's mind. Thoughts like women weren't respectable, only objects of lust…but he was ten.

"I'm not normal. Maybe I should be in Torrance."

"Luke, that's absurd. It's a psychiatric hospital. The doctor said you have a mild form of anxiety, not something serious. Remember what the doctor said; diabetics need insulin and your body needs other things?

Do you think diabetics aren't normal? Or Jeb, for taking heart medicine?

"But they act normal…"

Ruth got up and went over to the desk, and pulled a sheet of paper out of the bottom drawer. "I was over at Maryann's when Marge was there, the nurse who's buying the farm down the road from Granny. She started to act real irritated and her hands got shaky, so she took a sugar pill and sucked on it. Said she had low blood sugar, or hypoglycemia. She confessed she has lots of mood swings, so I asked her for more information. She gave me this."

Luke took the paper from Ruth's hand. "What's this got to do with me? A sugar pill isn't medicine."

"Read the list, Luke."

He read through the list, and then looked at her in amazement. "Fatigue, uneasiness, possible aggression, headaches, trembling. Ach, I had all these."

"I'm not saying you have low blood sugar, but emotional problems happen with other things too, like low sugar." She took Luke by the shoulders. "You're not crazy, understand?"

"But I have almost every symptom on this list," he said as he turned to scan the paper again.

"Well, you can't stop taking your medicine, but we could ask the psychologist about it at our next appointment."

Luke hunched over, as in defeat. "It's so embarrassing seeing a psychologist."

Ruth felt compassion well up and reached for Luke's

hand. "The doctor made me understand you have a physical problem. Luke, you're not crazy." She put her head on his shoulder. "What's the difference between you taking medicine and me taking all those herbs once a month for PMS? I'll admit, I acted crazy before Dan put me on something."

"But you're on herbs, not a medicine..."

"Herbs have chemicals in them though. Medicine's made of chemicals, *jah*? And remember, you have mild anxiety. The doctor told you how many millions of people take medicine for it."

Luke lowered his head again. "I'm just ashamed. Such a weak man."

Ruth looked at their interlocked hands. She didn't know the torment he felt inside until now. Being too focused on her own hurt feelings had made her blind to see his pain. For over two months she had to admit, she'd started to feel a trickle of love toward him, but stopped up the flow; it was like she was erecting a fortress around her heart.

"Luke?"

He looked up at her. "*Jah*?"

"I think I still love you."

"What?"

"If I didn't, I wouldn't care so much. I'm just afraid if I give an inch you'll –"

Luke leaned toward her and tenderly kissed her. "I haven't heard you say you loved me in so long."

Tears streamed down his cheeks, and she took a handkerchief out of her pocket and wiped them. It was a sweet kiss, not unfeeling, like in the past. But would this new man stay sweet if she gave more than an inch? She looked at Luke's blue eyes, hopeful she'd return his affection. She quickly got up to tend to little Mica…

~*~

Roman talked to Jonas as Lizzie ran out to get the mail. Buds were on the trees and he hoped spring would bring fresh changes to her life.

When Lizzie reappeared, she sifted through the mail. "So much junk mail. Well, *goot* to start fires with." She held up a letter. "Another letter from Amos." She plunked herself down in a rocker. "He's apologized enough, really."

Roman knew Amos felt he was in culture shock while in Smicksburg. He was also worried about his *kinner*, since he never left them for four days. Lizzie said she needed time to sort through her feelings, but it was more painful than Roman thought. He loved her and wanted to court her again. She was learning to trust, thanks to his girls and their weekly dinners. Child-like trust was rubbing off on Lizzie; it showed in her countenance. Every day she was turning into her old carefree self, the Lizzie before the assault so many years ago.

His eyes met with Jonas'. "I need a nap. Nice seeing you, Roman." He slowly got up and made his way out of the room.

"Lizzie, it doesn't get dark until six now. Want to take a walk in Smicksburg Park before knitting circle?" Roman asked.

She looked up from the letter and grinned. "I have a

kite put together already to fly."

Roman remembered how much Lizzie looked forward to March, kite flying time.

"I haven't flown a kite in eleven years," she said, triumphantly. "I'm learning to live again. Do the things I love."

"Is that a sign the grieving is over?"

"It's a step forward. Let me get my wraps and kite and we can head out."

Roman almost skipped out to the store and to the buggy. Thank you God! Lizzie is coming back! Now give me the words, and the courage.

Lizzie came out of the shop with a kite that had butterflies on it. Roman smiled at her. "Nice kite. The girls would like one."

"We have plenty in the store. I'll give them one."

When she started to walk to the buggy she started to slip on the mud, but found her footing. He offered his hand into the buggy and pulled her in. "Too warm for a buggy robe, don't you think?"

"Well, it's a bit nippy."

Roman pulled up the buggy robe. "Let's go." He pulled out and headed toward Old Smicksburg Park. How many times had they played hide and seek, even in their late teens, hiding behind those massive trees. "Remember when we played hide and seek at the park and you climbed the tree and you never found me?"

"*Jah*, I do. My laugh was the only thing that gave me away, after you looked for over an hour."

"It wasn't an hour, as I recall."

"You need to take the girls over to the park more. Why don't you?"

Roman knew the girls would love the park, but memories of Lizzie always came to the surface there, and the guilt that followed. When Abby was alive, she didn't see the need to go to the park, having a swing set in the backyard. He took Lizzie's hand. "We can bring the girls sometime."

Lizzie didn't say anything, just looked around at the beauty of early spring. "*Daed* said he heard peeper frogs the other night."

"So early?"

"*Jah*. Spring's coming on mighty fast. Next month we'll be putting in snow peas. Well, at least I will."

Roman couldn't help but notice the drop in Lizzie's tone. "What's wrong?"

"*Daed's* MS. The doctor thinks he might be having some kind of relapse. I'll be planting the garden alone."

"I can help," Roman said, squeezing her hand. "You know I'm here for you."

She put her head on his shoulder. "I know. *Danki.*"

Lizzie had always put her head on his shoulder when she was stressed. He remembered when her *daed* was diagnosed with MS, and times he'd just hold her and not say anything. It was what she wanted; what she needed. He leaned his head on hers and she didn't pull away.

They drove in silence for the next few minutes and then pulled into the park. Like a kid, she pulled down the buggy robe, grabbed her kite, and started for the vast open field. He jumped out the buggy and took the horse's reins and looped them to the hitching post. He ran to catch up and walked swiftly beside her. She was headed to the area they'd always gone when courting. She could have gone to other spots in the park. Was she doing this out of habit or desire to recapture the past?

She told Roman to hold the kite while she ran with the string. When she signaled, he'd let it go. He nodded and she ran and then looked at him and waved her hand. He let go of the kite and it soared into the air. He ran toward her and watched as she giggled, letting out string and watching the kite lift higher.

She looked over at Roman and smiled. "Remember all the kites I lost because you always got them tangled in the trees?"

"That's because I let the kite go higher than a rooftop." He gave her a wry smile.

"I can make a kite go high too…"

Roman watched as she looked up at the sky. God was healing her; it was so evident in her countenance. But like his *daed* said, she needed time. Move in pace with nature, Son. He looked at Lizzie like a flower that just needed a lot of sunshine to open up. He was pleased with the progress over the past few weeks, but she still hadn't said if she'd court him again.

Should he let his impatient, impulsive self- rule, or was it natural to want to know by now? The thought of Amos still writing made him insecure. He was confused, and the Good Book said God wasn't the author of confusion.

Lizzie came near him and took his hand. "Now you fly the kite. Make it go as high as you want."

Roman took the spool of string and smirked. "Now we'll see some real kite flying." He loosened the string and soon the kite jutted into the air. It was windier than he thought. The kite headed over to the trees across the field and he struggled to pull it back in, but it started to nose-dive. He ran back and the kite escaped the trees as he let more string. As he started to wind up the string to even the kite, it fiercely resisted. His jaw dropped when the string broke and the kite helplessly soared into the trees.

"I can get it down." He ran towards the trees but stopped when he heard Lizzie laugh harder than she'd done in years. He ran back and took her hand. "I'll get the kite, and you're going to help."

They ran across the field, Lizzie teasing him that he'd never get it down. He retorted that she forgot he could climb a tree like a raccoon. He looked up, figured out which tree it was in, and glad it was a maple with lots of low branches. He jumped up and caught the lowest limb and pulled himself up. He caught hold of the next limb and swung up.

"Roman, I think you made your point. That tree is too high."

Roman took a deep breath. How refreshing to hear that she cared for his safety. "I'll watch my step." He continued up the tree and soon retrieved the kite out of the top branches. He looked down at her, concerned etched on her face. How he loved this woman. He had to know. "I'll give you your kite back on one condition." In the past, that meant he wanted a kiss first.

"And what's that?"

Did she really forget all those kisses after he'd withheld something from her? "Remember when your cat got stuck in the tree? What did I ask for before I brought her down?"

He saw Lizzie put her head down. He should have listened to his *daed*. He was rushing things. He slowly made his way down the tree, not eager to get to the bottom. She'd tell him she needed time and that she wasn't sure of her feelings for Amos. How much longer could he endure this?

He looked at her from the bottom branch. Her back was turned and her head was down. He'd really gone too fast. Knowing all she'd been going through, she needed time. He swung down from the branch. "Sorry, Lizzie. Here's your kite."

She didn't turn around. He made his way to her, placing both hands on her shoulders. "I'll wait. As long as you need...I'll still be here waiting, okay?"

He turned her around and saw that she was beaming. She got on tip-toes and tenderly planted a kiss on his lips. "Can I have my kite back now?"

Roman gasped, not realizing he'd been breathing so shallow. He drew her to him. "Lizzie, I love you so much. Please say yes. Not to courting, but marrying me."

She threw her arms around him. "Yes. I'll marry you. I've never loved anyone else."

Roman twirled her around. He could call her his Lizzie again.

~*~

Granny bowed her head in silent prayer, and then looked up at the two men in her life; her dear husband, and grandson Nathan. "I can't tell you how much it means to me that you might stay."

Jeb chuckled. "I've survived almost fifty years of marriage. I'm not going anywhere."

Granny rolled her eyes. "I'm talking to Nathan…old man. And you take back what you said about just surviving."

Jeb made a straight face. "I've had almost fifty years of marital bliss."

Nathan hit the table. "*Yinz* make me laugh. All this bantering back and forth."

"It's your *opa*, Nathan. He's always trying to get my dander up," Granny said, eying Jeb.

"I'm just having fun. Not boring to live with, right?"

"*Jah*, never a dull day…" Granny turned to Nathan. "Can your *daed* spare you on the farm? Does he know you want to stay?"

"Well, to be honest, it was his idea that I come for a while. I have lots of money saved, but just can't seem to find the right girl to share it with."

Granny looked at Jeb and smirked. "A single man with a large fortune is in need of a wife."

Nathan scratched his head. "*Oma*, why are you talking so funny."

"To get up my dander," Jeb groaned. "She's quoting Jane Austen again."

"Who's she? Austen doesn't sound like an Amish name. Is she an *Englisher*?

"*Jah*, from England. Exactly. I read her books."

Jeb leaned forward. "*Jah*, and this lady thinks love is a feeling more than a commitment."

"No she doesn't." She gave Jeb the look that he knew so well. Let's change the subject.

Jeb poured gravy over his roast beef. "Nathan, there's lots of nice girls here in Smicksburg. Maybe go to a Singing."

"Will Lavina be going?"

Jeb's eyes grew round and searched Granny's. She held her fork full of granola up in mid-air. Silence followed and Nathan slouched back in his chair. "Is she someone else's girl?"

Granny put her head down, trying to compose herself. She loved Lavina, but she'd imagined a good moral Amish girl for her Nathan. But Lavina had kneeled and confessed to her immorality and they were to forgive.

"*Oma*, what's wrong?"

Granny hoped Jeb would say something, but he only looked up at the ceiling, as if deep in thought.

"*Opa*? What's wrong?"

Jeb slowly looked down at his grandson. "I've been asking the dear Lord to bring the right man in her life. Maybe you're the answer. So you like her?"

"*Jah*, we've talked for hours. She such a *goot* listener...and real pretty." He turned to Granny. "What do you think, Oma?"

Granny held her stomach. "I think this meat is bad... feeling sick."

~*~

Roman and Lizzie burst through the door, and Granny took the cold washcloth off her forehead, and leaned her head back down against her rocker. "What on earth?"

"We're getting married. Me and Lizzie. She said yes." Roman twirled Lizzie around again. "Can you believe she said yes?"

Granny looked at Lizzie, laughing and hugging Roman around the middle. But it wasn't long ago that she had quills up like a porcupine when around him. Over the past few months, since she went to Lancaster for counseling, she was transformed. God had heard all her prayers. The fast she did on Second Christmas, a day to pray for Lizzie while in Lancaster. God really heard her…her moaning at times, translated into a prayer, like the Bible said. When we don't have words, He heard her heart. She clasped her hands over her face, so touched at the thought. Cast your cares on the Lord because He cares for you. How could she have doubted.

Roman took the cold washcloth from her hands and put it back on her forehead. "Are you sick, *Mamm*? You aren't saying a word. "

"*Ach*, I'm sorry. Ever so happy." She reached out for Lizzie's hand. "It's been my prayer *yinz* would find love again. I watched you court before, remember?"

Lizzie looked at Roman, and then back to her. "So you don't mind? I mean, I know how much you loved Abigail."

"That I did, and we'll always remember her warmth and love. But I know my Roman's been a lonely man, and you've always had a place in his heart. "

Roman put his arm around Lizzie. "And I love her more than when we were young. "

"How so?" Granny asked.

"Well, I know what it's like to live without love, and know how much I need it, I suppose."

Granny pulled a handkerchief from her apron pocket and dabbed her eyes. "I feel a *goot* cry coming on. Tears of joy." She held the handkerchief up to her eyes and was silent, trying to absorb it all. But she had the knitting circle to get ready for. Cookie bars to put in the oven. She'd have a *goot* cry tonight. "So, we'll have two weddings this fall."

"*Nee*, we want to get married in May, before planting time."

Granny gasped. "It's hardly ever done in spring. Why the hurry?"

"We've missed too many years together already. Anyhow, spring is Lizzie's favorite season."

Granny knew many *Englishers* got married in the spring, but it was their custom to have weddings in November, and if necessary, December. But she wouldn't say anything to break this moment of joy. And she knew her son well enough; once he set his mind to something, it rarely changed. She looked at Roman. "You'll need to talk to your *daed* and the bishop, jah? To get their blessing?" She turned to Lizzie. "But if they're in agreement, looks like we have lots of work to do. Where will the wedding be?"

"Well, since my *mamm's* not with us, we thought maybe…."

"Ach, of course. You'll have it here," Granny said. "And your dear *mamm* would've been so pleased."

"*Jah*, she hoped I'd marry Roman someday."

"*Mamm,* a wedding can be whipped together in no time, *jah?*" Roman asked.

Granny tried to hide her shock. Men. They always thought big gatherings took such little time to prepare. Roman had no idea what he was asking. "I say you talk to your *daed* and the bishop and see what they have to say before plans are talked about, *jah?*" She tilted her head. "Aren't you forgetting something important though, Roman?"

"What?"

"Your bothers, scattered across the country."

"*Ach*, I forgot about them." Roman led Lizzie to the bench and looked at her. "I'd like my brothers to be here."

"We can wait until fall…" Lizzie said.

Roman put his arm around her. "You're worried about your *daed…*"

"*Jah…*"

Roman turned to his *mamm*. "Jonas seems to be having some kind of relapse. His MS treatments were going *goot*, but now he's having trouble with his legs. If it gets any worse, Lizzie will need more help. She can't lift him."

Lizzie leaned her head on Roman's shoulder. "It could just be the cold weather affecting his joints. That's why we're bringing up closed in buggies at counsel meeting on Sunday. "

Granny got up and went to sit by Lizzie. "Do you

really think it's wise?

"They have them in Lancaster. I don't see why not."

"The expense. " She took Lizzie's hand. "So many of us old folk have arthritis and it's painful in the winter. But to make everyone buy new buggies?"

"Maybe the bishop and elders can make an exception for my *daed* and elderly folk. "

~*~

Granny took the cookie bars out of the oven with the help of Lizzie. To think this girl would be living next door filled her with such joy. And the girls would have a *mamm* again. She and Jeb needed to take a long train ride out to visit their sons after the wedding, which would hopefully be in the fall. Knowing that her headstrong son was talking with Jeb at this very moment gave her another knot in her stomach. Roman was being so impulsive…She grabbed her middle.

"Granny, what's wrong?" Lizzie asked.

"Upset stomach."

Lizzie put her hand on Granny's forehead. "You don't feel feverish. But go sit down in your rocker. I'll finish up here."

Granny embraced Lizzie. "I'm so happy you'll be my *dochder*."

"And I'll have a *mamm* again," Lizzie said. "God puts solitary souls in families, *jah*?"

"*Jah*, like the Good Book says." Granny held Lizzie for a few moments, thanking God for Lizzie once again, and then turned and made her way to her rocker. She didn't know if turning seventy made her nerves be so unraveled. Was this part of aging? *Nee,* she knew what it was. Ever since Nathan said he took a liking to Lavina she'd felt sick, and she felt ashamed. But she didn't want Nathan to marry someone who'd been with other men. Nathan deserved a *goot* Amish girl. Ach, but Jeb seemed to encourage it? Of course Lavina told Jeb more than she did him, amazed that she found a man who was kind and listened to her. Yes, Lavina was finding healing through the love of Jeb. Would she find further healing with Nathan?

She picked up her knitting loom and started to knit. The feel of the yarn wrapped around her fingers always calmed her nerves. She looked at the black yarn in her basket. How the black wool made such pretty patterns on the shawls. She'd heard the English call someone the black sheep in the family, and she'd asked Suzy about it. It was a phrase for someone who'd done something wrong and shamed the family. She thought it was so unkind to black sheep; they were a beautiful animal.

She thought of Lavina. Would she be considered a black sheep in her family? Did she need to be spun together with another family? Lizzie had quoted one of her favorite Bible verses...God puts the solitary in families...but it was longer than that. She reached over to the little table where her well-worn King James Version Bible lived. She opened the back cover where she'd kept her notes. Under "Verses for Lonely Days" she'd written out several scriptures. She moved her finger down the list and found Psalm 68:6 written out. *God sets the solitary in families: he brings out those who are bound with chains: but the rebellious dwell in a dry land.*

Was Lavina someone bound, or was she someone who was rebellious? Her stomach tightened again. This was something she needed to cast off before she made herself sick. Only God knew Lavina's heart and the reasons she didn't want to go home. Lord I cast Lavina on you. Lead Nathan to a girl who's the one for him, and take the others away!

She heard the door open and she looked up. Jeb slowly walked in, face pale. He looked over at Lizzie in the kitchen. "Deborah, can we talk our bedroom? Private-like?"

"*Jah,*" she said, setting down her Bible. "Jeb, you alright? Need to see the doctor?"

He motioned for her to follow him, which she did. Obviously, Roman was being impulsive again and they had a divided house. She took a chair in their room while Jeb sat at the edge of the bed. "I told Roman he was being too hasty, and he said he thought I dragged my feet too much. He called me a turtle, when I told him to be in pace with nature. He said I was a turtle and he was a jack rabbit." He looked down at his clasped hands. "I'm getting mighty old…"

"Nonsense. You're gray hair is a sign you have more wisdom. "

"But Roman did bring up some goot points. A wedding in November gives the couple all winter to live with relatives to save for a house. But Roman has a house already. "

"Well, I've been praying those two would get married

for years, but I always imagined a fall wedding. " She scooted her chair up toward Jeb and took his hands. "What's really worrying you?"

"Well, Amos was here not long ago. I just don't understand women. Seems like Lizzie liked that fellow, and now she's marrying Roman? How's that possible?"

Granny's eye shone. "I saw through it all. Amos helped her when she needed a friend, after counseling. But when she got home, I saw how she looked at Roman, and I knew it."

"So she never cared at all for Amos? He came the whole way out here to see her? Hasn't ruled out moving here, neither."

Granny pursed her lips. "You know when you see those big orange detour signs when the English are fixing the roads? You go on a different road for a while, but end up back to the road you were on. It's the same thing. Amos was a detour, but Lizzie's heart is back to where it's always been, with Roman."

Jeb slowly looked up. "I see. Like when I'm fishing and the fish get distracted, but always come back to the worm?"

"*Jah*, Lizzie was distracted for a while. So, are we going to have a wedding in spring or fall? Does Roman have your blessing for a spring wedding?"

"We have Easter in three weeks, and the lambs will be birthing. It's birthing season for lots of our People. And May would be plowing time. We have weddings in November for a reason. "He sighed deeply. "And I'm supposing Roman wants you to plan everything. You're no spring chicken anymore."

"I'll have help…"

"*Nee*, it's asking too much. I'll be telling Roman he needs to wait until fall, but we won't be in agreement and we have communion coming up."

"*Jah*, you need to have no strife or unforgiveness, and knowing Roman, he'll be awful upset." She squeezed his hands again. "Let's cast this all on God. He can knit your hearts together in love."

Jeb moaned. "I see you spin that wool of yours. Sometimes it breaks. Let's hope Roman doesn't pull so hard he breaks the unity in the *Gmay*.

~*~

Ella raised the spoon to Vina's mouth. "Eat your grits, *wee boppli*."

"She's not so little anymore," Zach mused, sitting across the table. "Seven months old, right?"

"*Jah*, seems like a week ago we went up to Troutville and collected them."

"What's wrong, Ella?" Zach asked. "I can watch them while you're at the knitting circle. Why aren't you going?"

"Ach, tired, is all."

Zach leaned forward. "Tell me."

"Granny said Lavina is welcome to join. Going to our *Gmay* is enough; do I have to see her everywhere?"

"She's made it clear she doesn't want the twins back. I believe her and you said you did too."

Ella sighed and put some Cheerios on Vina's highchair tray. "Eat these, Sweetheart." I don't know Zach; I don't trust her. Has she really changed? I mean, she's making it very clear to Nathan she's available. Almost flirting."

"You've seen this?"

"*Nee,* heard it through the Amish Grapevine."

"Not a reliable source, *jah*?"

"Well, I see the concern in Granny's face too. She's struggling and with Easter approaching; we need unity. I can't be having these feelings toward Lavina and take communion."

Zach took a sip of coffee and gave Moses a spoonful of baby cereal. "He's a guy for sure. This is his second bowl."

Ella grinned. "Moses is my big boy. *Jah,* Moses?"

Moses clapped his hands and swung his feet in delight. "He knows his *mamm's* voice."

"*Jah,* he does. He's my big boy, who will need a haircut soon."

"*Nee,* it's not long enough for a bowl cut, but in a few months." Zach scratched the back of his neck. "It's not a feeling, Ella."

"What?"

"Forgiveness. You know that."

"If she hadn't followed Nathan around like a stray cat, I don't think I'd be feeling this way."

"He follows her around. Watch real close after church. He makes his way over to her and they take a walk outside."

Ella met Zach's eyes, seeking comfort and advice. "Do I need counseling?"

"Maybe talk to an older woman in the *Gmay,* who's raised *boppli.* I think you're tired.""

"But is it normal to have all this anxiety? And unforgiveness?"

"Ella, I know you. You take your walk with God real serious and fear you'll lose that closeness with Him more than anything. Am I right?"

Ella's eyes misted. "My faith means more to me than my life, I think. When we read the Martyr's Mirror and learn of all the torture our ancestors went through for their love for the Lord, I want to be like them. When I read the story of Dirk Willems, of him helping his enemy out of the icy pond, saving his life, only to be burnt at the stake when caught; well, I'm so ashamed."

Zach got up and kissed Ella on the cheek. "I picked you as my wife because of your love for God. And didn't Granny tell you she admired your faith too?"

Ella looked down, feeling heat rise in her cheeks. "*Jah*."

"Maybe your faith is being tested, as if in a fire. But we know the story of Shadrach, Meshach and Abednego. When they were thrown into the fire, everyone saw four people, not three. The Lord was with them in that fire."

Ella slowly looked up. "I forgot about that."

"And how about Job? A good example that we're small and God is too big for us to understand. You try to figure everything out, or do all women do that?"

Ella got up and put her arms around Zach's neck. "I don't know…" She felt Zach's lips on hers and then her head being cradled against his chest. Her tower of strength. "So what do I do?"

Zach kissed the top of her head. "Pray for strength to

forgive. We can't do it on our own. And think the best of Lavina. She's done a lot of things right. She could have done away with the twins but she wanted them happy, so she gave them up, even made sure she liked you first..."

"I almost forgot. She wrote and asked me lots of questions. Even little things, like whether we had a tire swing or not."

Zach cupped her cheeks and kissed her again. "I think they'll understand if you're late for knitting circle. Why not go?"

She beamed. "Because I want to spend time with my husband." She pulled Zach down and kissed him. "Let's put the twins down for bed early."

Zach scooped her up and kissed her until she was out of breath. He winked. "Let's all go to bed early. " He kissed her nose. "That proverb, 'Kissing wears out, cooking don't', isn't true for me."

Ella laughed and buried her face in his chest.

~*~

She heard buggy wheels and went over to the window. Lavina, Becca and Maryann had arrived. She saw Nathan shoot out of Roman's house like a rock from a slingshot, and head straight to Lavina, taking the pies from her hands. She hid behind the white curtain, pulled over on one side, and studied Nathan's face, especially his eyes. Did she see love? Another pain in her stomach. She turned and willed herself to not fret, casting her concerns on God. This was getting to be an hourly ritual.

When they entered she welcomed them, telling them to take some bar cookies. Nathan put the pies on the table and Granny got out plates and knives. Maryann protested to any desserts, and Granny suspected Dan, their herbalist, had convinced her white sugar was bad for her health. Granny shrugged her shoulders. She was seventy, healthy, and desserts full of white sugar were served daily after every meal. The meal wasn't complete without dessert.

She noticed that Fannie looked mighty down, and went over and put her arm around her, as the other women sat at the table eating pie.

"Lavina, did you make this berry pie?" Ruth asked. "The crust is so flakey and tastes different."

"I use butter, not margarine or Oleo. I think it makes a difference."

"She's teaching me things about baking I never knew," Maryann said. "Your *mamm* taught you well."

Lavina's eyes had a far-off look about them. "I miss her."

"Are you thinking of going back home?" Fannie asked.

"*Nee*, I talked to the bishop here. Told him why I couldn't go back and he agreed. He's glad I'll be a sheep in his flock."

"But where will you live? " Granny asked, turning toward Maryann. "With you?"

"*Jah*, she's a big help…"

Becca chimed in. "I can actually go out more with friends."

"And I can live with a family where I see lots of love in the home. I'm getting a vision of what I want my family to be like."

Granny couldn't believe what she was hearing. Maryann had been Lavina's biggest critic, but now offering a permanent home? She knew Maryann was a *goot* judge of character though. But the bishop usually encouraged reconciliation between families. Why wasn't he telling her to go back home and make amends? It was all such a mystery.

Lavina looked across the room at Becca. "I see Gilbert Miller was baptized too. *Yinz* seem like *goot* friends...and now being both baptized."

"What are you saying, Lavina? Granny asked. "Becca's only fifteen and not looking to marry soon. " She turned to Becca. "I didn't know you were taking baptism classes. So young."

"With everything happening with *Mamm*, I got real scared. Always thought *Mamm* would be out there watching my baptism. Now I know life's like a teacup, fragile."

"Maryann, you're going to be alright?" Fannie asked.

"I should be. Doctors say it looks *goot*. They caught it all...Becca just got nervous."

"But the baptismal vow is the most sacred and important. You had no doubts?" Ruth asked.

"*Nee,* not one. I'm Amish to the core." Becca said.

The side door opened and Lizzie soon appeared. "Sorry I'm a little late. Was over at Roman's."

"Seeing those precious girls?" Maryann asked.

Granny saw that Lizzie now looked pale. Maybe her stomach pains weren't from stress but a virus. "Lizzie, you feeling alright?"

She looked at Granny, sorrow in her eyes. "I feel fine."

Granny got up and took Lizzie's hand. "You girls can start to knit, now that you're almost done with dessert. I need to talk to Lizzie private-like."

The women all put their dirty dishes into the sink and went out into the living room. Granny put her hands on Lizzie's shoulders. "This should be the happiest day of your life. Why so sad?"

"Roman's awful upset, and so is Jeb. Those two are like sheep, butting horns. Neither will give in."

"Jeb's concerned about me. I can tell. April's birthing time and May for plowing. You know how he goes on about staying in step with nature."

"*Jah*, but Roman and I don't need the type of wedding young folk have who don't have anything. Roman has a house...."

Granny knew she had to talk sense into Jeb. As touched as she was that he hovered over her, protecting her, she could do this wedding if..."Let's go into the circle and you can give your *goot* news. At least you and Roman are together again and that's the important thing."

Lizzie followed behind her as they entered the circle. "Lizzie has some *goot* news." Granny said.

"*Jah*, Roman and I are courting again."

Silence filled the room, only the ticking of the pendulum clock and the faint sound of peeper frogs from outside could be heard.

"That's *wunderbar*, Lizzie. But why do you look so sad?"

Lizzie looked at Granny, bewildered.

"My son wants a spring wedding and my husband is against it. So they're not in unity and we all know what that means this time of year."

"Well, all year long, we need to focus on it," Maryann corrected. "But communion will be delayed if no unity. That hasn't happened in a while."

Granny looked around the room. "Jeb thinks it's too much work for an old woman like me. I have sheep that will be birthing their young. .."

Fannie stood up. "I have an idea. *Yinz* know Melvin and I are planning a spring wedding. Why not have a joint wedding. A double wedding?"

Lizzie slowly took a seat and put her loom on her lap. "I couldn't. It's your day, Fannie. But *danki* just the same."

Fannie put her hands on her hips. "I don't want to be the center of attention. It unravels me. This could be my answer to prayer." She sat down. "And my big day won't be happy anyhow…"

"What?" Becca blurted. "It's your wedding day."

"*Yinz* heard about the Coblenz's moving to New York? Well guess who wants to move there too? Melvin's *daed*." She looked over at Granny, tears welling up in her eyes. "I'd miss everyone so much, but he'll be my husband. "

Granny couldn't imagine Fannie being so far away, but then again, it was painful when all her sons moved away. "You'll be greatly missed. Melvin too."

"What will he do with his shop?" Lizzie asked. "He's always loved that place. What would he do in New

York?"

"Dairy farming," Fannie moaned. "We'll have to hand milk the cows too and it's freezing up there. But I love Melvin so..."

"So you tell him how you feel," Granny said. "A marriage has two people in it. And the husband should love his wife and care how she feels about big decisions."

"Really? I thought it would make Melvin think I didn't love him. I do love him enough to move to New York. "She turned to Lizzie. "But he loves his shop. His *daed's* selling it to buy the farm and cows."

"Fannie, *yinz* need to talk," Lizzie said. "And I need to talk to Roman. I told him how much I wanted a spring wedding, saying it was the prettiest time of year for a wedding. But if it causes dissention, it's selfish on my part. It's just so much warmer..."

"*Jah*, it's cold in November and most the leaves are off the tress," Ruth said.

"How's the unity between you and Luke?" Maryann asked. "Been reading the Bible and praying together? Remember what I told you?"

"*Jah*, we have and it's binding us together." Ruth's face slowly grew red. "I can say we should be in full unity to take communion on Easter."

~*~

Lizzie could see the girls' lights were out, so she headed over to Roman's after the knitting circle. He greeted her with a kiss that lingered.

"My Lizzie again..." He held her close. "We'll have a spring wedding, don't you worry."

Lizzie could hear the beating of his heart, and wished she could stay in his arms forever. "Roman, we can wait until fall. I don't have to have a spring wedding."

Roman led her to the bench and sat her on his lap. "So, you're having second thoughts?" He winked playfully.

"Roman, do you know how upset your *daed* is? He thinks we're being selfish, and I'm starting to agree. We can wait…"

Roman pulled her to himself. "But I have a house. There's nothing to prepare."

"Only the wedding and it takes a lot of work, and the women do it all." Lizzie sighed. "Fannie's been planning hers for weeks, since she got engaged."

"But we're not like the English, who plan theirs for a year. We just need to have the wedding feast."

"Which the women do and we need time to prepare…plus your bothers won't be here. I think that's bothering your *daed* too."

Roman kissed her cheek. "My bothers in Ohio can come."

"How do you know?"

"I called them. Used the neighbor's phone and called the numbers they gave me. They called back and they said just to tell them the date a week in advance. They have a driver who needs work." He kissed her again. "My other brothers can't come, but two can."

"Does your *daed* know this?"

"*Nee,* but he will tomorrow when we talk with the bishop."

Lizzie snuggled against Roman. "What about my *daed*? We need to see how he feels, moving into this house and giving up the store…"

"I talked to Nathan and he said he'd be happy to live with your dad. Maybe for a year, if need be."

Lizzie looked up at Roman and their lips met. "I'll be Mrs. Roman Weaver."

"I'll be the happiest man in town…"

~*~

"My neck hurts," the bishop blurted. "Turning to each of you as you hurl words back and forth."

"Sorry," Roman said.

"*Jah*, I'm sorry too," Jeb said. "I've just seen what Roman's impulsiveness has done in the past, and want him to wait until fall."

"*Daed*, I won't be changing my mind."

"But it wasn't long ago that *yinz* both had your dander up when around each other. All the time."

The bishop put his hand up. "And we know why, Jeb. Lizzie was a hurting woman."

"*Jah*, *Daed*, you know the whole story."

Jeb clasped his hands on the table. "I still think you should wait."

"Jonas is mighty happy for Lizzie. His legs are worse in the winter and he said Lizzie has to help pull him up and even tries to lift him at times. *Goot* thing he's a small man." He cocked his head toward Jeb. "Two of your sons will be coming. What's the real reason you want them to wait?"

Jeb raked his fingers through his hair. "It's too

sudden-like. And Deborah seems so tired at times. She'd be doing most of the planning, with Lizzie's *mamm* gone." He turned to Roman. "As for Lizzie, let's have Nathan live with Jonas now and help if his legs are bad."

"What do you think, Roman? Sound like a plan?" the bishop asked.

Roman's eyes misted. "You both don't understand, do you? Spring is Lizzie's favorite season. It reminds her of new life. Since the assault, the life inside her seemed to die. It's like she's been resurrected. And if she wants spring to be like a symbol to her, I want her to have that."

Jeb leaned toward Roman. "She told *yinz* that?"

"*Nee,* it's in little things she says."

Jeb rubbed the back of his neck. "You're more like your *mamm* than I thought. Always seeing things no one else is seeing."

"I'm not imagining this all up," Roman snapped.

Jeb put his hand on Roman's shoulder. "It was a compliment, Son. Calm down."

~*~

Fannie saw Melvin pull in the driveway and she closed her eyes. Lord, give me strength. She went to the wooden pegs where all the capes and shawls hung and decided on a shawl, since it was warming up. She met Melvin on the front porch.

"How's my peach?" he asked.

Fannie tried to talk but got tongue-tied. Embarrassed that she stuttered, she looked down.

"What's wrong Fannie? You're acting like you did when we first met, shy and all. It's me, Melvin. "

"Let's sit on the porch swing." She walked over to the white swing and Melvin sat next to her. "I have something to tell you."

"You're scaring me Fannie. So somber. Do you want to call off our wedding?"

Fannie noticed when Melvin was fearful, his green eyes seemed darker. "*Nee,* I want to be your wife, but I think I'll be a bad one. You may not want to marry me."

"Now that doesn't make any sense." He leaned away from her. "Are you saying there's something from your past that you haven't told me about? Some reason why I'd think you're bad?"

"*Nee,* only something in my heart."

Melvin looked straight ahead. "I saw you talking to Hezekiah. When I first met you, that's who you always talked about….."

Fannie remembered how she used to dream of Hezekiah and become upset when "skinny little Lottie" got his attention. She hadn't thought of her jealousy in so long. To think of how insecure she was and how the knitting circle helped her recondition her mind, when she thought of her love for Hezekiah, it made her laugh. No, Melvin was someone who she thought of only in a dream, not even attainable. She took his hand. "I see him in passing, and believe me, I feel nothing." She kissed his cheek. "See how it feels to be jealous. Remember how insecure I was about Lizzie?"

Melvin looked at her and grinned. "I suppose I'm doing the same thing. So what is it then? Why would you think you'd be a bad wife?"

"I don't want to move to New York. Granny said I should let you know how I feel. Said marriage is between two people and they need to both share their feelings."

Melvin looked straight ahead again. "We may need to postpone the wedding then. I was right. Daed had a buyer for the house and shop. If I don't go to New York, I'll have to find a place to work." He took her hand. "A fall wedding then. We can live with your folks, just like everyone else, and spend the winter saving to build a house in the spring. "

Fannie saw the dread on Melvin's face. Could she be this selfish? His *daed* had offered to build a shop next to the farm in New York. He wanted to turn the big farmhouse into a duplex, so they'd have their privacy. "Melvin," she blurted. "I'm sorry. I never should have said anything. Now you're not happy. If you're not happy, I'm not either."

"And the same here. I want you to be happy."

She leaned her head on his shoulder. "It's time I grow up."

~*~

Ella pulled the buggy into Maryann's driveway and noticed buds were on her azalea bushes, and daffodils were scattered across the yard. She stared at the tire swing; she'd forgotten her prayer long ago. To have *kinner* for the tire swing Zach had put up several years ago. God heard that prayer and now she had two little ones. God really did care about all the times she'd swung on the tire, crying her heart out to him. And Lavina was, in a way, an answer to her prayer.

She heard laughing and froze when she saw Lavina and Nathan walking in from the back field, holding hands. As they approached she could make out what they were saying...."Can't wait until the next singing..." That meant he was taking her home, after Sunday Singings, in the wee hours of the night. Was Lavina seducing Nathan? Is Nathan the reason she didn't want to go back home? But she said the bishop agreed that she stay in Smicksburg...or was Lavina lying? Nathan was the sweetest man and thought the best of everyone. Was he just plain naïve?

Ella put her head down and closed her eyes. She didn't like the Ella she was becoming, feeling anger every time she was around Lavina. In the past, she'd always thought the best of people, like Nathan. But when it came to Lavina, she always feared she was being lied to, and that she was naïve. She had to stop this. The Bible said love was thinking the best of others, not keeping a record of wrongs. She confessed her bad feelings about Lavina to the Lord, and felt a burden lift slowly lift. It was God's job to reveal the truth, not her. She was not to judge.

She looked up and her eyes met Lavina's. She looked at her with a puzzled expression. "Ella, are you okay?"

"Ach, just deep in thought. Well, prayer actually. You know, just talking to God."

"How are you Ella?" Nathan said. "And the little ones?"

"They're angels, really. A gift from God." She looked at Lavina, hoping she understood her meaning. If the kinner were a gift from God, so was she.

Lavina nodded. "*Jah*, they were a gift."

Nathan put his hand on her shoulder, as if lending strength. "I best be getting back to *Oma's*."

He nodded to Ella and she nodded back, mesmerized by what she was seeing. They acted like they were confidants or best friends. How odd? She fidgeted with the horse's reins. "Want to go to the Country Junction for some pie?"

Lavina looked startled. "Why? I mean, we have pie here…"

"I'd like to treat you and get to know you better."

Lavina mouth soon slipped into a smile. "I'd like that."

~*~

A red sports car splashed with mud appeared in Granny's window. Jack barked viciously, as if the people inside were strangers. Soon a short woman with light-red hair popped out of the passenger side. "Jack, don't you know who I am?" Suzy quipped. "Come here and give me a hug" Jack ran to her and put his front paws up on her shoulders, almost knocking her down. He proceeded to lick her face.

"Suzy," Granny chimed as she ran out on her porch. "When did you get home?"

"A few days ago. Oh, Florida is glorious in the winter: no snow, ice, gloomy days, only sunshine." She walked up the porch steps and gave Granny a hug. "And you'll never guess what I found?"

"Yarn shops. How many did you find?"

"Oh, plenty, and do I have some ideas for mine. No, I found an Amish settlement. Have you ever gotten a circle letter from Pinecraft, Florida?"

"*Nee*, never."

"Well, you're always telling me I don't need to go to be a snowbird, but I found Amish people who are. I couldn't believe it."

"Who milks their cows?" Granny pulled her shawl tighter.

"I don't know. Never thought of that." Anyhow, I bought you one of their cookbooks."

Granny embraced Suzy, her dear English friend. "I've missed you."

"Missed my van?" Suzy smirked.

"*Nee*, we all missed you. But where is your van?"

Suzy pointed to the car. "I came with Marge. She's in there talking on her cell phone to her husband. She told me all about meeting you, and the farm down the road." She put her hand on Granny's shoulder. "Are you alright? You look pale."

"I've been feeling drained. Did you hear about the engagements? Fannie's marrying Melvin and my Roman will be marrying Lizzie."

"Did Emma do that?

"Who's Emma? Don't know who you mean."

"You know. The Jane Austen book? Emma, the matchmaker? Jeb was calling you that."

"I've come to learn the Lord is the matchmaker,."

"But you don't seem happy about these weddings?"

Granny linked her arm through Suzy's and led her inside. "Want some tea?"

"No, I need to get back to the shop. Marge just

wanted to show me the farm inside...have to run. But tell me, what's wrong?"

"Well, you know how head strong my son is. Roman wants to get married the first week of May. Jeb thinks he's being impulsive and wants them to wait until fall."

"And you don't like it when people aren't getting along? Especially in the family?"

"*Jah.* I feel torn. I can see both sides."

"Why can't Roman get married in May? I mean, he is an adult. You Amish don't get wedding dresses, cakes, photographers. Only a big meal, right?"

"*Jah*, but it's a special meal. A large meal, sometimes a thousand people attend. There's no time for folks to come out of state."

Suzy sighed. "You're always telling me us "English" make you laugh, always keeping up with the Jones'. And here you are keeping up with the....Yoders."

"What?"

"Why does the wedding need to be big? Can't you have a small wedding with maybe only fifty people?"

"Fifty! If I invite Maryann's family I'd have nine already."

"Okay, how about two-hundred? Would that be too hard?"

"*Nee.* Suppose not...just used to attending big weddings in the fall. Hardly a wedding in spring."

"Well, I need to get back to the store, and I know Marge has to check on Maryann." She took a piece of paper out of her big paisley purse. "Read this, and think about joining."

Granny took the paper. Amish/English Knitting Circle. Classes starting in May. Learn to knit with needles. Classes Friday at 1:00. Stop into the store for more details. She looked up at Suzy. "Knit with needles and not a loom? Is it hard?"

"It's easy. And I've always wanted to offer classes to the Amish. Do you think any will come?"

"I don't see why not."

"Good. I'll stop by later in the week to talk. Have some ideas for Roman's wedding."

Granny smiled. "So *goot* to see you again."

~*~

Granny closed her eyes and listened to the peeper frogs. With Jeb's fishing hole in the back, they had so many, sometimes the noise was deafening, but they always sang the same song. Spring is here, and winter is over.

Everything did seem new in spring, and now two women from her knitting circle would be starting new lives, and for that, she was so thankful. But when would Roman's wedding be? And would Fannie be home to see Lizzie get married? She thought of the tall, awkward girl who thought she was ugly and fat: Fannie. Now she was transformed from a worm to a butterfly, but she'd fly away...away from her. It made her so sad, she couldn't even cry. She looked out the window into the spring sky:

Lord, I'm glad you're never weary and I can come to you all day long if need be. I come again tonight to cast burdens on you. I hate saying good-bye to loved ones, so I give Fannie to you. She's not mine, just a gift to keep for a while. Fill her life with joy, and fill

the hole that'll be in my heart when she leaves. And Lord, help Jeb and Roman come to an agreement about the wedding. Soften their hearts so they can see each other's point of view. I don't like discord in my family. Spin them together, like I do my wool. And Lord, I give Nathan to you. He's been seen with Lavina once too often, for my liking. I do love Lavina, but I don't see that she's the one for Nathan. Maybe you could open his eyes to Lydia Troyer or Lottie Hochstetler? You're the matchmaker, not me. Turn Nathan's heart toward the girl he's to wed. Lord, some days things seem spun out of control and I start to fret, even make myself sick with worry. I cast all my cares on you, knowing that you care for me.
In Jesus Name,
Amen.

~*~

Here is a recipe for granola that an Amish friend shared with me long ago. This was the first recipe that showed me how frugal the Amish are. Look at the recipe and see why. Enjoy!

Everything but the Kitchen Sink Granola

10 c. oatmeal and dry goods such as left over cereal (smashed in small pieces)

2 c. wheat germ or other dry ingredient on hand such as corn meal, sesame seeds, wheat flour,

2. c. coconut

2 c. brown sugar (light or dark)

2 c. nuts or seeds such as sunflower seeds, almonds, walnuts (whatever is on hand)

½ c. oil

½ c. honey

1 Tbs. vanilla

1 tsp. salt

Mix above ingredients together, put on cookie trays, and toast at 300 degrees until golden brown. Be careful to flip mixture to prevent burning. (20-30 minutes)

Raisins, dates, and other dried fruits can be added after granola is done baking.

EPISODE 10

New Beginnings

Granny looked across the table at the bishop. How she wished she'd agreed for this meeting to be at her own nest, but Sarah sat next to her husband, and it was a comfort.

"*Jah*, bishop. I have unforgiveness in my heart toward two people and I'm afraid I might ruin Easter for everyone."

Bishop Mast stared at his fiddling thumbs. "If I shed some light on the circumstances surrounding Lavina, it needs to be held in confidence. Jeb knows all about it because he's an elder."

Granny felt her heart jump. Jeb knew something about Lavina and her immoral past? He didn't tell her? Must be something awfully serious. "Go on Bishop. You have my word."

"Well, I won't be saying much more than Lavina comes from a very harsh home. Lavina's family has moved because her *daed* won't repent of abuse; Lavina's had blows to her body and heart."

Granny leaned forward. What was he saying? Thoughts of Marge telling her she would contact the law if Lavina told her one more thing ran through her mind…. She took a deep breath and slowly let the air out. "So her *daed's* a cruel man?"

"*Jah*, and I've reported it to his bishop. He's denying it, and accusing Lavina of lying. So it's hard for her to go home. I welcomed her into my flock."

Granny didn't know if it was right to ask, but had to. "But Lavina did have twins…so she was immoral?"

"I believe with her *daed* being such a hard man, it made her look for love in the wrong way."

"But to say she didn't know who the *daed* is, which makes it seem worse."

Sarah reached for Granny's shaking hands. "She knows who the *daed* is. Her old boyfriend who mistreated her too, just like her daed. They wanted her to marry this man, but Lavina refused, wanting a *goot daed* for the twins."

Granny pursed her lips, trying to fight feelings of rage and sorrow. "Doesn't she have any family in Troutville? Someone to speak up for her?"

"The little family that's there thought she should have married before she showed. Kind of sweep it all under the rug. When Lavina refused and confessed. Her old boyfriend threated her to say she didn't know who the *daed* was to save his skin. And her *daed* agreed with the boyfriend."

Granny felt like pounding on the table. "How about her *mamm*? Didn't she speak up for her?"

"*Jah*, she did. I've talked to her and she said she believed Lavina, but the woman is controlled by her husband who's mighty unfeeling toward women." The bishop cleared his throat. "Do you have more compassion toward Lavina?"

"*Jah*? Sure do."

"You said you had two people to forgive. Who else?" Sarah asked.

Feeling dizzy, she put her head in her hands. A sob escaped and Granny saw tears stain her mauve dress. "Jeb, but I understand now. I think I need to lie down."

~*~

Lizzie helped her *daed* sit in one of the rockers at Bishop Mast's. "*Danki* for seeing us, Bishop." Lizzie said. "I can leave if you want me to, *Daed*."

"*Nee,* stay here. You know what I have to say."

Lizzie took another rocker and tried to give Sarah a smile, glad the bishop's wife was present. Jonas hit his fist on the bent hickory arm rest. "I have to say I have some hard feeling, Bishop. The *Gmay* may not have voted in glass enclosures for our buggies, but I don't see why an exception can't be made for those who have an illness or are elderly. Arthritis is an awfully painful think to deal with in the winter."

Bishop Mast looked down, and Lizzie feared her daed had gone too far. The *Ordnung* was agreed upon by everyone three weeks ago. Her *daed* had voted to wait a year to think over the matter, as it was a serious change.

"Jonas, why are you changing your mind? What's really bothering you?"

"Pain. I'm in pain in the winter and being out in the cold is unbearable at times."

"The *Gmay* needs more time to make such a big

change; you know that. So, I'm asking again; what's really bothering you?"

Jonas looked at the bishop evenly. "I don't say things I don't mean. Pain, plain and simple."

"I have a suggestion," Sarah said. "How about we take up an offering so Jonas can have a driver? Be in a nice warm car?"

The bishop looked over at Sarah and a smiled slowly lit his face. "*Danki.*" He turned to Jonas. "What do you think? An English driver for a year when the weather gets cold?"

Jonas nodded. "I'd be grateful, for sure. So sorry to make a fuss."

"You're not yourself, Jonas. Is giving up the store bothering you that much?"

"*Jah*, I suppose. Don't want to be put out to pasture like an old cow. Need income too. But when Lizzie weds, she'll have *kinner* to tend…"

Lizzie felt a sting in her heart. "*Daed*, why not say something?"

"What's there to say?"

Lizzie groaned. "What you're feeling, that's what. I thought you were glad to move into Roman's house. We'll have a little *dawdyhaus* attached to the side, in time, so you'd have privacy."

"Well, I was excited. Jeb has a goot fishing hole and we'd be neighbors. But when the dust settled, well, I'll miss the store. But I've dealt with bigger changes, like losing your *mamm*. Losing the store is a little thing compared to that, and God gives us the grace we need."

~*~

Fannie sat across the table from the bishop and Sarah. "Lots of buggies coming to your place today? Are there other people who have unforgiveness? Think we'll need to postpone Easter?"

The bishop put his hand to his mouth, hiding a grin from the animated girl. "Fannie, we're working things out. So, who do you hold unforgiveness toward?"

"Ach, my father-in-law to be, Melvin's *daed*. It's like he pulled the rug up from underneath Melvin, giving him no choice but to move to New York."

"Have you talked to him about this?"

"*Nee*, I don't have the nerve. He'll be family and I want to get off on the right foot."

"Have you talked to Melvin?"

Fannie bit her lower lip. "I told him I'd be happy wherever he is, which is true. But I'd miss my family and friends here in Smicksburg. And, I don't want to hand milk cows, that's for sure."

Sarah chuckled. "How many cows?"

"I'm not sure, but I know Melvin would have little time to carve. He takes such pleasure in carving."

"No one makes cuckoo clocks like Melvin," Sarah said. "You just tell him what animals you want on it, and he can carve them." She pointed to her clock on the wall. "I picked squirrels collecting nuts, and they look real, *jah*?"

Fannie got up and walked over to the clock. "They do. Such *goot* work, but he'll have to give up this God-given talent because of his *daed*."

319

"Hold on now, Fannie. You don't know Martin's side of the story," the bishop said.

"What side?"

"I grew up with Martin. He's a buddy of mine since we were both *kinner*. He's talked about his love for cows since he was a *boppli*. I'll miss him, but he's finally getting to do his God-given dream. He never thought he could have a dairy farm and jumped at the chance when he could. Maybe he seems impulsive, but, none the less, it's done."

Fannie sighed audibly. "But he owns a shop with Melvin and should have told him the farm and shop were for sale."

The Bishop narrowed his eyes. "I helped Martin build that farmhouse and shop. I can see that he'd think he owned that place and had the say –so."

Fannie feared she'd have to confess unforgiveness toward the bishop because he was only defending his friend. But he did make sense, she had to admit. He'd built the house and had the right to sell. She just didn't want to leave Smicksburg.

"You need someone to blame, *jah*?" Sarah asked. "Feel like your life's ruined and it's someone's fault?"

"*Jah,* I suppose so."

~*~

Granny let Jeb hold her on his lap and rock her, like her *mamm* used to do years ago. "I'm so sorry I thought such awful things of you, Love."

"Too many Jane Austen books and not enough of the Bible."

"That's not true…"

"Only trying to make you laugh, Love." He cradled her head against his chest. "The church council agreed that no one's to know about Lavina's situation until her old boyfriend confesses his part. Hopefully soon so Lavina's name can be cleared of such immorality. Not knowing who the *daed* was…my eye." Jeb moaned. "So you understand now why I don't object to Nathan seeing her?"

"Jah, of course. We all make mistakes, "Granny said. "Ach, I'm wrung out like an old dish cloth. Too tired to make anything for knitting circle and need some rest. Do you think you can get word to the girls that the circle will be canceled tonight?"

Jeb held her tighter. "The Amish grapevine moves faster than that internet Suzy has. Not a problem. You take it easy and rest."

~*~

Jeb noticed the tiny blue hyacinths pushing their way up through the soil in Granny's flower beds. He'd planted the dead flower bulbs last Easter and here they were again, alive and new. Just like the resurrection, he thought.

He spun on his heels as he approached his buggy. He'd been a stubborn fool. Instead of heading over to the bishop's, he needed to head over to his son's and ask forgiveness. He knocked on the door and soon heard the scurrying of little feet. Tillie opened the door and smiled, revealing a lost front tooth. "*Opa*! Come in."

Jeb scooped up Tillie and kissed her cheek. "I never

get tired of your dimpled smile. Been kissed by angels, *jah*?"

"*Opa*, I'm too old to believe that. God made my dimples."

Jeb's heart sank. The girls were growing up too fast. He noticed Roman come to the door, and saw that he immediately put a wall up when seeing him. "Son, I'd like to talk to you."

"It's dinner time, *jah*?"

"I can come back then…"

Roman motioned for him to come into the kitchen. "Sorry, *Daed*. I'm being rude. Let's talk, again."

Jeb sat at the table across from Roman. "I take it you're tired of our talks."

"*Daed*, Lizzie and I agree to abide by your counsel. We'll wed in the fall, like you want. Don't want to sound blunt, but what's the matter now? Something else?"

Jeb saw something in Roman he'd missed before. He'd agreed to wait patiently. Lizzie was *goot* for him, showing him the advantages of moving slower, keeping in pace with nature. "Son, I think your *mamm* needs a party."

"What? We had a birthday party not long ago…"

"*Nee*, I mean a different type party."

"*Daed*, is *Mamm* okay? She looked mighty sad this afternoon and now she's canceled knitting circle. I know she saw the doctor. Was it bad news?"

"She's a fit as a fiddle, but I've noticed something. Ever since she started that knitting circle, her love for the girls makes her tired. It's like she takes on their burdens too much."

"She helps carry burdens, *jah*? Like the Good Book says to do?"

"But I get worried. Now she's joining an Amish and English knitting circle, and what problems will that bring? More problems to be loaded on your *mamm*." Jeb swatted the air. "That's not what I came over to talk about..."

Roman got up and poured coffee into a mug and sat it on the table in front of his *daed*. "You look serious. What's on your mind?"

"I was a stubborn mule concerning your wedding, and I'm asking for forgiveness. I do move like a turtle and I guess it comes with age."

"So, *Mamm* wanted us to have a spring wedding?"

"I'm learning to read between the lines, like *yinz* do. *Nee,* she never came right out and said it, but I know she'd be mighty happy if you had a wedding to plan in a few weeks."

"But *daed*, you said it was putting too much on her and now –"

"I'm afraid of change, Okay. There, I said it." Jeb pulled at his beard. "And I wanted all my boys at the wedding too. But if three out of five are together, I'll be happy."

Roman shook his head. "*Daed*, what are you saying?"

"Get married in the spring, in a few weeks, is what I'm saying. They only need a week's notice in Ohio to get a driver, *jah*?"

Roman shot up. "*Daed*, are you sure?"

"*Jah*, I'm sure son." Jeb got up and went around the table to embrace his son. "I should have thought better of you. You're not impulsive. I'm sorry."

"You only wanted the best for us." He pulled away. "I need to go tell Lizzie. Can you stay here with the girls?"

"*Jah*, you go run along and tell your bride the *goot* news."

~*~

"Married in a few weeks?" Jonas barked. "What on earth?"

Lizzie put her arm through Roman's. "Jeb was the only one against it, and he confessed to being stubborn. *Daed*, aren't you happy?"

"My head is spinning is all…"

Roman knew he was attached to his store, and had even offered for the family move into his place. Was he being stubborn by insisting his girls not be uprooted? "Jonas, you don't look *goot*. It's your store, *jah*? You're attached to it, like I am my rocker shop? Too much change?"

Jonas lowered his head. "*Jah*, but life goes on."

Lizzie ran over and knelt by her *daed*, taking his hand. "You won't be leaving this place in a few weeks. Nathan's agreed to come live here until the house and store are sold."

Jonas looked up with misted eyes. "That would be *goot*. Make things move a little slower."

Roman knew how distressed Lizzie had been over her *daed's* health. It was good news his MS wasn't getting worse, only his arthritis. But none the less, his bride to be was as attached to her *daed* as he was to his girls. Was he being selfish?

"Lizzie, can I talk to you, private-like?"

She took his hand and led him back to the kitchen. He drew her close. "I'm sorry. I didn't see how hard this was on you and your *daed*."

Lizzie planted a kiss on his lips. "*Daed* is fine, really. Once he starts fishing with your *daed*, he'll be fine."

"But he loves his customers; that's for sure. When you were in Lancaster, I helped run the store. He loves it."

"I trust your judgment, Roman. You love me and my *daed*." She put her arms around his neck. "So we can wed in a few weeks?"

"*Jah*, that's what *daed* said. But *Mamm* will need lots of help."

"I need to sew a new dress. And pick attendants. We can't delay or it'll be plowing time." She put her head on his chest. "I'm so happy."

Roman lifted her chin and kissed her gently. "Me too." He rested his head on hers, wondering what to do about Jonas.

~*~

Ruth asked the bishop if he wanted coffee, but he declined. "This is my fifth house to visit this morning, and my nerves will get too jumbled up." He took off his black wool hat and looked over at Luke. "Soon we'll be wearing straw hats again, but it's nippy today."

"*Jah*, it's windy." Luke said. "The pinwheels are spinning and keeping birds out of our peas. Nice having a garden with Ruth's family."

"They're your family too, *jah*?" the bishop asked.

"They treat me like a son, and I'm grateful."

"So *yinz* are in full forgiveness? We can plan on having Easter service on Sunday?"

"*Jah*," Ruth said. "Like you said, it's an act of obedience, not a feeling." She turned to Luke and smiled. "But since Luke and I have been reading Psalms and praying together, it's helped us open up what we've been keeping secret. I know Luke much better now."

"And I know Ruth," Luke said, beaming. "She's a *goot* woman, for sure."

"I feel like I've walked into a different home," the bishop said. "There's peace and contentment here now. We'll continue with this arrangement though?"

"*Jah*. I like living here and working here in the woodshop," Luke said. "We're planning on adding on to this house."

"Why, it's not too small...for a small family."

"This family will be growing," Luke said.

The bishop gaped at Ruth. "You mean –"

"*Nee*, I'm not with child. *Nee*, in time, *jah*, but now...*n-nee*."

Silence filled the small kitchen, only the chirping of birds at their birdfeeders could be heard. "You love birds, don't you Ruth?" the bishop asked.

"*Jah*. It's something Luke and I both do together now."

"And once you said you wished people got along like finches. I remember that. Be praying for our *Gmay*. We need to take part in the Body of Christ with no sin of unforgiveness on Easter. Pray we'll be like finches." He put his head down and stared at the floor.

Luke went over and put his hand on his shoulder. "Bishop, you seem worn out. Can we do anything for you?"

"Pray. You know there's power in it. Pray for unity in our church district and others around here too. All the bishops got together and prayed. Most powerful thing you can do."

~*~

Roman walked into the store and saw Jonas talking to Fannie and Melvin. "Looks like the old shop keepers are here again."

Fannie smiled. "*Jah*, we held the store together real *goot*, when Lizzie was gone. So much fun playing checkers and Dutch Blitz."

"I've been coming to this store since I was a *kinner* to get gum or some other candy," Melvin said. "Sure am sad to see it close."

"Well, I'll have it open for a while. Nathan and I will be here until fall, and then we'll just have to see what happens. "

Jonas looked down, and Roman could see how hard he was trying to hide his pain. "Maybe the house can be rented and you keep the store," he said.

Jonas shook his head. "*Nee*, it's time to move on. Handwriting's on the wall."

"Jonas, can I talk with you, in private?" Roman asked.

"We're leaving. Just ordering candy for our wedding. Jonas gets a *goot* bulk price," Fannie said. "Danki Jonas." She kissed his cheek.

Melvin nodded and they went out to their buggy.

Roman kept his eyes on Jonas. "You're fond of Fannie, *jah*?"

"Lives right down the road. Knew that girl when all she did was make fun of her weight. That knitting circle helped her in many ways. Now she'll be married and… gone too."

Roman scratched the back of his neck. "Look at what you'll be gaining. You'll be living with us, only a door separating us for your sake. My girls won't leave you alone, once they get asking questions. Especially the 'why' ones. 'Why's the sky blue?' 'Why don't birds have noses?' Why, why why…"

"Birds have nostrils on their beaks, don't you know?"

Roman grinned, hoping Jonas would cheer up. "*Jah*, I know that. Just saying you'll have other people in your life; maybe you won't miss Fannie so much."

Jonas made his way over to his chair and sat down. "What did you want to talk to me about?"

Roman pulled up a chair. "Jonas, Lizzie's torn up inside. She wants you to be happy. So, if it's too much change too fast, us getting married in a few weeks, we'll postpone the wedding until fall."

Jonas' face softened. "You mean that? Don't you?"

"It's my word. Course I do."

Jonas bowed his head. "I'm being selfish. Holding on to my wife like I've been…"

"How so?"

"Well, all the *goot* things in my life happened in this here spot. Building a house for my new bride, with my own hands, before MS took over. And then the *Gmay* building a business for me. Even after the fire, they helped rebuild it all. This house is like my life. No matter how much life can scar us, we still have others to help us heal. To rebuild us. This house tells a story, and it means so much to me…too much I'm afraid."

Roman tried to take in all Jonas was telling him. He never realized this house, this business, kept Jonas' spirit fresh. It filled him with hope because it was built with love, twice. Maybe he and the girls needed to move in. They were young and could adjust, but he had his parents to look after.

"I think if we wait until fall, we'll better understand what to do," Roman said. "For now, I need to know if you have any hard feelings for me, turning your life upside down so sudden-like."

"*Ach*, you'll be my son sooner or later, and I couldn't be happier. I'm not upset at all. Just getting old, I suppose, and having a hard time with change."

"Well, maybe it's because we're rushing things." Roman put his head down, praying for strength and wisdom. His dream of marrying Lizzie in a few short weeks was unlikely…And when they wed, where should they live? "Jonas, we'll all be fasting and seeking God until noon tomorrow, since it's Good Friday."

"*Jah*, open hands and hearts toward God. I'm willing to receive anything he's in charge of. I've learned from the past; God can be trusted."

~*~

Ella took her well-worn Bible and sat in her rocker, watching the sunrise. She loved these holy days, a time to reflect. An image of Lavina showing up at her door on Old Christmas, ruining her day of solitude, ran through her mind. How angry she was and what progress they'd made, since Lavina told her everything about her past. She bit her lower lip, thinking that if Lavina showed up today, they'd pray and read aloud together, and her day would be the better for it.

But she did crave solitude, and got up especially early to have this time alone to reflect on the cross, and the passion of Christ. She opened her Bible and found the scripture she felt the Lord imprinting on her heart all week, 1 Peter 2:21-24:

"For to this you were called, because Christ also suffered for us, leaving us an example, that you should follow His steps:

Who committed no sin, Nor was deceit found in His mouth who, when He was reviled, did not revile in return; when He suffered, He did not threaten, but committed Himself to Him who judges righteously; who Himself bore our sins in His own body on the tree, that we, having died to sins, might live for righteousness—by whose stripes you were healed."

Ella's eyes misted as she thought of the healing in her heart over the past few weeks. Christ had died for her to be emotionally whole, not cringing with fear over losing the twins.

She looked up at the first verse and skimmed the words over and over. Suffering, example and follow in his steps pulled at her heart. She was to suffer living in the same town as the biological *mamm* of her twins, but Christ had given her an example to live, so she could walk in his steps.

She hugged her Bible. There was no suffering anymore though. The Lord had healed her heart, so God really did all the work. She just needed to stay on the path, close to him; for she knew his burdens were light and easy, with him to help carry them.

~*~

Jonas looked at the cover of his devotional book, My Utmost for His Highest, by Oswald Chambers. He didn't feel like reading it today, his heart torn over too much change. But he stared at the book, and realized he never really thought of the title. Christ had given his utmost, being crucified to make a clear path to God. Was he acting in a Christian manner, giving his utmost, for the sake of all? Living in community always meant sacrifice, and giving up selfishness. Was he giving his utmost to his daughter, who'd finally be married? And to the man she'd always loved.

He looked at the end of the title again...for His Highest. Was his unhealthy attachment to his house and store keeping him from some higher good? His Highest implied a plan God had in the mixing. He needed to give his utmost, all he had, to find this new higher ground.

He'd told Roman he'd learned from the past that God could be trusted. Did he really believe it though? If so, why was he holding on to the past, afraid of change? If God has a higher path he wanted to take it; why was he gripping so hard onto the past? Yes, he'd miss all his customers, seeing so many people, and being handicapped, he didn't get out a lot.

Anxiety filled him. He didn't want to ruin his

daughter's hopes. She'd always dreamed of an early spring wedding, when blossoms were in full bloom. He bowed his head and asked God to calm his nerves so he could think clearly.

~*~

Granny got up to make lunch, her stomach growling. She was glad the fast for Good Friday was only until noon. She spent more time in casting off prayers than reading scripture and meditating on the cross. No, she thought of her own cross, Jonas not agreeing to a spring wedding, shattering both Lizzie and Roman. But she'd hold her tongue and pray for the best.

A van pulled into the driveway, Jack barked, and Suzy quickly got out, but ignored her dog, not playing with him as she usually did. She went out on the porch. "You're just in time for lunch?"

"No, not today. Just stopped by the give you more leaflets for the Amish Friends Knitting Circle. I changed it since no one knows you call us *Englishers*. So it's Amish and their friends." Suzy shifted. "Actually, not much response from the Amish. You're the only one signed up and thought you could get your girls to invite friends?"

"Suzy, slow down and come in to eat −"

"I can't. And I'm late for church already."

"Church? On Friday?"

"Good Friday, remember. And I fast from noon 'til three."

"Why then?"

"Well, it's the time Jesus hung on the cross, so we don't eat and have a church service. My store's closed too."

Granny had to admit she felt like a heathen. Here was an *Englisher* who was fasting and intently reflecting on the crucifixion, and her mind wandered all morning while trying to meditate. But then, she'd come to see there were many *Englishers* who were as devout a Christian as some of the most earnest Amish. "I'll pass these out. But I may get a big response. What if we can't all fit in your store?"

"We could have it here? Let curious Outsiders into an Amish home?" She quickly embraced Granny. "You think about it. Really have to run. It's so embarrassing being late for church."

Granny waved from the porch as Suzy pulled out and tore down the driveway, kicking up gravel in Jack's face as he chased in hot pursuit. Slow down! You English need to slow down. Maybe they'd learn a slower pace from her, if she had another knitting circle at her place.

She thought of Fannie and how much she'd enjoy spending time with a circle of Englishers, but would be moving to New York. She swallowed the lump in her throat; she'd become too attached to all her little women in her circle.

She went over to her breadbox and got out a loaf of homemade bread. She slowly sliced it, and an idea formed in her mind. What if...Ach, why hadn't she thought of it sooner? She laid the knife down and grabbed her shawl and bonnet. She needed to talk to Jonas, and fast.

As she ran out to the buggy, Roman yelled for her to watch her step, the mud being slippery. He went over to the buggy and took the horse's reins. "Now, where are you going? And what's the hurry?"

"Roman, I think I have a wunderbar goot idea. I need to talk to Jonas."

"Jonas?"

"And Fannie and Melvin too…"

Roman narrowed his gaze at her. "*Mamm*, when I was fasting and praying, I got an idea. I wonder if we're thinking the same thing?"

"Go fetch your *daed* and make sure he can watch the girls. Then hop in the buggy and we'll talk."

~*~

Jonas saw a buggy pull up to the store. No, it was Good Friday and he wouldn't open the store for anyone. He was shocked when he saw it was Deborah and Roman Weaver. "More pressure to have a spring wedding. He thought about giving his utmost; he'd do it so he could find this new, higher ground the Good Lord had for him in this new life, living among the Weavers.

He opened the store door and couldn't help but notice the flush on Deborah's cheeks. "Are you ill? Need some medicine from the store?"

"*Nee*, just worked up," Granny said. "We need to talk."

Jonas knew she wasn't a quiet woman, so he knew that meant he had lots of listening to do. He asked them to follow into the kitchen, where Lizzie was making lunch. "Are you hungry?"

"*Nee*, I'm fine," Roman said.

"Well, I missed lunch, so I'll have whatever Lizzie's making"

Lizzie greeted them warmly, her eyes lingering on Roman. "Since it's Good Friday, we're only having cold cuts and soup I made yesterday."

"I'll just have a sandwich," Granny said.

"Me too," Jonas said, turning to Roman. "Last call. Are you hungry?"

"*Nee. Danki.*"

Jonas, Granny and Roman took a seat at the kitchen table. Lizzie looked out the window. "*Daed*, you did put the 'closed' sign on the store door?"

"*Jah*, I did."

"We invited Melvin and Fannie over. We all need to talk." Roman said, smiling at Lizzie. "Stopped at Fannie's before we came here, and glad that Melvin was visiting."

Jonas kept thinking he needed to give his utmost, not knowing what to think, but he did feel more change was in his future, and his head started to spin. He closed his eyes. Lord, give me strength.

Lizzie led Melvin and Fannie into the kitchen, offering them a sandwich, which they both denied, having already eaten lunch.

Roman cleared his throat. "This morning, during fasting time, I had an idea. A plan that would involve all of you." He looked over at Lizzie. "When my *mamm* had the same idea, I knew it was some kind of sign that I was on the right path."

Jonas tilted his head back, bracing himself for the blow. "Go on…"

"Well, I think we have a solution to everyone's problems. Fannie and Melvin, do *yinz* really want to move to New York?"

"*Nee,*" they said in unison.

Roman turned to Jonas. "Do you want to keep the store and run it?"

"*Jah*, but I was being selfish."

Roman looked at his *mamm* and grinned. "Well, just hear us out, because we have a *goot* plan, if everyone's in agreement." He looked around at everyone, hopeful. "Jonas, what if Melvin and Fannie bought your house and you kept the store part." He turned to Melvin. "We could get some buddies together and build a shop for your clocks on the other side of the house."

Jonas gawked. "Roman, are you still fasting? Need something to eat? You're not making sense."

Fannie walked over to Jonas and put a hand on his shoulder. "I think I understand. Jonas, you want to keep the store, *jah*?" She turned to Melvin. "If we bought this house, Jonas could live with us, or in a side *dawdyhaus* and keep his store."

"But with my handicap, I'd still need Lizzie."

Fannie kissed his cheek. "I have store experience. I can work in the store."

Melvin cracked his knuckles one at a time. "But I told my *daed* I'd be moving up to New York and would be helping him."

Granny stood up. "He can hire milkers, *jah*? And so many Coblenz's moving up there, he'd have help."

Fannie went over to Melvin and put her arm through his. "It's your *daed's* dream to farm, not yours."

Lizzie put her hand up. "Let me understand this.

Fannie and Melvin would buy this house, and my *daed* would live with them? And not us?"

Roman got up and put his arm around Lizzie. "This could all be temporary-like. If Jonas doesn't like it, he has a home with us."

Melvin sighed. "I don't have money to buy this place."

Jonas knew this was an answer to prayer. He felt like skipping, if he could. "How about *yinz* sign a land contract? No interest. Say, for twenty years?"

Melvin stared at Jonas for a long while as silence filled the room. "You're serious, aren't you?"

"*Jah*, course I am." He turned to Lizzie. "Darlin' I know it's hard for you to care for me. I need a man who can lift."

Melvin spun Fannie around. "I can help, Jonas. Not a problem."

Granny got up and put her arm around Lizzie too. "Your *daed* will be fine. You're not losing him, remember?"

Roman kissed Lizzie's cheek. "You'll be gaining a new *daed* and *mamm* when you become Mrs. Weaver."

Fannie kissed Melvin and jumped up and down. "I didn't want to move, and God heard my prayer."

Lizzie looked at Roman. "Where will I live when Fannie and Melvin marry? Here in the house too? It's not that big. And is Nathan still coming?"

"Nathan isn't needed anymore, since Melvin will be here. And there's nothing stopping us from having a spring wedding, since your *daed* won't need to make any changes. "He looked at Jonas. "Isn't that right? With you happy here, with your store, there's no reason for Lizzie and me to wait until fall."

"*Nee*, there isn't."

Fannie ran over to Lizzie, still jumping. "We need to start working on your wedding, now."

Jonas saw the shock on his daughter's face. "I say we all pray about this and sleep on it. If we're all in agreement on Easter, I say let's do it. But if anyone feels too rushed or confused as to what to do, we'll know it's not right, and need to wait further, until everyone's in unity. Agreed?"

Everyone nodded.

"Wise words, Jonas," Granny said.

"I'm trying my utmost, "Jonas mused, "to see a higher path."

"What are you talking about, *Daed*?" Lizzie asked.

"Ach, something between me and the Lord."

~*~

Fannie and Lizzie got out of Marge's red sports car. "I still don't see why the Amish get married with an apron on." Marge said.

"It's a reminder our hands are always ready for work," Lizzie said. "Anyhow, a nice white apron is pretty."

"*Jah*, I can't wait to wear mine." Fannie nearly skipped as the three made their way into Punxsy-Mart. "My dress is mint green to bring out my eyes."

Lizzie gawked. "You shouldn't talk like that."

"Why?" Marge asked.

"Because it sounds vain."

Fannie rolled her eyes. "*Nee* it does not. I want to look

pretty on my wedding day. Took me long enough to think I wasn't fat and ugly."

Marge put her hand on her massive hips. "You thought you were fat? How come?"

"Comparing myself to others and looking at magazines here in the store. Suzy showed us how the computer changes the images."

Marge clasped her hands. "But you thought you were ugly? You're gorgeous."

"*Danki*," Fannie said. "I still work on that. The not feeling ugly part. Still compare myself to others, but it's getting better."

Lizzie walked immediately over to the mauve material. "Do you think this brings out my eyes," she teased. "How silly."

Marge guided Lizzie over to the mirror and held the material up to her face. "See the burgundy flecks in your eyes?"

Lizzie leaned closer. "*Jah*, I do."

"Mauve brings out that color and makes your eyes look bigger. Of course, since they're brown, a brown dress would do the same."

"*Nee*, not brown," Lizzie said. "So you think mauve would be *goot*?"

Fannie brought a bolt of wine colored material over. "I think this would look best. Your eyes are dark and so is this shade."

Lizzie held the material up. "I see what you mean." She turned to Fannie. "Who have you picked for attendants?"

"Can you believe I still haven't picked anyone? Can't choose one friend over another."

"But your wedding's in three weeks, *jah*?"

"Well, I wanted you in it Lizzie, but not with you getting married too."

Marge sighed. "I'm confused. Are you talking about your bridesmaids?"

"What that?" Lizzie and Fannie asked in unison.

"You know. The girls who walk down the aisle before you."

"We don't walk down the aisle." Fannie chuckled. "Why would we do that?"

"So everyone can look at the bride...see her gown...I see. You don't want attention because it shows pride?"

"*Nee*. We sit in the front with our attendants. We have two, and the groom has two. Sometimes we pick couples we'd like to see together, since the attendants spend most of the day with each other."

"So it's like being a matchmaker?"

"If you want to," Fannie said. "But it's usually just best friends. I just can't narrow it down. Don't want to hurt anyone's feelings."

"Why not narrow it down by groups? Say you're going to ask only sisters or friends who all do the same things together," Marge said.

Fannie's eyes grew round. "Knitting circle friends. But I can only pick two..."

"You better pick them soon." Lizzie said, still looking in the mirror. "Sure wish we could put flowers in our hair like the English."

"Why don't you?" Marge asked.

Fannie gawked. "Only our husbands are supposed to see our hair, not other men."

"You're kidding, right?" Marge asked, eyes wide.

"It's our custom," Lizzie said. "It says in the Bible that a woman's hair is her glory. We never cut ours or show it to anyone, but save it for our husbands."

Marge sighed. "That's kind of romantic...I like that. So what do you wear on your wedding?"

Fannie pointed to her head. "A prayer *kapp*, like this one, but always white."

"And where's the wedding?"

"At the bride's house. Her *mamm's* usually the one who puts on the wedding feast..."Fannie took Lizzie's hands. "I know you miss your *mamm*."

"I'll have Granny as a *mamm*, when I'm married."

"So will your wedding be put on by Granny?" Marge asked.

"Roman and I are trying to figure things out. For now, we're just hoping by tomorrow we'll all be in agreement so we can wed in a few weeks."

~*~

Luke shielded his eyes from the sun pouring into Mica's room. The same question went through his mind, like it did every morning. When will Ruth and I share the marriage bed again? A woman's heart, once betrayed and broken, took longer to heal than anything. But it was the nature of Ruth's heart he loved, and it was something he knew to cherish and protect in the future; to serve her like Jesus did the church, like Jeb told him....like the

Bible said to do.

The smells of coffee and bacon drifted from the kitchen. He hoped to get up sooner and make her breakfast on Easter, but she was always up early with the birds, binoculars in hand to see her feathered friends. Well, at least he finished the white gourd feeder, just like the one Jeb made for Granny. Ruth hinted that she wanted one, saying purple martins eat mosquitoes. Yes, he was learning to pay attention to the little things she said, and he hoped soon, her wounded heart would be healed.

One thing about morning he didn't miss was the dark dread that rushed at his mind. Anxiety always showed up at the crack of dawn, but since he was on medicine, he woke up thinking clearly. His doctor was right; medicine allowed him to be himself. How isolated he used to live, never telling a soul his struggles. He'd isolated Ruth too, remembering Zach telling him she was a bird in a cage. It was like he used to cling to her like a child his favorite toy when sick. But now he and Ruth had lots of family and friends. He needed to stop looking backwards, like Granny said. If you look back, you'll turn into salt, like Lot's wife.

He quickly got dressed, being careful not to awaken Mica and headed out to the kitchen. "Happy Resurrection Sunday, Love." Luke kissed Ruth on the cheek. "*Danki* for breakfast. Quite a feast."

"Easter's my favorite day. Flowers coming up from the ground, just like the resurrection."

"*Jah*, God gives us all a second chance...a new

beginning?"

Ruth wrapped her arms around his neck. "*Jah*, he does."

Luke gently kissed her lips and told her to sit down. He took a basin out of their pantry and filled it with water. He knelt at Ruth's feet. "We'll all be washing each other's feet at the *Gmay* today, but I've never washed yours. Men only wash men's feet...."

Ruth leaned forward and cupped his cheeks in her hands. "You don't have to do this."

"You don't want me to?"

"*Nee*, I'm just saying you don't have to do everything Jeb tells you he does for Granny."

"Jeb never said anything about washing his wife's feet..."

Luke took her black knee sock off both feet and put them in the water. How petite and beautiful her feet looked. He thought of Christ washing the disciples' feet, an act of a servant. He silently prayed that as he served his wife she would open up just like the blossoming trees all around them.

Tears filled Ruth's eyes. "This must be the sign I was praying for."

"What?"

Ruth took his hand and led him back to her bedroom. He was not prepared for what he saw. She had the bed covered with the double-ring wedding quilt he bought her for a wedding present. He remembered the very day she ripped it off the bed and told him that the overlapping rings on the quilts stood for unity, and she didn't see it in their marriage. The quilt was a constant reminder of what their marriage lacked. But now?

She put her arms around his neck. "Luke, I've been so afraid of getting hurt again. You know, if I let you get too close. So I asked God to give me a sign. Something to let me know we should share the marriage bed again. By washing my feet...well." She kissed him fondly. "That was it. I'm not afraid anymore."

Luke scooped her into his arms and twirled her around. "I love you, Ruth."

"I love you too..."

~*~

Granny sat on the front bench at church. She knew if she sat in the back she'd fret, not being able to help notice Nathan looking over at Lavina. No, she would not fret about Nathan, having cast her love for him on God. Her love for Lavina too.

This would be Lavina's first time celebrating this long yet wonderful day, when unity was celebrated with communion. She thought back to the day she wrote the letter to her knitting circle. She feared no one would come and word would get out that she was a lonely old woman. She didn't realize she was a little lonely, now that her life was so intertwined with the girls. Roman and his girls filled her days, and she was grateful Jeb was still in good health. But when all the other sons moved, there was a void, and her knitting friends filled it. Yes, she had many reasons to sing the first hymn with all her strength.

~*~

As the second hymn, the *Loblied*, was sung, Maryann

closed her eyes to keep her tears from spilling over. How she praised God that He was her provider, like the song reminded. She'd stared death in the face and God provided the grace she needed, and the friends.

With Lavina on one side, and Becca on the other, she felt blessed beyond words to have two girls from the knitting circle as constant companions. Granny was right all along, women were stronger spun together, just like her wool when made into yarn. What would she have done having cancer without the help of her knitting friends?

When her favorite part of the hymn was sung, asking God for wisdom, she concentrated on each word, sung slowly, intentionally. As a *mamm* of eight, and trying to advise Lavina, she sang it often.

Open the mouth of Thy servants, Lord,
And give them wisdom also,
That they may rightly speak Thy Word
Which encourages a devoted life.

She couldn't help but notice Lavina sang louder, as if praying for wisdom. Yes, Lavina needed wisdom. No progress yet between their bishop and the one in Troutville. Her old boyfriend would not confess to immorality or say the twins were his. How could this man remain Amish? How could Lavina's *daed* not be plagued by nightmares of his daughter confessing to the whole congregation to not knowing who the *daed* was, as if she'd been immoral with more than one man?

Well, Lavina was welcome to live with them as long as needed. Cancer had taught her many lessons. Life was short and love was needed. She aimed to live each day extending love to anyone in need, and not listen to her judgmental mind. She was grateful her knitting friends had shown her a better way to live.

~*~

When Jeb preached the first sermon, reading from Exodus about Moses leading the Israelites out of Egypt, Ella held her own baby Moses tighter. She'd read that the Nile was full of crocodiles, and for the mother of Moses to let him float down it in a basket took lots of faith. She looked over at Lavina. She'd done the same thing, giving her twins to strangers so they'd have the life she never had. Hers was filled with violence and abuse, and it took courage to stand alone and do what her heart demanded.

How thankful she was to be the home the twins floated into. Seven years of being barren made her love them even more. They were a gift from the Lord Himself. Sermons from the Old Testament would fill the morning, and most likely Abraham and Sarah would be spoken of. How she used to fret that she'd never have *kinner,* just like Sarah. She pursed her lips to hide a smile. Sarah had a *kinner* at ninety and called him Isaac, which meant laughter. She'd laugh too if she got pregnant, and she was young.

But thoughts of being barren didn't plague her anymore. She had her twins and it all started when she let other women know how distressed she was; she needed more help than she'd thought. Through the long journey of finding the twins to her fears of losing them, she couldn't have made it through if it wasn't for her knitting circle friends. She thanked God for them daily, and especially Granny, who saw her pain and invited her.

~*~

Fannie sat next to Granny, her stomach rumbling. Since there were no formal breaks today, a meager lunch was provided; nothing was to stop the seriousness of this holy day. She elbowed Granny as she pat her stomach.

Granny's brow furrowed. "Are you sick?" she whispered.

"Starving. Want to go back and get something to eat?"

Granny turned to Lizzie and asked her if she wanted to join them. She agreed, so the three made their way to the back of the large barn where a table of light refreshments were being served. After a few bites, they made their way to the outhouse.

Fannie clenched her fists. "I can't concentrate on the preaching."

"Why?" Lizzie asked. "Jeb preached *goot*."

"I keep thinking of New York. We'll have to move if we're not all in agreement." She took Lizzie by the elbow. "Has your *daed* made up his mind?"

"He didn't say anything to me. Just keeps reading his Oswald Chamber's book and saying he's trying his utmost to make the right decision."

"He said we'd all talk after the service," Granny said, before she shut the outhouse door.

Lizzie took Fannie by the shoulders. "Now take a deep breath. Enjoy this day and we'll all talk in a few hours."

She crossed her arms and looked down at the ground. "I'm anxious too, not knowing when my wedding will be. I've really thought about what Marge and Suzy said. Sometimes we get *goot* ideas from the English."

"*Jah*, who would have thought of such a thing," Fannie grinned.

"Thought of what?" Granny said, exiting the outhouse.

"Just a silly idea from an *Englisher*." Fannie said. "They have strange notions." She winked at Lizzie. "But sometimes *goot* ones too."

Granny eyed Fannie. "You're supposed to be preparing your heart for communion, remember?"

"Just have a lot on my mind about the store and having to move to New York-"

"Cast it off, Fannie. Cast your cares on God. Who knows? Maybe New York will be *goot* for you and the Lord knows it."

Fannie gasped. "Why are you saying that? You know something, don't you? I saw Jeb talking to Jonas before the meeting."

"The men always talk before they enter the service." Granny said. "They're all waiting outside to file in."

"But they looked real serious-like."

"It's a serious decision," Granny said. "I'm praying mighty hard."

~*~

The bishop lifted up the loaf of bread, reminding the congregation that bread is made up of grains of wheat. Every grain had to be crushed to make the loaf. If one grain is not crushed it can not only be a part of the bread, but also brings attention to itself. This would not be submission but pride. Then he talked about grapes and how they all needed to be crushed to be a part of the wine. In like manner, all present had come to a place of unity, though some had felt they were being crushed. But he gave a strong reminder that Christ's body was broken and His blood spilt because of love. Are we to do less?

Then everyone filed to the front to take a piece of the bread and drink wine from the same cup, all a sign of unity. Then people paired up, women with women, and men with men, and they took basins to wash each other's feet. Granny went over to Lavina and asked if she could wash hers, and she quickly nodded in agreement. Zach went over to his brother, Luke, to ask if he could wash his feet. Luke beamed and hugged his brother.

After the foot washing, the bishop thanked everyone for not only their desire for unity, but hard work to maintain it. He said it was a day to celebrate, but also a warning that unity was something to yearn for daily. This took a lot of patience, but encouraged everyone that this was a fruit of the Holy Spirit, who was ever present to help; He would maintain unity if leaned upon.

Three weeks later.

The loud pounding work Granny up. What on earth? She turned to Jeb, but he wasn't in bed. The racket was coming from the back of her house so she made her way to the back window to look out. Lizzie and Roman were talking to Suzy. But that didn't startle her. It was the sight of Suzy's big white tent she used at craft show, going up in her yard! And the church bench wagon pulled in, and Melvin was driving it.

Granny ran to get her robe and knit slippers, since the first day of May was still chilly. She walked out to see Roman, who was now helping erect the tent. "What's going on?"

"Go ask John and Harry."

Granny frowned. "Why should I pay *goot* money and walk to the phone shanty if you know the answer."

Roman turned to her, eyes beaming. "They came in last night. Real late. John's staying with me and Harry with Jonas."

Granny felt like she needed to wake up. Her sons from Ohio were home? She looked down at the green grass, trying to make sense of what Roman said. Then it dawned on her. "Ach, they came home for Fannie's wedding?"

Roman grinned at her. "*Jah.*"

"That's real nice. Well, I need coffee. Heading back in." She turned to go into the house, puzzled. Neither Fannie or Melvin were kin. She never sensed a special bond between them, either. So why would they come to their wedding? She shook her head, still trying to wake up and make sense of it all. A big white tent was in her backyard and her sons from Ohio were home. What did it mean? Was Roman planning a gathering while they were home?

When she got to her kitchen she heard the pendulum

clock strike seven. She needed to get over to Fannie's in a few short hours to help her on her wedding day. She got the coffee out of its container, putting extra grounds into her blue speckled ware coffeepot. She needed it to be strong this morning. A long day ahead.

"So, are you surprised?" Jeb asked her as he came in the side door.

"About what?"

"The huge tent going up in your backyard." Jeb's one cheek slid up to form a crooked grin.

"I've seen tents before. So you're planning a gathering?"

"*Jah*, I am, along with Roman and Melvin…"

"That's the part I don't understand. Melvin's getting married today and he's here helping with a tent? And drove the bench wagon here, instead of over to Fannie's." Granny moaned. "Don't tell me Fannie's renting pretty chairs with covers, like the English. She's been talking quite a bit to Suzy about English weddings."

"*Jah*, she has, and Suzy has *wunderbar goot* ideas."

Granny's head shot up. "Old man, we are Amish and have our own ways. It's the traditions that bind us from one generation to the next. Humph! Fancy chairs. What could Fannie be thinking?"

Jeb sighed. "Just sit there, Old Girl. I'll get your coffee. I don't think you're awake, cause you're not putting one and one together."

Granny squinted. "What are you talking about?"

~*~

At two o'clock, Granny sat wide-eyed at the front

bench looking up at the top of the tent. It was prettier than the inside of a barn. The sun shone through better, and with open sides, it was much brighter. She thanked God for this day. She'd read Pride and Prejudice twice this past year and always sighed at the end. She'd always ended by placing the book to her heart and inwardly groan. How she longed to have what they had: a double wedding.

She watched as the two brides and their attendants, Ella and Ruth, sat across from the men; the groom and their attendants Zach and Luke. The love in Ruth's eyes was similar to the brides'. How she'd fretted about all her little women and how faithful God was, though He worked in such mysterious ways.

With the three hour church service almost complete, the bishop asked the couples to be married to come and stand by him. He then asked the men:

"Do you promise that if she should be afflicted with bodily weakness, sickness, or some other circumstance, that you will care for her as is fitting for a Christian husband?"

Both Roman and Melvin nodded in agreement, and said yes. He then asked Lizzie and Fannie if they could make the same vow, and they also nodded and said yes. Then the bishop asked:

Do you solemnly promise with one another that you will love and bear and be patient with one another, and not separate from each other until the dear God shall part you from each other through death?"

Both couples looked at each other fondly and said they

promised, sealing this sacred covenant. Then they returned to their benches. Granny felt like pinching herself, this being too *wunderbar goot*. It was better seeing a double wedding that just reading about one, although she had to admit, in Jane Austen's time, being able to carry flowers and wearing a fancy dress would have been nice, but she quickly dismissed the notion. No, she loved her Amish life. An English wedding looked pretty, but if it took a year to prepare, and the couples were so busy they had little time to think about their vows, then the centerpiece of the wedding was not in place. Though they had no flowers, they sure had their centerpiece, Christ, the head of the married couple, as the focal point.

~*~

The singing got louder and louder as faster praise songs were sung. Granny took Jeb's hand and looked over the sea of people that filled their back field, barn and Roman's house. Such merriment all around her only heightened her own and she wondered if a person could burst from happiness. She woke up this morning, thinking she was helping Fannie at her place. Granny bit her lower lip and chuckled. Fannie feared she'd be overwhelmed and so everyone kept the secret from her.

She looked over at Jonas as he talked to Melvin and Fannie. They would make a *goot* team to run the dry goods store. Jeb had always been so fond of Fannie, and seeing her move to New York was simply too much.

Granny heard the girls laughing, and turned to see them jumping up and down, all vying for their new *mamm's* attention. Lizzie glowed like a full moon, as she patiently answered their questions. She was a born *mamm,* just like Ella.

She felt Jeb's hand do a nervous twitch. "What's wrong, Love?"

Jeb leaned down and whispered. "The fish are calling to me. When are they all leaving?"

Granny gasped. "Jebediah Weaver, of all things to say on your son's wedding day."

Jeb chuckled. "Don't get your dander up, Deborah. Only joking…kind of."

~*~

Granny was exhausted, but too happy to sleep. Since the time she'd opened her eyes this blessed day, she marveled at all God had done. She was blessed. Her girls were blessed. Seeing all the new lambs birthed over the past week made her wonder if there were new girls that needed to come to the knitting circle. Maybe not Amish, but English. She thought of Suzy's idea to have a knitting circle at her house. But was she over doing it, as Jeb feared? Did she need to slow down? She didn't know, but learned to bow her head and cast it all on God, for He cared for her.

Dear Lord,

I can't believe Lizzie is living right next door. Be with Jonas as he makes the necessary transitions. If he's to live with Fannie and Melvin permanently, show him, but give him peace. And Lord, thank you for not taking Fannie from me and providing a way for her to stay in Smicksburg. I'm ever so fond of her. I thank you I felt so carefree today, not fretting over any of my girls. They've all become so strong, being knit together in your love and in each other's

354

company. *Show us if we need to reach out to Englishers, if we're supposed to. Help Jeb not worry about me. Help him learn to cast his cares on you, too, for you truly do care for us all.*

In Jesus' name,
Amen

~*~

Well, dear friends, we're at the end of the *Amish Knitting Circle*. It's been fun writing this with so much input from readers. Fannie stayed in Smicksburg, by popular demand, as did the book end in a double wedding.

I need to reiterate that this is a work of fiction. Concerning Luke and Ruth getting back together, it's a dream for anyone in an abusive marriage. If you feel unsafe or threatened in your marriage, please seek help from a pastor or a social agency.

I'm leaving you with a recipe but also a challenge. Are there women on your hearts who you feel would be stronger if spun together, like Granny did? Why not start a knitting circle or other group activity? Maybe a scrapbook club? How about a reading circle where you can read Amish fiction? You don't need six women, maybe only two or three. God bless your efforts to reach out to each other and be spun together, becoming stronger. And why not start by asking some friends over for shoo-fly pie, to discuss your plans. God bless you all!

~*~

Shoo-fly Pie

Syrup:
1 c. molasses
1 c. hot water
½ c. light brown sugar
½ tsp. baking soda

Crumbs:
2 ½ c. flour
1 c. light brown sugar
½ c. shortening
¼ tsp. soda
¼ tsp. cream of tartar
1 tsp. nutmeg (optional)
1 tsp. cinnamon (optional)

Mix all syrup and crumb ingredients separately in different bowls. Syrup should be dissolved completely. Divide syrup evenly into two unbaked 9 inch pie crusts. Divide the crumbs on top of each pie. Bake for 10 minutes at 450 degrees, then 30 minutes at 375 degrees, and finally 30 minutes at 350 degrees. Let cool and enjoy

ABOUT THE AUTHOR

Karen Anna Vogel is an author on a mission to use stories to entertain and encourage, but most of all to help heal the hurting...and she does it masterfully! **Kathi Macias author of over forty novels, including** Unexpected Christmas Hero

A trusted English friend among many Amish in rural Western Pennsylvania, Karen wants to share about these wonderful people she admires. Karen writes full-length novels and short story serials and hopes readers will learn more about Amish culture and traditions, and realize you don't have to be Amish to live a simple life.

She's a graduate from Seton Hill University with a B.A. in psychology and elementary education, and a Masters from Andersonville Theological Seminary in Pastoral Counseling.

In my spare time she enjoys knitting, birding, and photograph. Karen also loves old houses, and has helped her husband of thirty-three years restore a century old farmhouse (with the help of Amish workers). They have four married adult children, and one granddaughter they've nicknamed *Precious*.

Karen is represented by Joyce Hart of Hartline Literary Agency.

Recipe Index

Thanks for taking the time to read this story
by Karen Anna Vogel; we hope you enjoyed it.

You may also enjoy other works by Karen Anna Vogel
published by
Lamb Books www.lambbooks.com

Amish Knitting Circle: Smicksburg Tales 1
Amish Friends Knitting Circle: Smicksburg Tales 2
Amish Knit Lit Circle: Smicksburg Tales 3

Coming in 2014, ***Amish Knit & Stitch Circle: Smicksburg Tales 4***

Full length novels with Lamb Books
Knit Together: Amish of Smicksburg Romance
The Amish Doll: Amish of Cherry Creek Romance

Novellas with Lamb Books
Amish Knitting Circle Christmas: Granny & Jeb's Love Story
Amish Pen Pals: Rachael's Confession

Novella with Murray Pura
Cry of Freedom Civil War Series: Christmas Union: Quaker Abolitionist of Chester County, PA

Made in the USA
Middletown, DE
01 December 2022

16621885R00199